either by taking over one of the closed shops, fulfilling a role in the community such as a doctor or teacher, or providing some kind of service. And while candlemaking couldn't exactly be described as something vital like being a doctor, she still felt that she had something to offer. And clearly so did the new owners of the castle, Kitty and Ken, who had practically snapped her hand off, offering her a place in the village within a few hours of her applying. She was excited about the change.

A jaunty little sign on the side of the road declared she had finally reached her destination.

Welcome to Harmony Castle and the Village of Happiness.

She couldn't help but smile as she swept through the gateposts and drove past the castle. It looked a bit tired in places and one poor turret seemed like it had crumbled away to nothing. It must be very expensive to maintain these kinds of places. She drove round the front of it and came to a row of four houses, though she could see the road wound away down the hill and included several more houses and shops. She had been allocated Sunrise Cottage but she had no idea where to look.

She pulled up on one side of the green and got out.

The four houses here were grey. There was no other word for it. These were not the whitewashed cottages she had seen in the poster. Some of the windows were broken, one house had its shutters hanging off and the flowers in the hanging baskets were dead. Two of the houses actually looked like they were sinking into the ground. The sun dipped behind the clouds, leaving a dullness that made the light in her heart go out. Was this what the whole village was like?

Why hadn't she visited before she packed up all her worldly goods and left the little town of St Octavia behind for the Cornish coast? Her mum always said she was too impetuous, the kind to rush in and ask questions later. That had been her trouble throughout her life. She made snap decisions and then often regretted them later. She was already second guessing this decision.

Her eyes scanned across the houses; they didn't even look habitable let alone like anyone lived there. In fact there didn't seem to be a single other person in sight. Was she literally going to be the only person to live in the village of Happiness?

A roar came from the castle and a man appeared on a quad bike. He was wearing a sky-blue baseball hat, a paint-splattered t-shirt, and faded cargo shorts. His dark curly hair stuck out in different directions from underneath his hat. He bumped down the hill towards her and came to a stop, flashing her a small cautious smile.

'Hi, I'm Andrew Harrington, I'm the estate manager here.'

She tried to recover herself from the shock of the state of the village. 'I'm—'

'Willow McKay, yes we've been expecting you. I'm sorry I wasn't here to greet you when you arrived, I would have stopped you from seeing that shambles behind you.'

'How would you have stopped me from seeing it, by blindfolding me?'

'It crossed my mind,' he grinned.

chapter 1

Willow McKay swerved across the road to avoid a pheasant and checked in the rear-view mirror to see it stumble safely back onto the grassy verge and disappear into the tall bushes that lined the road. What was it with this place? That was the fourth animal that had almost been squished under the wheels of her car. Maybe the animals round here were particularly stupid or they just weren't used to cars. She had been driving along this little country lane for what seemed like an hour, going up and down hills, and hadn't passed a single vehicle. The village of Happiness really was in the furthest corner of nowhere.

But that was exactly what she needed.

Six months ago she had proposed to her boyfriend of four years and he'd said yes. The very next day, he'd changed his mind.

In hindsight, she hadn't really wanted to marry Garry with

two Rs, which was how he introduced himself to everyone. She'd just wanted something to change between them. They had stagnated for far too long. She'd kind of thought a marriage proposal would be the make or break of them. And in reality she wouldn't have cared too much if he'd said no, she just wished he'd done that before she had announced the news on Facebook and told all her friends and family. The texts and Facebook posts reporting the change in her status the next day were more than slightly awkward.

Although she and Garry with two Rs had parted fairly amicably, her friends and the people in her town couldn't seem to let it go. The looks of pity, the sniggers; she'd had enough.

She needed a fresh start and Happiness was just the place to make it happen. The illustrated poster on the advert had showed glittering seas and the little whitewashed Cornish village tumbling down the hillside. It had looked tranquil and inviting.

Brightly coloured flowers danced and bobbed on the roadside as she passed, the warmth of the sun seeped into the car like a cosy blanket and up ahead she could spot the sea sparkling like a turquoise-sequinned carpet spread out beneath her.

It filled her with hope.

The opportunity to move to Happiness had seemed too good to be true. The privately owned village lay nestled in the grounds of a castle and, in an attempt to fill some of the empty houses, the new owners had offered free accommodation for a year to anyone who could give something back to the village,

He had a nice smile. Although Garry with two Rs had a nice smile and look where that had landed her.

'Come on, hop on, I'll take you down to your cottage,' Andrew said.

'What about all my stuff?'

'I'll give you a hand with all that after, I'm sure you're dying to see your new home. I promise, it's nothing like this.'

Willow eyed the back of the quad bike dubiously and then climbed on.

'You might want to hold onto something, it gets a bit bumpy in parts,' Andrew said. 'Wouldn't want to lose you on the way.'

There was nowhere to hold onto except Andrew himself and from the smile on his face, he knew that.

'I normally insist on dinner before wrapping my arms around a man.'

'Well if you insist, I'll let you take me out for dinner later,' Andrew said.

She smiled. 'Any weird spellings to your name that I should know about?'

'Only the silent K in the middle,' Andrew said.

She laughed and wrapped her arms around him. Maybe life in the village of Happiness wouldn't be so bad after all.

chapter 2

They bumped down the little cobbled road, passing shops and houses that appeared not to have been lived in or used for years. A couple of the shops looked like they might be open during working hours but at the moment all the doors were closed and the lights were off.

'How many people live here?' Willow asked.

'Forty-seven in the village, well forty-eight now you've arrived. That doesn't include the housekeeper up at the castle or Kitty and Ken.'

'What are they like?'

'Lovely, really wonderful people. You'll like them,' Andrew said, loyally.

She would have to pop in and introduce herself properly.

'And how many houses are in the village?'

'Including the four where you parked your car, one hundred and twelve. Seventy-five of them are empty.'

That was a bit depressing.

'How many of the shops are in use?'

'Four at the moment, five when you open up yours.'

That really was a sad state of affairs. It wasn't the thriving village that she'd expected.

'That's the only pub in the village,' Andrew pointed at a tall stone building with a battered old sign swinging gently outside: *The Welcome Home.*

They took a right at a little fork off the main road and travelled down a tiny track lined with overhanging trees. There were a few more houses down here.

'That's my house,' Andrew pointed to a pale blue little cottage, hidden under a mountain of thatch. It was tidy and well maintained and the garden was blooming with flowers. 'Feel free to pop in at any time and if you have any problems, you know where to call.'

They passed a few other houses and then the trees fell away and Willow was treated to a glorious view of the sea. Andrew pulled to a stop outside a bright yellow house.

'This is Sunrise Cottage,' Andrew gestured grandly.

Although it was very small, it at least looked like it wasn't going to fall down any time soon, which Willow supposed was a bonus, and it had an amazing view. Her view from the front of the house she had shared with Garry had a view of the houses on the opposite side of the street and a graveyard from the back. It hadn't exactly been inspiring.

She climbed off the bike and Andrew rushed forward to open the little gate, which almost fell off in his hand as he did.

'I'll fix that,' Andrew muttered, as he tried to shove it back onto its hinges and failed.

The lawn had been recently mowed and there were a few flowers trying to bloom in the overgrown borders; there was potential here. And the newly painted bench, angled to take in the view, was a lovely touch.

'The door is open,' Andrew said.

Willow pushed it, feeling the tackiness of freshly painted wood. So tacky in fact, her hand actually stuck to the wood. She peeled it off, leaving a lovely handmark on the front door.

'Ah sorry, I thought that would be dry by now. Don't worry, I'll paint over the handprint.'

She walked in and was faced with a tiny lounge with a bright red two-seater sofa, a tiny coffee table and an old cube-shaped TV in one corner. There was also a little log burner. She could see the kitchen through an archway. There was a slightly tatty feel to the place, but it had obviously been cleaned and patched up and painted recently. Someone, probably Andrew, had tried to make it feel like a home. There was even a vase of freshly picked flowers above the fireplace.

She looked at him and he was watching her hopefully.

'It's lovely,' Willow said, truthfully.

'I'm glad you like it. Now the shower has just been grouted so I'm afraid you can't use it until tomorrow night to be on the safe side, but you're welcome to pop up and use mine if you want one before then.'

'You're inviting me to use your shower, that's very forward,' Willow teased.

He smirked. 'It's not like I'm offering to scrub your back for you. I'll be downstairs, with my eyes closed for good measure.'

Willow giggled at the thought of him sitting on his sofa with his eyes firmly closed just in case.

'Well that's very kind of you.'

He shrugged. 'Now, I wouldn't recommend bringing your car down here, the lane is too rocky for that and probably too narrow. So if you give me your keys, I'll hook the trailer up to the back of the quad bike, load your stuff into that and bring it down here myself. Why don't you go out for a walk, get to know the place, and by the time you get back, all your stuff will be here. I'll park your car in the car park behind the castle and leave your keys here too.'

'Wow, that is good service. Let me give you a hand loading the trailer, there's quite a lot of stuff.'

'There's no need. As many of the elderly folk say, I'm a big strong lad, I can cope with a few bags. Please, go and explore, meet the locals.'

'OK, if you're sure.' Willow couldn't deny that she wanted to see her new home.

'You can go back to the village the way we just came. Or if you follow the coastal path to the left along the cliff path, you'll come to some steps that will take you down to the beach. You can go left at the top of the steps and the path will take you to the bottom of the main high street. Keep following that and you'll come to the pub again. The village is kind of laid out in a big triangle so it's not too hard to find your way around.'

'Thank you,' she said, handing him her car keys.

He smiled and ducked back out the door. He really was rather huge. She watched him walk down the path, shaking his head at the gate as he passed through it, and then he climbed on the quad bike and roared away, giving her a wave as he disappeared up the lane.

She stepped outside and pulled the door closed behind her. She hadn't seen a key but she supposed Andrew must have that. As there was nothing of hers in the house and she was really in the back end of nowhere, she wasn't too bothered. She walked out of the gate and took the coastal path that wound its way past the cottage and along the cliff tops.

The view from up here was utterly spectacular, the sea a gorgeous turquoise green glittering with gold-crested waves. She could see the cliff tops and meadows that hugged the coast stretching out for miles ahead of her and, other than the rooftops of the houses from the village of Happiness, she couldn't spot a single sign of life as far as the eye could see.

The idea of solitude appealed to her but the isolation of Happiness meant it was just a bit too quiet. At least in St Octavia, she would pass people on the streets she had never seen before, she could walk into a shop without everyone knowing her name. She got the sense that here, in the village of Happiness, if she so much as sneezed the whole village would know about it.

Her phone rang in her pocket and she smiled when she saw it was her best friend Ruby. She answered it.

'Hey Rubes, how's it going?' Willow said as she walked

along the little cliff path.

'Shouldn't I be asking you that question?' Ruby laughed.

'Well I've arrived in the village of Happiness.'

'And is it happy? Are there little lambs gambolling everywhere, children dancing round the maypole, flowers blooming from every surface?'

'Not quite,' Willow said. 'It looks pretty dead, some of the houses don't even look habitable.'

'Ah Willow. You know that famous expression?'

'Only fools rush in?'

'No, you're not a fool, you're an optimist. Which is a lovely thing to be. I was going to say, "Look before you leap." Maybe you should have checked this place out before you decided to move there.'

Willow sighed; she knew Ruby was right. She was definitely a fool.

'It's only for a year,' Willow said, trying to defend her decision. 'I have to start paying rent to the owners of the village after a year. I'm not staying if I hate it, but at least I can save some money while I'm here so I can buy or rent somewhere if I come back. But I think I need this. I don't think it was just mine and Garry's relationship that had stagnated, I had too. I want adventure and change and, while I've only met one living person so far and the village looks half in ruin, maybe Happiness is the place to find it. I've always wanted to live near the sea and now my house is right on the edge of the cliff. The view is startling.'

'Always the optimist,' Ruby said, fondly. 'You know you

didn't need to run away just because of what happened with Garry.'

'I'm totally fine with what happened with Garry,' Willow said, with exasperation. 'We were never meant to be together. What I'm not fine with is the constant comments, giggles and looks of pity. I bought a cake from Linda's cake shop the other day and she asked if I was drowning my sorrows. It's been six months. Let them talk about something else for a while, maybe they will have forgotten all about it by the time I get back.'

'OK, OK,' Ruby sighed. 'I hate to say you probably made the right decision because I'm missing you already, but I think this could be good for you.'

'You can visit anytime,' Willow said as she approached the steps to the beach.

'I may hold you to that.'

Willow smiled as she imagined Ruby with her brightly coloured clothes. She would be just what Happiness needed to brighten the place up.

'You'd be very welcome.'

'Are there any hot men there?'

Willow thought about Andrew. He was good-looking and had those huge shoulders she liked in a man. He had wonderful Mediterranean-blue eyes, which seemed to sparkle with permanent amusement. He made her laugh too. She shook her head with a smile.

'Not for me, I think I need some time to find happiness on my own for a while, not fall into bed with a handsome stranger with a nice smile.'

'Ah, so there is someone?'

Willow laughed. Ruby wouldn't let it go if she thought there was even the remotest chance of romance in the air.

'Ruby, you're breaking up.'

'Don't you hang up on me.'

'The reception is really bad, I'll call you later,' Willow said, making some crackly noises with her throat for good measure and then she disconnected the call as Ruby gave another squawk of protest.

She slipped her phone into her back pocket and looked out over the view for a moment. The tide was out, leaving a long horseshoe-shaped beach at the bottom of the steps. Steps that seemed to go on and on down the side of the cliff. The beach was completely deserted even though it was a warm sunny day. Clearly none of the residents of the village fancied a long trip down the steps either or the journey back up. Maybe she'd leave that bit of exploring for another day.

She turned up the path and headed back towards the village. She passed a few houses that were no more than crumbly stone walls, probably hundreds of years old. She hoped the rest of the village fared better than this. It didn't take her long before she reached the bottom of the main high street where there were little houses either side of the cobbled road. Some of them were boarded up but, she noticed as she made her way further up the high street, even the ones that seemed lived in looked worse for wear with peeling paint, tiles missing from the roofs and broken fences.

She just felt so disappointed. Happiness was supposed to

solve all her problems. She was going to start a new life here, and now that new life was looking bleak and dismal. She had been completely misled by the beautiful painting and she couldn't help feeling a little angry about that. But it was just an advert, of course it was going to try to show Happiness in its best light. A crumbly, broken old castle and a village in ruins was hardly going to make anyone want to come. And really, she was more angry at herself. She was an idiot. How could she not have checked this place out first? How could she let herself get so easily swayed by an advert? Could she really stay here and build a new life for herself amongst the tattered ruins? But then what was the alternative? There was no backing out now. She could hardly go back to St Octavia with her tail between her legs. The gossips would have lots to say about that.

She carried on up the high street and curtains twitched as she walked past. She gave the occupants a cheery wave. But other than that she didn't see another sign of life anywhere, the street was deserted. It was only half past six, was everyone really tucked up in their beds already?

She passed a row of shops that looked as though many years had passed since they had sold anything. One shop had an abandoned teddy in the window which looked sad and lonely as it stared out through the dusty glass.

She spotted the post office, the only splash of colour in what was otherwise an almost entirely grey affair. The front door was painted a bright red as was the sign above the shop window, the words *Post Office* painted in gold, written in a rather ornate handwriting. Someone clearly took pride in their place of work. In fact the three other shops that were clearly in use were all clean at least, their products ranging from cheese to paintings displayed cheerfully in the windows, even if the paint was peeling on the outside. There was hope here – not much, but some.

She decided to go to the pub, if it was still open. She was hungry and hopefully they might be serving food so she wouldn't have to cook. If she was lucky she might even find someone to talk to in this little ghost town.

chapter 3

She pushed open the door and was met with the kind of quiet you find in a library, so much so that for a moment she thought the pub might be closed. But there were people inside, a scattering of customers, maybe no more than ten, most of them sitting by themselves, a few talking quietly in small groups.

Ah, finally there was life here, after all. Albeit very quiet life.

Although what little conversation there was quickly died off to silence as everyone spotted her and gawped at her like a rare exhibit in a museum. She stood there awkwardly for a moment taking in her neighbours. Almost every one of them looked like they were over the age of ninety.

'What can I get you, love?' came a voice from the bar and Willow looked over at the barmaid who was at least in her forties. She was wearing a bright red polka-dot dress that matched the shade of her hair completely.

Willow cleared her throat and walked up to the bar with a confidence she didn't feel as slowly quiet conversations resumed around her.

'Don't mind these guys,' the lady said. 'They're just curious and all completely harmless. I'm Tabitha and my husband Connor is around somewhere. We're newcomers too, although we've been here about a month now.'

'I'm Willow. How are you finding it here?'

Tabitha let out a big breath. 'Well, it's very peaceful and quiet, everyone keeps themselves to themselves.'

Willow smiled at Tabitha's attempt to put a positive spin on it. 'Can't be good for business.'

'We do OK, mostly because Connor is a demon in the kitchen and some of the residents prefer to come in here for their lunch or dinner than cook for themselves. But we're not exactly the social hub we hoped we would be.'

'I know. The place feels so tired. I just expected Happiness to be a bit more… happy,' Willow said.

'So what will you be doing here?' Tabitha asked, handing Willow a menu.

'I'm having one of the shops, I'm a candlemaker.'

'Ah that sounds nice,' Tabitha said, though she didn't seem totally convinced. Willow wasn't convinced either. People loved her candles, the scents and different shapes and sculptures she made from the wax, but it certainly wasn't going to bring anything great to the village.

Willow glanced down at the menu.

'I can recommend the curry,' Tabitha said.

'Curry it is,' Willow said. 'And a half of cider.'

Tabitha poured her drink and Willow paid and went and sat in the window so she could look out on the street.

No sooner had she sat down than she was joined by a lady of about seventy years old who plonked herself down on the seat opposite Willow. Maybe Willow's earlier assumption that everyone was over ninety had been a bit harsh.

'I'm Dorothy.' The lady stuck her hand out, her eyes shining with happiness. 'I'm the village's resident artist, I own the painting studio out on the high street.'

'Willow,' she said, shaking Dorothy's hand.

'Did I hear you say you were a baker?' Dorothy said, excitedly.

'No, sorry, I'm a candlemaker.'

She watched Dorothy visibly deflate. 'What good is that to the village?'

'I'm sorry,' Willow said, awkwardly.

'We used to have a wonderful baker here when I was a little girl. His name was Sam and he would have the most delicious cream cakes in the window, freshly baked every day. He would only have the best cakes on display and, if any of them got broken, he would take them off display and give them to the kids to take home at the end of the day. There used to be quite the queue of children outside his shop at five o'clock each night. Sometimes I think he used to break some of the cakes deliberately, just so he could give them to us at the end of the day. He made the most delicious apple cake too, great big slabs of it. We would have it every Sunday in our house throughout the summer and autumn.'

'You've lived here your whole life?' Willow asked, keen to distract Dorothy from the shortcomings of her being a candlemaker.

'Yes, born and raised.'

'What was it like here when you were growing up?'

'Oh, it was thriving. Neighbours would walk in and out of each other's houses, borrowing sugar or vegetables or just stopping for a chat. The children would play in the streets. Everyone helped each other out. We used to have dancing here in the pub or up at the castle. It was a wonderful place to live.'

'What happened?'

'The old lord of the castle, Rupert, was a wonderful man, as was his father before him. Rupert looked after everyone in the village and was very much part of the community. When he died, his grandson took over the castle and he was everything his grandfather was not. He was rude, arrogant, and had no time for the villagers. He partied away his inheritance, squandered it all on fast cars and alcohol until he was completely bankrupt. In a desperate attempt to get more money he tripled the cost of the rent of the houses and shops. Most of the people in the village couldn't afford to pay those kinds of prices and, within a few months, over three-quarters of the village had packed up and left.'

'That's so sad,' Willow said.

'The grandson sold the castle on then but we never saw the person that owned it after that, I'm not sure if he even came here. The place fell into ruin and more people left. We had some new people come, like Roger and his sister Liz from the cheese shop,' Dorothy nodded to an older couple sitting quietly in the corner. Roger had a splendid red flowery cravat knotted neatly at his neck. Liz had gold-rimmed spectacles that were balanced precariously on the very end of her nose and was wearing a blue fluffy cardigan despite the heat of the day.

'But most of the newcomers didn't stay long,' Dorothy went on. 'The castle and village passed through several hands over the last few years until Kitty and Ken bought it. They're trying to build the village back up again but I think they've bitten off more than they can chew.'

Willow sighed. The village needed people to make it thrive again, young families to breathe life into the shops and houses, but when most people came and saw the state of the place they wouldn't be stopping even if the accommodation was free.

The atmosphere, at least in the pub, was one of defeat. The villagers didn't care any more and she didn't know what she could do to change that.

A man who she presumed was Connor came over with her food and she picked up her knife and fork hungrily.

Just then the door was pushed open and Andrew walked in. He had changed into jeans and a clean white shirt that was rolled up at the elbows, revealing strong tanned arms. The sleeves around the shoulders were taut around muscles she hadn't really spotted before. His curly hair was a little damp at the ends, but it was a bit more tamed now it wasn't sticking out at all angles from underneath his baseball cap. She wondered idly what it would feel like if she were to stroke her fingers through it. He had those wonderful crinkles around the sides of his eyes when he smiled, clearly showing that he smiled a lot. She liked that.

Immediately, Roger stood up and came over to talk to him, obviously bemoaning some problem or other, pointing and gesticulating as Andrew listened intently. He gave the impression of taking Roger's complaints seriously and that he had all the time in the world to listen to him, despite it being already way past normal working hours. Clearly, whatever Andrew said made Roger visibly relax. Eventually, after Andrew had taken the time to reassure him, Roger went and sat back down with his sister. But Andrew had only taken two more steps to the bar before a lady approached him. But again Andrew didn't look annoyed, he was nodding thoughtfully as he listened patiently. Willow found herself smiling; it was clear he genuinely cared about the villagers.

'He's easy on the eye, isn't he?' Dorothy said.

Willow realised she had been blatantly staring at Andrew ever since he'd walked into the pub and Dorothy had noticed that. Willow's food had been forgotten.

'Oh no, I was just watching how much in demand he is. He's not… I'm not looking for a relationship right now.'

'You could do a lot worse than Andrew Harrington.'

'I'm sure he's lovely.' She had a feeling that was an understatement. 'But I'm quite enjoying being single at the moment.'

'Hmm.' Dorothy was clearly unconvinced.

Finally Andrew got served and Willow forced her attention away from him to focus on her food. The last thing she needed was the villagers to get the wrong idea and try to matchmake between them.

She looked up to see him striding towards her, a big smile on his face.

'How are you finding the village so far?' Andrew said, sliding into the booth opposite her, next to Dorothy.

'It's lovely,' Willow said automatically and then berated herself. She wanted to moan to Andrew about what a state it was and how she had been misled. But none of it was Andrew's fault and it seemed he had enough problems to deal with without listening to her complaints. Andrew smirked though, because it was quite obvious that the village wasn't lovely. Dorothy grunted; even she clearly thought otherwise. 'It will be lovely once it's finished,' Willow said carefully.

Andrew was staring at her intently, a small smile on his face. He really did have the most amazing blue eyes. She focussed on her food again and looked up to find he was still studying her. She glanced over at Dorothy who gave her a theatrical wink.

'I'll be up and out early tomorrow so if you want to come for a shower and I'm not there, just let yourself in and help yourself,' Andrew said. 'My door is always open and not just in the metaphorical sense.'

'Oooh,' Dorothy chuckled. 'You going to scrub her back for her?'

'You'd love that, wouldn't you, you saucy little minx,' Andrew laughed, nudging her. 'Dorothy here, and quite a few women in the village actually, have been trying to set me up for months with their daughters and granddaughters and friends' daughters. They all think I need a nice woman to look after me, when I'm more than happy on my own.'

'Oh come on, Willy's lovely,' Dorothy gestured towards her like she was showing off a prize cow.

Andrew smirked at Dorothy getting her name wrong.

'*Willow* is very lovely, but we're not going to get together just because we're the only two people in the village below the age of forty,' he said, gently. 'And I'm way too busy with the renovations of the village and getting ready for the open day to be getting involved with someone anyway. So you can stop your meddling.'

Dorothy held her hands up innocently as if she wouldn't dream of doing so. Willow smiled slightly at the not-so-subtle warning to her too. Andrew was simply sitting here chatting to her to be friendly and she wasn't to get any ideas that it was something else. She had received that message loud and clear. Well, that suited her just fine.

'What's the open day?" Willow asked, trying to change the subject.

'There's an open day in eighteen days, we've put invites out with all the local estate agents and renting agencies. We're hoping that loads of people will come and be encouraged to apply for one of the houses. So we're trying to get all the houses ready in time for that.'

'That's a big job,' Willow said, thinking of all the houses she had seen so far that looked like they had seen better days.

'It is,' Andrew said, frowning. 'Anyway, it's pub quiz night, want to make a team?'

'Oh, don't you have other friends here that you normally team up with? Don't feel you have to look after me.'

'I don't, and no, I just team up with whoever wants me.'

'Everyone wants Andrew to be on their team.' Dorothy rolled her eyes with amusement. 'The boy knows everything.'

'Is that right?' Willow laughed.

'I have a head full of completely useless facts. Are you in, Dorothy?'

'Of course, it'd be nice to win for a change.'

Tabitha came round with quiz sheets as Willow finished off her dinner. She looked around the pub as people shifted around to make up teams. One team seemed to be Liz, Roger and another man who had pulled out a huge magnifying glass to read the quiz sheet. There were two ladies on another team; one seemed to be having a little nap. No wonder Andrew always won if this was the competition.

'Shouldn't we wait for more people to arrive?' Willow said.

Andrew shrugged. 'We don't get a big turnout. Most of the villagers prefer their own company. So we need a team name, how about… Young at Heart?' He gave Dorothy a playful nudge and she giggled like a schoolgirl.

Willow thought about that name and what Andrew had said a few moments before. She looked around at the small scattering of villagers again. 'Are we really the youngest in the village?'

'Yes, by a mile,' Andrew said.

'No children?'

He shook his head.

There was something sad about that too. The village needed children and young families to give it some energy and oomph. But what could they do to encourage families to live here?

There was no time to think about that as Connor suddenly switched on the microphone and tapped it a few times to get everyone's attention. 'OK, are we all ready for round one, question one?'

There were a few murmurs of assent but Connor ploughed on regardless of whether people were ready or not.

'Question one, who is the Prime Minister of New Zealand?'

'What's her name? Oh it's Jacinda, Jacinda something,' Willow said, desperately trying to find the name in the depths of her memory.

'Jacinda Ardern,' Andrew supplied helpfully.

'That's it.' Willow quickly wrote it down.

'Question two, continuing on with the head of countries theme, who is the King of Belgium?'

'That's King Philippe,' Andrew muttered.

'Are you sure?' Willow asked, pen poised over the page. He nodded and she quickly wrote it down.

'Question three, who is the Prime Minister of Canada?'

Connor went on.

'Oh, I know this one,' Willow said. 'Justin Trudeau.'

'Are *you* sure?' Andrew said, a smile playing on his lips and she knew he was teasing her.

'OK smart-arse, I'm sorry for doubting you over the King of Belgium question.'

'You're forgiven.'

'That Justin Trudeau is a hot bit of stuff, isn't he?' Dorothy said. 'Clever too, he knows stuff about quantum technology that would blow your mind. I always think intelligence is a highly attractive attribute, don't you?'

Dorothy gave Willow a look and then gave a not-so-subtle nod towards Andrew, as if Willow would find him attractive simply because he'd answered two questions, well one and a half.

Willow turned her attention back to Andrew. He was an attractive man, there was no denying that, but she wasn't going to leap into a relationship with someone just because they had a lovely smile, strong arms and incredible eyes. And she meant what she'd said to Dorothy and Ruby: she wanted time to just find herself again and to find what made her happy.

chapter 4

Willow stepped outside the pub and stared up at the starlit sky. It had been a good night during which she'd gotten to know Andrew and Dorothy a bit better. Even Roger and Liz had come over to say hello during the break.

As predicted, Andrew had known the answer to almost every question, even some of the most bizarre ones. Willow had known the answer to many of them but she had nowhere near the general knowledge that Andrew had. And Dorothy had been right, the fact that he was so smart was an attractive feature. He had a playful sense of humour too, which she really liked.

And despite his earlier protests, she had a feeling he quite liked her as well. The way he had stared at her as they had talked over the last few hours had been almost a bit… intense. He hadn't taken his eyes off her all night except to write down some answers on the sheet. There had also been quite a number of times when he'd glanced down at her mouth as she talked instead of into her eyes and she'd wondered if he was thinking about kissing her, which seemed a bit forward considering they'd only just met a few hours before. She wasn't entirely sure she wanted that. He seemed nice, sweet, and yes there were certain things she found very attractive, they got on well too, but she really wasn't looking for a relationship right now, with anyone.

Halfway through the last round of questions, an elderly man who Andrew had called Joseph had arrived in the pub, clearly in a bit of a state, and hurried over to Andrew to tell him of a leaky ceiling. It had been close to ten o'clock, Andrew had just bought himself another pint and still he'd rushed off to help poor Joseph as if he was a doctor attending a medical emergency. There had been no sign of frustration or annoyance from Andrew that his evening had been disturbed and she liked that too. He was clearly a very patient man.

She turned down the little lane heading back towards her cottage. Within a few minutes, the lights of the main part of the village fell away and she found herself walking in almost complete darkness, the only illumination coming from the moon. It picked out the houses, silhouetted in the darkness, a few of them with warm golden light pouring from the windows.

The trees swallowed her, the glow from the moon going out completely, and she fumbled in her pocket for her mobile phone, switched on the flashlight app and shone it around so she could find her way.

Dorothy had told her that there were fifteen people, including herself, who had grown up in the village and had spent their entire lives there. The other thirty-odd people had all moved there later on in their lives, but most of the villagers had been there while Rupert had been the lord of the castle, before it had all gone wrong. But they had stayed there regardless, this was their home. Although at some point along the way, they had stopped caring. The owners of the village hadn't cared for them or the houses and so the villagers hadn't cared either. They had withdrawn from the community way of life. Willow wanted to be able to give them back the village they fell in love with but she couldn't do that alone. The villagers had to start caring again and she wasn't sure what she could do to make that happen.

She cleared the trees and could see her little cottage on the cliff tops, the twinkly black sea behind it, seemingly stretching out for miles. Little solar stars and dragonflies dotted the bushes and trees around her house glowing gold in the darkness. It looked magical. This was her home now too, she wasn't going to leave because it hadn't turned out how she'd imagined in her rose-tinted view of the world. If she wanted it to be rose-tinted, then she was going to have to make it that way.

Willow woke the next morning to sunshine sparkling on her face. She got out of bed and went to the window. The sea stretched out in front of her before disappearing into an early morning pinky haze on the horizon. The water was an inky blue today, crested with gold. She could stare at that view forever.

She quickly brushed her teeth, got dressed and then gathered her shampoo and toiletries together so she could go and have a shower at Andrew's house. She felt like she had a lot to do today.

She walked up the track and waved cheerily to Joseph. He was tending to his garden, bending over to prune the bushes, and as he straightened up to wave, he stretched his back out to ease the discomfort from all the bending.

She passed another house and stopped, noticing that it had been painted all the way round the outside but obviously only as far as whoever lived there could reach. There was easily three foot of wall above the new paint that hadn't been painted, leaving the house looking like it was stripy. The top part of the new paint wasn't even in a straight line, it was wobbly and there were different levels to it. Willow almost wanted to laugh except it was just a little sad that someone had tried to paint their home but made such a bad job of it.

She carried on to Andrew's house and knocked on the door. There was no answer. She waited a moment or two then knocked again. Still no answer. She opened the door and called out to him but the house seemed to be utterly silent.

She hesitated for a moment, but he had said that if he wasn't there she was welcome to let herself in and use his shower. She walked upstairs to where there were only two doors. One was obviously the bedroom as she could see the bed, so the other closed door must be the bathroom.

She went into the bedroom and undressed, leaving her clothes on the bed. The bedroom was neat and tidy and smelt of his wonderful scent. There was a large photo of the aurora borealis on the wall over a snowy mountain range. It looked beautiful.

There was another photo in a frame on top of a chest of drawers and she moved to pick it up. It was of Andrew and a small girl of about five who had her face painted like a butterfly. They were both laughing with big grins on their faces.

She put the frame down just as there was a movement near the door. She looked up to see Andrew stark naked staring at her in shock. She registered a stunning phoenix tattoo in yellow, orange and red with hints of blue and purple flying over his chest and shoulder. It looked magnificent. She also noticed how strong his arms were and how broad his chest was. Her eyes drifted lower before she remembered they were both standing there naked. She yelped and turned away, clamping her hands over her eyes for good measure before realising she was now giving him a fabulous view of her arse. She dived onto the floor behind the bed.

'I'm so sorry,' Willow said, but there was no answer.

She heard him moving around and she peeked up over the bed. She watched him, still naked, pick up two small flesh-coloured bullet-shaped objects from the top of the bedside drawers. He saw her watching and scowled so she quickly ducked back down below the height of the bed. Her cheeks were burning with embarrassment. A few moments later she felt him lean over the bed.

'Here, put this on.'

She looked up and saw that he had placed a hoody on the bed for her to wear. She quickly slipped it on and peered over the bed again to check that he was now suitably attired. He was wearing a pair of knee-length cargo shorts although his fabulous chest and tattoo were still on display.

He didn't look happy at all.

'I'm so sorry, I did knock twice and I called out to you. Did you not hear me?' Willow said as she stood up, the hoody coming down to almost her knees.

'I was in the shower,' he muttered. 'I wasn't expecting you so early.'

'I thought you were out. I'm really sorry.'

He still seemed pissed off, which hardly seemed fair. 'You did say to just come in and help myself if you were out.'

'I know.'

She frowned. They had chatted for hours the night before, but now he could barely look at her. Why was he being all weird?

She scooped up her clothes and grabbed her soap bag. 'I think I'll leave the shower.'

She walked out of the room and down the stairs. She'd got as far as the front door when she heard Andrew running after her.

'Wait, just wait a moment,' he said, slamming the door

shut just as she opened it.

She turned round to face him and he was right there in her space as he leaned against the door.

He stepped back and pushed his hair from his face. It was wet and curly and stuck out at all angles but it just made him look cute and dishevelled.

He sighed. 'I didn't hear you knock or call out because… I didn't have my hearing aids in.'

She stared at him. She hadn't been expecting that. 'You're deaf?'

'Yes, not completely. I can hear fairly well with my hearing aids in but without them I'm pretty much next to useless.'

'You're not useless,' Willow said, defensively.

'No, you're right. That's the wrong word. My therapist would crucify me if she heard me say that.'

'Your therapist?'

He stared at her for a moment as if deciding whether to talk to her about this.

'Yes, I had a therapist when I was a kid just because I was deaf. Or maybe she was some kind of motivational life coach, I don't know. She was supposed to convince me that I was just like everyone else, that I could do anything that all the other children could do. The ironic thing was I'd always thought I was just like everyone else, until I wasn't allowed to play outside with my friends every Saturday because I had to sit in my therapy sessions and listen to how my *condition* shouldn't hold me back. What kind of weird twisted logic was that?'

'It doesn't seem like the best way to convince you,' Willow said.

'My mum knew that there was a very good chance I would be deaf as her sister was, so she had me tested at a very early age and I had hearing aids fitted even before I could talk. I think having it diagnosed so early helped my speech to develop almost at the same rate as other children my age.'

He chewed on his fingernail for a moment and Willow realised that he wasn't exactly comfortable talking about this.

'You don't like people to know,' she said.

He shook his head. 'This *special needs* label followed me throughout all my education no matter what, so when I left school I decided I wouldn't tell anyone I was deaf. I can hear just fine with my hearing aids in and they are very discreet so there was never any need for anyone to know. Of course people find out and when they do they speak louder, enunciate their words, they try to mouth what they are saying more clearly so I can lip-read, when in fact that always makes it harder. Inevitably a lot of the people that find out always treat me like I'm stupid and I hate that.'

'You are far from stupid, you knew so much in that pub quiz.'

'I read a lot. You don't need to be able to hear to enjoy a book. I can take as much time as I need with a book and I don't need to be able to concentrate to keep up like I do with a conversation.'

'Books don't judge you.'

He smiled slightly. 'No. Look, I'm sorry. I've been here

three months and no one knows and I was annoyed that you've not been here twenty-four hours and you've found out already.'

'I didn't find out, you told me.'

'You saw me pick up my hearing aids, you shouted out for me and I didn't hear you – you would have figured it out. Besides, I wanted to tell you because I was annoyed at the situation, not at you. This isn't your fault. I'm sorry if I was an arse up there.'

'You weren't.'

'No?'

'Well, maybe a little.'

He smiled slightly.

'Look, I'm not going to tell anyone. Why should anyone be defined by the things we can't do? Your secret stays here,' Willow said.

'Thank you. I really appreciate that.'

She glanced down at the phoenix tattoo again and suddenly it made sense. He'd felt like he had to fight to prove he was good enough. The phoenix had risen from the ashes and Andrew must have felt that he'd done the same, that he'd fought to be something, to be accepted.

'I like this.' Willow gently touched the phoenix.

He stared at her and she watched his eyes cast down to her lips again.

A sudden realisation hit her, making her cheeks flame red. 'Oh god, you can read lips can't you?'

'Yes I can. I find myself studying people's lips when they

talk even though I can hear perfectly well with my hearing aids in.'

Willow laughed in embarrassment.

'What?'

'Oh nothing.'

'I've just told you my secret, I think you can share yours.'

Willow sighed. 'Last night you kept looking at my lips and I thought…'

He smiled. 'That I wanted to kiss you.'

'Yes.'

Andrew grinned and looked down for a moment. 'There might have been an element of that.'

Oh god. Her heart leapt as the chemistry sparked between them, until he took another step back away from her.

'Please, go and have a shower. I promise, I'll stay down here the whole time,' Andrew said.

'With your hands over your eyes?'

'Yes, that too. And I'll even make you breakfast to sweeten the deal. How does a bacon sandwich sound?'

'Now that sounds like a plan.'

chapter 5

Andrew had left Willow to finish off her breakfast with the excuse that he had work to do. It wasn't a lie, he had a list a mile long of things he needed to do to help turn the village around and a very short time to do it all. But mainly he'd left because Willow clearly wanted to talk some more about being deaf and he didn't want to go into that.

Willow was incredibly easy to talk to. He hadn't talked about his struggles with growing up deaf with anyone, preferring to leave that part of his life behind. He knew a lot of deaf people who would berate him, saying he shouldn't be ashamed of his hearing loss, and he wasn't, but he didn't exactly want to make a big deal of it either. It was a part of him, not who he was. He was someone who was deaf, not the deaf kid, which was how he'd always been labelled at school. To him, there was a big difference. But he'd known Willow less than twenty-four hours and already he'd found himself opening his heart to her, telling her about his childhood. And that bothered him a bit. While there was something lovely about being able to share that with someone, he had now closed that box back up. He didn't want her sympathy, didn't want her to think of him as different. He didn't want to give that vulnerable side of him to her, or to anyone.

But he liked that she had treated him exactly the same after she had found out he was deaf as she had before. She had chatted to him as normal over breakfast about the village, the different villagers and about Kitty and Ken. She had not made her voice louder or tried to mouth the words more clearly like a lot of people did.

He really liked Willow, there was something about her that made him feel warm inside and he hadn't felt like that in a very long time.

He had a feeling life was about to change in the little village of Happiness.

After Willow had left Andrew's, she wandered into the village to explore some more. She felt a bit happier about it all now. The village might be in a state of disrepair and over half the houses empty, the locals might prefer to keep themselves to themselves and her candlemaking skills might not be totally appreciated by the villagers, but waking up every morning to the incredible view she saw from her bedroom today was going to be hard to top. She mentally started ticking off all the positives. Having the beach right on her doorstep was something she had dreamed about all her life. She now lived in a beautiful part of the world with rolling hills and pretty meadows as far as the eye could see. The villagers she had met – Dorothy, Liz and Roger – seemed nice. And then there was Andrew. He seemed to deserve a tick box all of his own. He was… lovely and he made her smile a lot. And although she stood by not wanting to have a relationship right now, she did think they could become very good friends.

But she had decided that if she wanted the village of Happiness to change then she was going to have to be that change. And while she could hardly renovate a whole village, she knew there must be something she could do to help make the village shine.

She looked at the cluster of little shops, which were already open and selling their wares. What was going to be her candle shop was standing on a corner opposite the pub and she smiled to see that it was painted in the same bright yellow paint that Sunrise Cottage had been painted in. Obviously Andrew had bought a job lot of paint and decided to go with the theme.

She didn't really plan to go in there today, she was waiting for more of her stock to arrive. She had a few bits and pieces here but as she had fulfilled all of her online orders before she'd left, she wanted a few days to explore the village and get to know the place before she settled into work again.

She pushed open the door to the post office and stepped inside. Andrew had already told her that she could pick up a few groceries here. She had brought a few bags of food with her, and she had a big grocery order being delivered in the next few days, but she needed a couple of things to keep her going. She hadn't quite been expecting the huge and eclectic range of things to buy. There were buckets and spades, mops, irons, picture frames, cuddly toys, sandals, cooking utensils, pyjamas, envelopes in every size, indoor fountains, paddling pools, cushions, blankets, disposable barbeques, outdoor lights, dog leads, board games and several aisles of groceries, all jammed into a shop that appeared so tiny and unassuming from the front. Willow had no doubt that whatever she needed or wanted at any point in her life, it would be found here.

'Hello, can I help you?' came a voice from somewhere in the depths of the post office emporium.

Willow moved forward through the overcrowded shelves. 'Hello, I was just… looking for something for my lunch.'

She would save the other groceries she needed to get for another time. The whole place was a little overwhelming and she felt sure if she stayed too long then she might come out with a jacuzzi and pet husky named Blaze.

A small elderly lady appeared round the end of one of the aisles. She had big puffy candyfloss-pink hair that seemed to shimmer and shake as she walked.

'Ah, you must be Willow McKay. I'm Julia Dalton, the postmistress. I've been waiting for you.'

Willow smiled. She didn't realise she had an appointment.

'Let me show you how the postal service works here,'

Julia said, ushering her to the till. 'All the post for the village comes to me and I make a record of it here in this book, see. That way you can come in and, if I'm busy with customers, you can check the book to see if there is any post for you without having to queue up to ask me.'

Willow looked around the shop. There was not a single soul in there apart from her and Julia. It was hard to believe that Julia ever got busy in here or had even seen a queue.

'OK, that's good to know,' Willow said.

'When you collect any post, you'll have to sign to say you've collected it,' Julia went on, showing the signatures of all the villagers in her special book. 'I keep all the post locked in a cupboard out the back, so it's quite safe here if you can't get in to see me every day.'

Willow wondered if Julia was expecting her to come in every day. She never got that much post at home so she wasn't suddenly expecting an influx here. 'OK.'

'Now,' Julia clapped her hands together loudly. 'What can I help you with today?'

'Well just something for my lunch, perhaps a sandwich or the means to make one. Maybe a bit of fruit.'

'There's a bakery in the next town that delivers a small selection of sandwiches here every day. Let's see.,' Julia gestured for her to follow her to a small open fridge. 'We have egg and cress and umm… oh yes, another egg and cress.'

Willow resisted pulling a face. 'Oh, how about those sausage rolls, they look nice. And I'll take a few bananas and some grapes if you have them.'

'Of course we have bananas. We have lots of fruit. We even had a pomegranate in here the other day. Didn't sell though, I had to throw it away in the end. This way, dear.'

Julia bustled off and Willow grabbed a packet of sausage rolls and followed her.

The fruit display was a bit sorry-looking. There was certainly a wide range, but most of it looked a little past its best. Willow picked up a banana that wasn't too freckly and a packet of grapes at least two days past its sell-by date.

'I think that's everything for now,' Willow said, hoping Julia wouldn't try to persuade her to buy the wrinkly kiwi fruit or the strange orange fruit that most definitely wasn't an orange.

'Are you sure there's nothing else I can help you with?' Julia asked, hopefully.

'This is fine, thank you,' Willow said.

She followed Julia back to the till and she rang up her purchases.

'Well, do pop in again,' Julia said. 'If I don't have what you need, I can get it.'

Willow had no doubt of that. 'Thank you.'

She turned to leave and walked straight into Andrew, literally headbutting him in his hard chest.

'Hello,' he said, gently, steadying her with his hand on her bare shoulder.

'Hey,' she said. He had such a lovely smile. He hadn't taken his hand from her shoulder and something about that touch, the heat of his skin against hers, did something inside her that she hadn't felt in years.

'Just getting some lunch for later,' Willow said, gesturing unnecessarily to her sausage rolls.

'So I see.'

This seemed a bit too polite for two people who had seen each other naked about an hour before. She blushed at the glorious memory. He had an amazing body. Her eyes cast down and caught the edges of the phoenix tattoo peeking out from underneath his t-shirt sleeve. She wanted to see that again. She caught herself and looked back up at him. He was smiling as if he knew exactly what she was thinking. But he couldn't possibly know. He might be good at lip-reading but not mind-reading. She comforted herself with that thought, although the spark of amusement didn't fade from his eyes.

'Well, must dash, there's lots to do, nice seeing you again,' Willow said and hurried off, her cheeks burning. She was so silly. They had chatted just fine over breakfast, so why was she suddenly embarrassed about seeing him now? She knew why. Because her mind was going to all the places it shouldn't with those memories and that simple touch.

She moved off down the main high street until the houses that were homes gave way to the houses that were most definitely not. She could see that Andrew had started work on some of these but there was still so much to be done.

She passed an old shed-type building. The doors were open and inside were stacks of tins of paint amongst other things and she paused for a moment as an idea came to mind. Before she became a full-time candlemaker she used to buy old wooden shelves, chests, chairs and tables and give them a new lease of life, painting them pink or blue or sunshine yellow, some with flowers, butterflies, suns or stars, some with fish jumping out of the waves. She wasn't particularly skilled or artistic but the simplicity of her designs appealed to some people. She had stopped doing it after she had started going out with Garry. He always moaned that it took so much of her time and paid her so little, but the money had never been the reason why she did it. She just loved giving these old bits of furniture a second chance, to see what they could become with a little bit of love and care. Garry had insisted she focus on something that could actually pay the bills and she'd known he had a point. Initially it was a hobby instead of her main focus, but when her candlemaking business started to take off her hobby had soon stopped altogether because Garry didn't like their home cluttered with old bits of furniture. She did miss it though.

But maybe she could have a chance of doing that again here. Only not with furniture this time, but with the houses themselves. Maybe that was what the village needed. A little bit of love and a lick of paint could go a long way. Maybe that could be the thing she could give to the village, maybe she could help it shine again. Garry always said she was a fixer, a doer. If a bulb needed changing, a shelf needed fixing, a picture needed putting up, she would just get on and do it. She looked around the village and sighed. This was a bit bigger than a broken shelf or a chest of drawers that needed painting, but maybe she could help in some small way.

She stepped inside the shed and looked around at the tins of paint. It was mostly white paint but there were some colours there too. Andrew had started decorating large ceramic plant pots different colours – purples, pinks, greens. He had seen what she had seen, that the village needed a bit of colour to brighten the place up.

She could paint some flowers around the door of one of the houses, emerald-green leaves and curly stems with flamingo-pink roses. She could see it in her mind and she knew it would look great.

But would Andrew be annoyed with her for doing it? Should she go and find him and ask him if it was OK? Although seeing Andrew and imagining seeing him naked again was enough to veto that idea. If he hated it she would personally paint over it herself.

She grabbed a few pots of paint and some brushes and went back outside, excitement bubbling through her. She paused outside one of the houses that had already been painted white, although a quick look through the windows confirmed this particular house was a long way off being finished.

She popped open one of the pots of green paint, dipped a brush inside and painted a beautiful winding stem up the side of the door. She was surprised at the rush she got from that simple act. It had been too long since she had done something like this and she loved being able to do this again. She curled the stem over the top of the door and down the other side.

The green paint gleamed in the sunlight. She added some curvy leaves at different places around the door and then stood back to look at it. It looked better already. It made the house come to life and, once she added the pink flowers, it was going to look really rather special.

It was such a tiny thing when the village needed so much work, but at least she was doing something to help. She only hoped Andrew would love it.

chapter 6

Andrew walked down to the end of the village. He had spent most of the morning trying to fix Joseph's leak. He hadn't been able to find the cause of it the night before so had just turned off the water after filling up a few saucepans so Joseph could still have his cup of tea. And he had now spent the last few hours trying to find the problem and then fixing it. Honestly, it was time he simply didn't have. With the open day coming up in just under three weeks, he knew that even if he worked every hour of the day he wouldn't get all the houses finished on time, so he really didn't need setbacks like this. He loved the villagers and he wanted to do everything he could to help them, but he really needed some help and he had no idea how to approach Kitty and Ken to ask them.

Although there was one man who always seemed to have time on his hands and who might be willing to come and help him for a few days.

He pulled his phone out of his pocket and gave his brother a call.

'Andrew, how's it going?' Jacob said.

'All good here, the sun is shining, the beach is glorious. Why don't you come and stay for a few days?'

'Well, isn't that sweet, my little brother wants to spend time with me,' Jacob said, sarcastically.

He knew very well Andrew had an ulterior motive. He and Jacob weren't exactly close. Jacob was sarcastic, interfering, confident to the point of cocky and quite honestly a pain in the arse, but he was also protective, loyal and generous with his time. If Andrew told him he needed his help, Jacob would be there, no questions asked. Although he might bitch and moan about it, Andrew knew he didn't really mean any of it.

'And what would I be doing on this little holiday of mine?' Jacob said. 'Picnics on the beach perhaps?'

'Well if that floats your boat, sure. But I'm sure there's plenty of inspiration here for your next *masterpiece*,' Andrew said, sarcastically. Jacob was a scrap metal artist and a very good one. But Andrew would never tell him that. 'And maybe you can give me a hand with a tiny spot of painting.'

'Well that sounds like a wonderful way to spend my holiday,' Jacob deadpanned. 'But as luck would have it, I do have a few days spare to come and get my brush wet.'

'If that's a euphemism, you've got no chance.'

'What about that new woman, Willow is it? The one who came to live there without even coming to see it? That shouts "woman trying to escape" if ever I heard it. I could be the fortress in her storm. What's she like?'

Andrew tried to find the words to describe Willow McKay. 'She's… nice.'

That was a gross understatement. *Nice* didn't even come close to describing what she was like.

'Oh, is she hideous?'

'You're so shallow. There's more to someone than just their looks.'

'Ah she is.'

'She isn't actually, she's…' Andrew trailed off because he didn't need to give Jacob any encouragement where Willow was concerned. 'She's off limits.'

'Oooh little brother, are you staking a claim? Because I definitely need to come and check her out if you've got your eye on her.'

'No, it's not like that.' It most definitely was like that. 'I just think she can do better than you.'

'Well, that's probably true. I'll be there in a few days and I'll see for myself.'

Andrew sighed as his brother said his goodbyes and hung up.

He thought for a moment about what Jacob had said. He wondered if Willow was escaping from something. He thought about how she'd been before in the post office, she'd practically run away from him when she'd seen him. He wondered if she felt awkward around him now she knew he was deaf, but that didn't seem to make sense when she had chatted to him just fine over breakfast.

He stopped suddenly and backtracked a few steps to the house he'd just passed. He stared at the flowers growing up the walls around the door which certainly hadn't been there yesterday. But as he stepped closer he realised they had been painted on. Who the hell had done that?

He looked around and saw three more houses, all with the same flowers growing up the sides of the door, and then he spotted the culprit working on house number five, only this one had stars of different sizes.

He stared at Willow as she painted. He didn't know whether to be angry that she had done this without checking it was OK, delighted that she wanted to help or frustrated that, of all the ways she could help, painting little flowers was not going to be anywhere near his top ten. He supposed the flowers did look quite nice, they gave the houses a bit of colour, but he couldn't believe she had done this without asking him. He marched over to tell her that this wasn't appropriate.

As he approached she looked up at him and he faltered in his stride because she had the biggest grin on her face he had ever seen on anyone in his entire life. She looked like a child whose Christmases had all come at once and to be angry at her felt like he would be kicking a puppy.

'Oh, I'm so sorry. I was just going to do one house and then come and find you to see if you liked it and if you didn't I was going to paint over it. But then I enjoyed doing it so much that I thought I would just do one more and now I've done five. I'm sorry, I just got carried away. If you hate it, I'll paint over them all myself. Do you hate it? Please don't tell me you hate it,' she laughed, nervously.

She had such exuberance and enthusiasm for what she was doing. He felt his anger just fade away.

He cleared his throat and looked again at the flowers. It really did help the houses to stand out and maybe even detract from any other little faults.

'It looks lovely,' Andrew said.

'Really? Oh god, I'm so relieved. I thought you might hate it or hate me for doing it.'

'I don't think it's possible to hate you, Willow McKay,' he said, softly.

'My old boyfriend, Garry, used to hate me doing stuff like this,' Willow went on. 'I used to paint old bits of furniture in bright colours and little designs like this. He said it was a waste of my time.'

'How can anything be a waste of your time if it makes you this happy?'

Her ex-boyfriend sounded like an arse. Christ, he'd let her paint the whole goddamn village with flowers and stars if it meant it kept that huge smile on her face.

'I did love it,' Willow said, wistfully.

'You shouldn't let anyone stand in the way of your happiness,' Andrew said.

She stared at him. 'I think you're right. Is it really OK, you don't mind?'

'I don't mind,' Andrew said, and he really didn't. It wasn't her job to paint or fix things in the village so he could hardly expect her to pick up a roller and start painting. The fact that she wanted to help at all was actually wonderful. Many of the other villagers had no interest in contributing to village life. And it did look lovely. The white houses looked smart and uniform but this added a little bit of character. 'Feel free to paint as many houses as you want.'

'Can I? Well, that's exciting.'

Her eyes lit up at the prospect of painting the whole village and he smiled. He'd definitely done the right thing.

'I can get more paint for you if you wish. Just let me know.' He paused as he watched her paint another star. 'Why does this one have stars?'

'Oh, I found this,' Willow said, picking up a broken name plate that had obviously hung outside at some point: *Starlight Cottage*.

'Very appropriate. I can fix that.'

'I bet you can, but why don't you leave that to me. I'm sure you have lots of other things to do.'

He nodded. 'And on that note, I really must crack on.' He took a step away and then turned back. 'Can I ask you something?'

'Sure.'

'Why did you run away before, when we were in the post office?'

He watched her cheeks flush bright red. 'You really don't want to know.'

He pursed his lips. 'Yeah, I really do.'

'But then you'll think terrible things of me.'

'Well now, I'm intrigued.'

'I was remembering what you looked like naked,' Willow blurted out.

He stared at her and then burst out laughing. 'I love your honesty, Willow McKay.'

'I couldn't help it, I headbutted your hard chest and your hand was on my shoulder and suddenly my mind was going to all the places it shouldn't. And just to be clear, I know you're not looking for a relationship right now and there's no way I'm looking for one, but it doesn't stop my filthy mind from wandering every now and again. But now you think I'm a pervert.'

'Oh no, I wouldn't think that.'

'No?'

'OK, maybe a little bit.'

She laughed.

'I really had better get on. I'll be over here if you want to perv over me again.'

She laughed again. 'Stop it. There'll be no more perving.'

'Good to know.'

He smiled and walked over to the shed to collect his tools and some paint. She made him feel warm inside.

Willow was feeling deliriously happy right now. Painting was such a simple thing but it did bring her so much happiness. And although it was such a tiny piece in the grand scheme of things, she really felt like she was doing something to help the village. She wanted to talk more to Andrew about the village, the open day and everything that needed doing, but she got the sense he just wanted to get on with his work today. She had stopped for lunch but Andrew didn't. She had offered him one of her sausage rolls which he gladly took but he didn't come and join her as she sat on the grass outside the latest house she had painted. He just carried on with his work, painting, hammering, fixing. He was diligent, that was for sure.

She stood back to inspect the latest house she had finished. This one was called Dragonfly Cottage so she had painted some dragonflies amongst the flowers that were winding and curling their way around the door. She hadn't done dragonflies before, but they were relatively easy.

She looked round as a voice called out for Andrew. Dorothy was hurrying down the hill towards them.

'Andrew!' Dorothy called, waving her hands to attract his attention. 'Andrew.'

Willow glanced over at Andrew and saw his shoulders droop the tiniest bit as he climbed down the ladder to come and talk to Dorothy.

'Andrew, all the lights have just gone out in my shop. I turned the light on in the kitchen to make a cup of tea and all the other lights went out. I didn't want to bother you, but I can't paint in the dark now, can I?'

'No, of course not,' Andrew said. 'I'll come and have a

look for you. Did you happen to notice whether the other shops or houses still have lights?'

'All the rest of the shops seem fine, think it's just mine,' Dorothy said.

'Come on then,' Andrew said.

'Why don't I go?' Willow said, wiping her hands. 'And you can stay here and carry on with your work.'

Andrew looked at her dubiously.

'It's likely that the bulb has blown and it's tripped all the other lights. I can easily reset the switch on the fuse board and replace the bulb for her and if it's anything else then I can come and get you,' Willow said.

'OK, if you're sure,' Andrew said. 'Thank you.'

'No problem,' Willow said and turned to Dorothy. 'Let's have a look and after you can make me a nice cup of tea and show me all your wonderful paintings I've seen in your window.'

Dorothy blushed with pride as she took Willow's arm.

Willow looked over her shoulder to see Andrew watching them with a smile before he turned and went back to his work.

'I hate to disturb him,' Dorothy said as they walked back up the hill. 'He works so hard, always rushing from one job to the next. Everyone in the village thinks he's at their beck and call for every little thing. He never says no to anyone but he is stretching himself too thin. I try to do everything for myself but when the lights all went out, I didn't know what else to do.'

'It's OK. I'm sure Andrew would want you to come and get him, rather than standing in the dark worrying. I'm sure I can help you.'

'You're a good girl, Willy.'

Willow didn't have the heart to correct her. She walked with Dorothy back into the main part of the village. There was so much that needed doing, but a lick of paint could fix a lot of the village's problems. The shops especially could do with some bright colours on the signs above the doors. Maybe she could do them too. Or was she getting too carried away?

'Here we are, dear,' Dorothy said, gesturing to the painting shop as if Willow wouldn't be able to find it on her own.

Willow let herself inside and sure enough the place was in darkness apart from the light streaming in through the main window.

Luckily the fuse box was by the front door so she didn't have to hunt around for it. As she suspected, one of the switches was down and she flipped it back up again and all the lights came back on in the shop.

'Oh you are clever,' Dorothy said, clapping her hands together.

'Now, which light were you turning on when the lights went out?' Willow said, closing the fuse box door.

'The kitchen one,' Dorothy said, pointing to the little kitchenette out the back.

Willow followed her to the back of the shop. 'Do you

have a spare bulb?'

'Oh yes, I always keep some in the cupboard. I can change the bulb myself, I always do,' Dorothy said, getting a wobbly-looking stool from behind the door.

'Why don't I do that for you this time,' Willow said. 'And you can make us both a cup of tea.'

Dorothy set about making a pot of tea in the limited light from the shop and Willow quickly changed the bulb.

'There we go,' she said, climbing down from the stool and flicking the switch.

'Oh thank you Willy,' Dorothy said as light filled the kitchen.

'No problem. Mind if I have a look around?'

'You go ahead, dear.'

Willow wandered out into the main shop area and started looking at all the paintings. There were some portraits of various members of the village but mostly they were of landscapes, hills, meadows, fields of flowers, beaches, the sparkling sea. They were all so pretty.

'Your paintings are lovely,' Willow said, as Dorothy came out with two pink china cups on matching saucers. 'I bet people come from all over to buy them.'

'Oh, not in here. I almost never get any customers in here,' Dorothy said. 'But I have a steady income from selling my paintings on Etsy.'

Willow wanted to laugh that this sweet little elderly lady, who couldn't even work out how to flip a switch in a fuse box, was a successful businesswoman on Etsy.

'Oh I sell my candles on Etsy too, amongst other online shops. In fact all of my business is online, I've never had a bricks-and-mortar shop before so that's a new step for me. Look at us, two young entrepreneurs of Happiness.'

Dorothy giggled.

Willow carried on moving around the shop and looking at all the paintings. Her eyes suddenly fell on a very familiar painting. It was the poster she had seen of Happiness, the little village, the thatched cottage on the cliff side, the sparkling blue of the sea, the little pink flowers around the sides. The only things missing were the inviting words, '*Start a new life in the village of Happiness.*'

'This is the picture they used for the advert,' Willow said.

'I know. Kitty and Ken asked me if I would paint something for it, make Happiness look warm and inviting. I based that little cottage on your Sunrise Cottage,' Dorothy said.

Willow stared at the painting. She didn't want to tell Dorothy that it was a complete misrepresentation of the village because, really, who in their right mind would uproot their whole life based purely on a painting? It was hard to believe this little painting had changed her life completely. She supposed only time would tell if that change was going to be for the better.

She moved the painting out of its stack to get a better look at it, revealing a portrait of Andrew behind it.

It was so realistic it was like looking at a photo. Dorothy had even managed to capture the little twinkle in his eye and the laughter lines around his eyes. He was laughing at something and the painting just captured his gentle, patient and mischievous personality perfectly.

If there was one person in the village who could help her make Happiness the vision of loveliness she'd seen in the painting, then Andrew was definitely the man for the job.

chapter 7

Andrew was just getting a cake out of the oven when there was a knock on the door. He gave a little sigh. He loved living here and he loved the villagers but his time never seemed to be his own. There was always something wrong, something else that needed fixing, something else to be added to the long list of repairs and maintenance he needed to do. There simply weren't enough hours in the day to do it all. Kitty and Ken were looking at hiring him an assistant and, honestly, it couldn't come soon enough. It was just starting to get dark now as well, so unless it was a real emergency, the problem would have to wait until the morning.

He plastered on a smile and answered the door. He was surprised to see Willow standing on his doorstep. Surely she hadn't found fault in Sunrise Cottage just yet?

'Hello. Have you come for another shower?' Andrew said, quickly clamping his hand over his eyes.

She laughed. She had this wonderful infectious giggle and he couldn't help smiling at the sound of it. There were many beautiful sounds in the world and sometimes he liked to close his eyes and just listen to the birds or the waves crashing onto the beach. He liked to commit them to memory. Willow's laugh was one of those he already wanted to play again in his head.

He peered through his fingers at her and she laughed even more.

'No peeking.'

'Sorry,' he put his hand back over his eyes again.

'I'm not really here for a shower. Just thought I'd come by and say hi.'

He lowered his hand in surprise. 'Not many people come by here to say hi. They come to me with a list of problems.'

'Well, I thought we could talk,' Willow said.

'That sounds ominous, you better come in,' Andrew said, stepping back to let her inside. She squeezed past him into the hall, she smelt of sunshine and holidays and coconut.

'Something smells amazing,' Willow said as she walked through into the kitchen.

He had to agree but then he turned his attention to what she was saying and realised she was talking about the cake.

'Rhubarb cake, it was growing in an abundance up at the castle, thought I'd make the most of it. Would you like a slice?'

'I've just had the biggest burger in the world, courtesy of the pub, so maybe a very small slice,' Willow said, sitting down at the breakfast table.

He smiled and cut off a big chunk of cake, placing it on the table in front of her. He cut himself a slice and sat down opposite her.

'I thought you might be there actually – at the pub, I mean. Not that I was waiting for you. Well, I kind of was but just because I wanted to talk. Not because I wanted to see you naked again.'

He laughed loudly. 'I'll try not to be offended that you don't want to see me naked again.'

'Oh no, don't be offended. I don't want to see you naked again purely because I really do want to see you naked again.'

She made him smile so much. 'Well, that's perfectly clear.'

Willow blushed and took a bite of cake, clearly as a distraction. 'Mmm, this cake is fantastic.'

He watched her for a while, tucking in. He'd never really considered himself to have a type. But his past girlfriends were all blondes so he supposed he must have. Willow was definitely not his type. She had this gorgeous brown wavy hair which seemed to shimmer with copper and bronze as she moved. He had never dated a girl with freckles before but Willow had them all over her nose and cheeks and, with her large green eyes, she was cute. She had this energy about her that made her shine. He straightened in his chair. But definitely not his type. In fact he wasn't looking for a relationship at all right now, so no woman was his type. And with everything else going on in the village, he didn't have time to start anything.

'What did you want to talk about?' Andrew asked.

'I don't know. This village, it's just…'

'Depressing, I know. I'm sure Kitty and Ken would understand if you've changed your mind.'

'I'm not leaving,' Willow said, defensively.

'Oh.'

'I just think it needs… something.'

'OK,' he said, slowly. He wasn't sure where she was going with this. By the look on her face he didn't think she knew either.

'How many people have taken Kitty and Ken up on their offer of free accommodation for a year?' Willow asked.

'Including me, you and Tabitha and Connor at the pub, seven.'

'You're new too?' Willow said in surprise. 'I've been hearing from all the locals how wonderful you are. From the sound of it, you've been here for ages.'

'Three months. I was the first. Kitty and Ken hired me as estate manager, maintenance man, Man Friday, odd-job man and the house came as part of the job. The whole free incentive was actually my idea. You can see how well it's working out,' he said, dryly.

'Are you getting lots of interest?' Willow asked, popping another chunk of cake in her mouth.

'Oh yes, but once they visit, they don't come back.'

'Those four houses near the entrance to the castle don't help.'

'No they don't,' Andrew admitted.

'You need to spruce them up.'

'They're not safe to live in – there's an old passage that

led from the castle out to the beach and it's collapsed. Those houses are built right on top of it. The ground isn't stable, two of the houses are actually sinking into it. We've had the rest of the village checked out though, you're perfectly safe where you live, it's just up there that's a bit dodgy.'

'Well you need to either knock those houses down or tart them up, make them at least look pretty, even if they aren't available to rent. Or we could cover them up, put something in front of them so they can't be seen when we have visitors to the village.'

He thought of his friend, Morgan, an idea bubbling in his mind. But he pushed it away. There was too much else to do rather than worry about houses that no one was ever going to live in.

'You make it sound so easy,' Andrew said.

'No, I appreciate it isn't. Sorry, I didn't mean to imply you're not doing your job properly. I'm sure you have tons to do.'

'I have, there's so much that needs doing ready for the open day, so many houses need repainting or renovating.'

'You can't do all that alone.'

'They are going to get me an assistant.'

'You need a team. A big one.'

He sighed, because he had to agree with her. He was reluctant to ask that of Kitty and Ken because they were so generous with their money and he didn't want to take advantage of them. The free home incentive had been his idea and since then he'd felt like he was constantly asking them for money for one thing or another. But they had no idea how much everything was going to cost, how long it was all going to take. It was a massive project to overhaul the village and they had no idea how big it really was. He had been trying to do things on the cheap for them, but maybe that was worse than not doing anything. He needed to have a serious conversation with them and he had been putting it off for too long.

'They don't have any money, do they?' Willow said, misunderstanding his reluctance.

'They do, I just don't think they appreciate how much this is going to cost them and I feel bad because all of this was my idea.'

'But they must have wanted to do it,' Willow said.

'They've always talked about doing the right thing for the village, of making it like it used to be. I think they'd like to bring that kind of community spirit back to Happiness, but I'm not sure we'll ever get that back.'

'We have to try,' Willow said. 'This village has so much potential. It could be great again. I appreciate seventeen days is such a short amount of time to get everything finished but there's still a lot that can be achieved in that time. Do you have a list of everything that needs doing and an idea of how much it will all cost?'

He nodded. 'In my head. Although the list gets bigger every day.'

'You're thinking of the bigger picture, but in reality you need to think on a smaller scale. You just need to make the village look nice from the outside. Make, say, five houses look good on the inside and those can be our show houses for the open day. If we suddenly get an influx of people wanting to move here then we can hold them off for a month or two until we can get more houses ready internally. No one will expect to move in the very next day. They will need to sell their house or at least give a month's notice if they're renting. But if the whole village is aesthetically pleasing from the outside that's going to be a huge step forward in getting people to want to move here.'

He hadn't thought about it like that. He looked at his rhubarb cake; if he wanted to sell it, he needed to add some icing, put some pretty leaves and flowers on it. He had been trying so hard to get everything finished but he had to prioritise and Willow was right, getting the exterior looking good was the most important. No one ever needed to know that the village was falling apart on the inside because, by the time they moved in, all that would be taken care of.

'OK.'

'Well, let's work through the list together now, make it as detailed as possible and prioritise what needs doing before the open day. Then we can go to Kitty and Ken tomorrow and tell them what we need, including a team of builders and decorators.'

He smiled, slightly. Willow was clearly-the-take-charge-and-get-things-done type.

'We?'

'I need to meet them anyway and I'd like to help. I might

not be good at any of the practical, renovation-type stuff, but I can help with a bit of the aesthetics, painting around the doors, painting the shop signs. I want this move to work, I can't go back. Everyone thought I was an idiot for packing up all my worldly goods and moving hundreds of miles away but then they all thought I was an idiot anyway so…' She shrugged as if she didn't care what anyone thought, but he could see straight through that bravado. 'I really want this to work. I want the village to be wonderful again.'

'I want this village to be a big success too,' he admitted.

'Then let's get started.' Willow shrugged out of her jacket, clearly meaning to stay for some time.

Andrew stared at her for a moment and, as he got up to get his notebook and pen, he wasn't sure whether to be pleased or annoyed that he'd opened the door.

Willow yawned and stretched her arms above her head.

'Well, I think we've made good progress,' she indicated the list.

Andrew nodded grudgingly. 'Yeah, it's quite extensive. But I know a good team who can help me if Kitty and Ken are willing. Thank you for your help.'

She smiled. She wanted to be able to give something worthwhile to the village. She loved making candles, she had a very successful online business and her candles made people happy so she wasn't going to give that up, but even she could see that pretty candles were not what this village needed right now. So she was pleased to be able to help in some small way. And decorating the houses felt like a step forward too.

'My pleasure. Right, I think I'm going to call it a night.'

She pulled on her jacket and was surprised to see Andrew slipping his on too.

He saw her surprise. 'I'll walk you back.'

She smiled at that gentlemanly gesture, but it was hardly necessary. She had walked home in the dark just fine the night before.

'I don't think I'm in fear of being attacked or mugged on my way home.'

'No, but it's pitch-black out there and the track is hardly smooth and bump-free. Plus I have a good torch.'

Willow nodded to concede that. She certainly didn't want to break her ankle and there were parts of the track back to her house that were in almost complete darkness.

'Oh, and take a cake with you.' Andrew offered her a large round cake, wrapped up in foil.

'I'm not going to eat a whole cake on my own.'

'Take it anyway, I always make too much. You can invite your neighbours round for coffee and cake.'

She took it, a great big heavy slab of a thing, and tucked it under her arm.

They left his house and she noticed he didn't lock the door behind him.

'No key?'

'Ah no, it's not really that kind of place. You have one for your door, but I don't think it's necessary for myself.'

He flicked on his torch and a silvery beam spread over the track in front of them. Without the lights of the city she was so used to, she could see millions of stars in the inky canopy above them, twinkling like tiny crystals.

'So what's your story, why are you here?' Andrew asked.

She didn't know what to say to that. She wasn't hung up over her break-up with Garry, she wasn't pining over him or nursing a broken heart. Breaking up had been the best thing that ever happened to her. But she had come here for a clean slate, to get away from the comments and looks of pity. She certainly didn't want to bring them with her.

'I guess I'm here for a fresh start. What about you?'

He shrugged. 'I suppose we all are.'

They walked on in silence for a while, probably both contemplating their own mistakes and experiences which had led them to being here.

'That's Elsie's house,' Andrew pointed to the little white cottage which was very badly painted. 'That's Joseph's and that's Dorothy's.'

Willow nodded, trying to remember where they all were so she could find them if she needed to in the cold light of day.

She shifted the large cake into her other arm. Then she had a sudden thought.

'Hang on a second.'

She turned and ran up the little path of Dorothy's house. It was in complete darkness so she was either tucked up in bed asleep or still in the pub lamenting the loss of her favourite baker.

She placed the cake on the doorstep and ran back to join Andrew.

'Didn't want my cake after all?' Andrew teased.

'I think Dorothy's need is greater than mine. She was telling me all about life in the village when she was growing up, especially how much she used to love the baker here and his amazing cakes. I take it we don't have anything like that amongst the shops that are in use?'

'We have a knitting shop, a post office, a cheese shop and an art-gallery-type shop. Not exactly huge, pivotal roles in the community. What is it you'll sell in your shop?'

The stars above them had disappeared as they walked through the trees and Willow cringed a bit in the darkness. 'I'm a candlemaker. Sadly, nothing huge or pivotal, I'm afraid.'

'Ah, I didn't mean…'

'It's OK, I know what you meant.'

'Everyone has their role to play in the community, I'm sure you'll be a valuable part of it,' Andrew said, clearly trying to make her feel better about her contribution.

She didn't have time to think about what she could offer the village as just then she saw Andrew stumble, the torch smashed into the ground and everything went black.

chapter 8

'Andrew?' Willow said, frozen in the darkness.

Silence. It was completely and utterly black here, the moon and stars above them not penetrating through the trees.

'Andrew!' Her voice was higher, filled with anxiety.

A groan came from nearby and she quickly rushed over towards the source of the sound, and then went flying as she tripped over him and landed with a thud on her front.

'Crap, are you OK?' Andrew said and she heard him feel around with his hand for her before it landed on her bum.

'I'm OK, are you?' Willow asked, frowning slightly that his hand was still on her bum. Either he hadn't realised or he didn't care. She really hoped he wasn't the sort to try to take advantage of this situation.

'I'm fine, I think,' Andrew said, moving his hand around in what he probably hoped was a comforting way but he was now stroking her bum.

Suddenly he must have realised where his hand was because he snatched it away as if he had been burned.

'Sorry.'

'It's fine.'

'No it isn't. I would never—'

'I know, don't worry.' She rolled over and sat up. 'Can you stand?'

She heard him shuffle around and grunt and then, judging from the sound of his breathing, he was clearly standing up.

'Here, give me your hand,' Andrew said, from somewhere above her.

She reached out and quite obviously grabbed him in the groin.

'Ah sorry,' Willow said.

She heard him chuckle and then burst out laughing and she started laughing too. This whole thing was completely ridiculous.

She clambered to her feet herself and realised that she was standing just inches away from him. She could feel his warmth, smell his wonderful tangy scent. The laughter died in her throat.

He placed his hands on her shoulders, clearly needing some connection with her in the darkness.

'Sorry about all this, I just tripped over. I think we still have quite a way to go to get to your house, so we really need to find that torch. Unless you have one of your candles stashed about your person?'

'And a means to light it,' Willow said. 'Sadly I don't but if we can find our way to mine I can provide you with a lantern to get you back home. I don't even have my phone with me as I left it to charge. I think that torch is probably ruined, it looked like it smashed before the light went out. Look, there's a clearing up ahead, it's a lot brighter there and I can hear the sea so we can't be that far away. We can make it.'

'OK, hold my hand,' Andrew instructed and her heart leapt a little as the warmth of his hand enveloped hers. They moved forward tentatively together, feeling around the ground with their feet for anything else that might trip them up as they inched towards the clearing. Finally they made their way out of the trees, and they could see Willow's little cottage standing on the cliff tops ahead of them, glinting in the moonlight.

She smiled as Andrew continued to hold her hand as they picked their way down the rest of the track.

Andrew walked her right up to her door.

'Here, let me get you a lantern to get back home,' Willow said, letting go of his hand to push open the door. She flicked on the light and went to one box, pulling out a small copper lantern with a large white candle inside. These were very popular with her online customers, having that antique feel. She lit the candle and then closed the little glass door, before returning to Andrew who was still waiting on her doorstep. In the light of the house she could see he had a leaf in his hair and, without thinking, she reached up to remove it.

He stared down at her and, for the briefest of seconds,

there was this… spark between them before he stepped back into the shadows.

'Thanks for this,' he held up the lantern.

'No problem,' she said, watching him as he walked out the gate. 'And Andrew?'

He turned back to face her.

'You might want to add some kind of lighting down that track to your massive list.'

She watched him smile and nod and then he disappeared into the darkness.

After a shower followed by breakfast outside in her garden the next day, Willow went off into the village to have a look at her new shop.

At the fork in the road, just outside the pub, there seemed to be quite the gathering of villagers, huddled together, with Dorothy holding court in the middle.

'It was just there this morning when I got up, no note, no explanation. And let me tell you, it was the most delicious rhubarb cake I have ever tasted. Tangy and moist and fresh.'

'Who do you think left it there?' Julia asked, her pink candyfloss hair wobbling as she talked.

'I'm not sure,' Dorothy said smiling, although she looked like she had a fair idea.

'Maybe it was Connor,' Liz said. She nodded her head

towards the pub. 'He knows his way around the kitchen and some of his puddings in there are divine.'

'Why would Connor leave me a cake?' Dorothy said, rolling her eyes at the stupid suggestion. 'I'm old enough to be his mother.'

Willow wondered if she should step forward and admit it was her but Dorothy seemed so excited by the mystery of it all that maybe she should keep her guessing for a bit longer.

'Why does it have to have anything to do with age?' Roger said, today sporting a dashing yellow polka-dot tie.

'Because I think it was a token of love,' Dorothy said, her face beaming.

Willow couldn't help but smile at this wonderful optimism.

'Maybe it was one of the newbies,' Julia said, practically, clearly dismissing the love theory.

'Maybe it was Andrew,' Liz suggested. 'I saw him carrying a load of rhubarb from the castle yesterday.'

'Maybe Andrew is in love with you,' Roger teased.

'Andrew is not in love with me,' Dorothy snapped.

'Look, there's Willow,' Julia pointed in her direction. 'She lives in Sunrise Cottage near you. It could easily be her.'

All eyes swivelled in Willow's direction.

'It wasn't her, I know who it was,' Dorothy insisted.

'Ask her,' Liz said.

Dorothy huffed. 'Fine, I'll ask her. Willy, Willy dear. Did you make me a cake?'

Willow moved closer to the group, ignoring the fact that Dorothy had got her name wrong again. She didn't like lying but she could answer that question with complete honesty. 'God no, I'm shocking in the kitchen. I couldn't bake a cake if Jamie Oliver was standing next to me and telling me how to do it.'

'Oooh, I like that Jamie Oliver,' Liz said.

'Give me Gordon Ramsay any day,' Julia said, fanning herself.

'I prefer that Paul Hollywood, with his twinkly eyes,' Roger said.

'See, it wasn't Willy,' Dorothy said, trying to bring the conversation back round to the mystery cake.

'Who do you think it was?' Willow asked.

'I think it was Joseph,' Dorothy said, dreamily.

'Joseph?' Julia said in surprise. 'Why would Joseph leave you a cake?'

'Because we grew up here together. He moved away, I got married, he got married, but I think he's always had a thing for me. Now he's back and we're both young, free and single again, maybe he's decided to make his move.'

'Well, not exactly young,' muttered Roger, which Dorothy clearly heard and decided to ignore.

'His house is just opposite mine, so it would be very easy to leave the cake there. And I think he's been giving me the eye.'

'That's probably cataracts,' Liz said and Roger snorted.

'Plus his grandfather owned the bakery here, I bet Sam

must have showed him a thing or two about cakes growing up,' Dorothy carried on regardless.

'I still think it was Andrew,' Liz said. 'Everyone knows how kind he is. He probably heard you moaning on about wanting a bakery in the village and decided to make you the cake.'

'I was not moaning,' Dorothy snapped.

Right on cue, Andrew roared into the village on his quad bike. Willow wondered how the villagers would react to him ruining their tranquil little haven with the noise of its engine but he had clearly already won them over with his charm and likeability. If this was a cartoon, love hearts would be coming from all of their eyes.

'Why don't we ask him?' Willow said, hoping he would play along.

Julia waved him down and he came to a stop and cut the engine.

'Andrew dear, how are you?' Liz fussed around him, removing imaginary bits of fluff.

'I'm fine, thanks Liz.'

'Did you have company last night?' Julia said, her eyebrows wiggling mischievously. 'I was walking my Colin and Rufus down the little lane behind your house and I could hear you laughing and talking with a girl.'

Willow frowned slightly. That was a little creepy.

'Yes, I did,' Andrew said, vaguely.

'A friend or someone *special*?' Julia asked.

He grinned at the digging; clearly he was used to this kind

of attention.

'I think I'd have to say both.'

Willow smiled at that.

'Andrew,' Willow said, meaningfully. 'Someone left a cake on Dorothy's doorstep last night. Do you know anything about it?'

Andrew hesitated for a fraction of a second before he shook his head.

'No, sorry, as Julia already pointed out, I was entertaining my guest until late last night.'

They all collectively *oooohed.*

'That kind of night, was it?' Roger laughed, clapping Andrew on the back.

'It was a good night, but I definitely didn't have time to go about the village leaving cakes on people's doorsteps,' Andrew said.

'See, I told you it wasn't Andrew,' Dorothy said.

'Dorothy hopes it was Joseph,' Julia said.

Andrew smiled. 'Really?'

'I think it's his subtle way of letting me know he has feelings for me,' Dorothy said, knowledgably.

'Well maybe you should subtly let him know that you have feelings for him too,' Andrew said.

'Oh, I couldn't do that,' Dorothy said, suddenly blushing.

'Maybe you could leave *him* a gift,' Willow said, loving the way this was unexpectedly going.

Dorothy clearly thought about this. 'Maybe I could.'

Willow smiled. A glimmer of an idea was forming in her

head. She needed to talk to Andrew about it but maybe this could be the very thing that Happiness needed.

Andrew drove his quad bike towards the castle. He had agreed to meet Willow at the entrance at one and they were going to meet Kitty and Ken together. He was glad she was coming with him, he was a little nervous about asking for so much money in one go, but if this open day was going to be a big success then it had to be done. As he rounded the corner and came up to the castle entrance, he smiled when he saw that Willow was waiting for him.

He didn't know what mischief she was up to with the cake she had left for Dorothy and then pretending she didn't know who had left it there, but there was one thing for sure: this girl was going to be trouble.

He liked her. Willow was sunshine personified. She sparkled with her over-the-top exuberance. He liked her honesty too.

He pulled to a stop in front of her and she climbed on behind him without any hesitation, wrapping her legs and arms around him. The warmth from her spread inside him like drinking a hot cup of tea on a cold day.

'Have you had a productive morning in your shop?' Andrew asked, raising his voice slightly to be heard over the noise of the engine as he drove through the castle gates. 'Or have you been too busy causing mischief and mayhem?'

'How dare you,' she laughed. 'I am a very righteous and upstanding member of this community.'

'Of course you are,' Andrew said, dryly.

'You'll be pleased to know, I've been in my shop all morning and not spoken to anyone since you roared off on your quad bike after that impromptu village meeting. I've cleaned the shop from top to bottom and this afternoon I'll be ready to move some of my stock in.'

'Do you have a lot of stock?'

'Not with me, it's on its way. I have enough to make an impressive window display but it won't take me long to start making some more, once the rest of the stock arrives. It's exciting really, this is the first time I'll have my own shop. Everything I've sold before has been online so I've never had to think about displays before. But I thought the main attraction of my shop could be that tourists might want to watch me work. Some of the candles are quite elaborate to make and I thought any visitors to the village might be interested in seeing the process. So I'm going to set up a workshop area in the middle of the shop to make my candles and visitors can browse the shelves and watch me work too. If nothing else, I will have a proper area to work in to sell my online stuff. Before I came here I made all my candles in a shed in the back garden.'

He smiled. She had so much energy and enthusiasm. He didn't know whether to burst her bubble now or later. Maybe he'd start the ball rolling.

'We don't get too many visitors here.'

'Yeah, Dorothy was saying she doesn't get many customers in her painting shop. But I find that hard to believe. That big old castle, the cute little village, no one wants to see that?'

'The village isn't that cute right now.'

'True,' Willow said. 'But it could be. And I know the castle is crumbling away but I bet people would still want to come and see it. Castles are big draws. Is it open to the public?'

'No, not really.'

'Well, maybe that's another thing I can talk to Kitty and Ken about. Bringing visitors to the castle would also bring them to the village, and if nothing else it would be good custom for the pub, even if it doesn't bring any visitors to my shop.'

He marvelled at her spirit – it would not be dulled no matter what.

'The castle is not in a good shape. Kitty and Ken are basically living in the old servants' quarters and the rest of the place is falling into ruin,' Andrew said.

'But people love castles. Kenilworth Castle in the Midlands is largely just a few old walls and turrets, it hasn't been lived in for hundreds of years, and people still flock there in their thousands. If they open it to the public, regardless of the state it's in, people will come.'

He pulled the quad bike to a stop next to Ken's Range Rover and turned off the engine.

'You really are a glass-brimming-over kind of girl, aren't you?'

She clambered off the back and he climbed off too.

'Better that than be the glass-half-empty kind. What type are you?'

He thought about that for a moment. 'Probably three-quarters full. All the good stuff is still there, but room for a little improvement.'

'I'll take that.'

She looked up at the castle, and he wondered what she saw. Up close it really was in a sorry state but she certainly didn't seem to be put off by it.

'So what was going on this morning with Dorothy and the cake?' Andrew asked. 'Why not just tell her that you left it for her?'

'Did you see how excited she was about the mystery of who it could be? I didn't want to take that away from her,' Willow said.

'But now you've encouraged her to think that it was Joseph.'

'She was thinking that before I came along and a little harmless matchmaking won't hurt.'

'It will if Joseph doesn't feel the same way. She'll end up embarrassed,' Andrew said.

'Dorothy doesn't seem the type that would embarrass that easily. I have an idea, actually. Maybe you can help me with it.'

Andrew pulled the huge five-page list from his pocket. 'I'm a bit busy with the last idea you wanted help with.'

She laughed. 'Oh shush, as if all of that was my fault.'

'Go on then, tell me your wonderful idea,' Andrew said, dryly, as if he was less than thrilled about anything she was going to suggest. But the truth was he could listen to her talk all day and not get bored of it.

She didn't take him remotely seriously.

'I'll tell you later, it'll be something for you to look forward to. Besides, I want to meet Kitty and Ken.'

She moved off towards the door and he rolled his eyes as he shoved the list back in his pocket. But an idea suddenly sparked to life. 'Wait, before we go in, you need to know that you're expected to curtsey to them.'

She turned to look at him in shock. 'Are you kidding? You said they were lovely.'

'They are but you know, they're royalty, and they're a bit old-fashioned like that.'

'They're royalty? I've never heard of a Princess Kitty before,' Willow said, doubtfully.

'Kitty is actually Lady Katherine, the Queen's third cousin and I believe thirty-fifth in line to the throne.'

She stared at him. 'Are you serious? Oh my god, I've never met royalty before.' She looked down at what she was wearing in horror. 'Why didn't you tell me, I would have got changed.'

He bit his lip. 'It's fine, they really are rather normal.'

'Apart from that they live in a castle and like people to bow and curtsey to them.'

'Well, yes, apart from that. Come on, let me introduce you to them.'

He opened the door and let her go ahead into the large kitchen. He stepped inside after her, ducking his head to get through the door. Willow held back for a moment.

Kitty and Ken were both sitting at the table reading. Ken looked every inch the royal lord with his splendid red waistcoat and walrus moustache. They both looked up as they entered and smiled at him.

Ken spotted Willow and shot out of his seat to greet her.

'Kitty, Ken, this is Willow McKay who arrived a few days ago.'

Ken held his hand out to greet her and Willow took it and duly bobbed into a perfect curtsey. She was going to kill him for this.

'My Lord,' Willow said, clearly having watched films like *Pride and Prejudice* too many times.

Ken looked flummoxed for a moment. Kitty stared in shock, and Beryl, the housekeeper and cook, let the mug she was washing up clatter back into the bowl, sending little bubbles flying through the air.

Andrew's shoulders were shaking from suppressed laughter as Kitty stood up and came round the table towards them.

'Oh you rogue, Andrew Harrington,' Kitty said, shaking her head fondly. She turned her attention back to Willow. 'Did he tell you that you had to curtsey to us?'

Willow straightened, dropping Ken's hand in confusion. 'Yes, on account of you being royalty.'

Ken chortled. 'Royalty, eh? Now that would be nice.'

'You're not Lady Katherine?' Willow said.

'Oh no, although that does have a nice ring to it. Beryl, I might start getting you to call me that from now on,' Kitty said.

Beryl snorted. 'You know what you can do if you think I'm going to start walking round here with airs and graces.'

Willow looked up at Andrew. 'You were winding me up?'

The laughter burst out of him and he wiped his eyes. 'I'm sorry, I couldn't resist.'

Willow's cheeks flushed bright red and then she smiled and started laughing too. 'Oh, is that how it's going to be? I'm going to get you back for that.'

Andrew couldn't contain his laughter. 'Of that, I have no doubt.'

'Willow, let's start again, I'm Kitty and this is my husband Ken, it's lovely to finally meet you.'

'Would you like a cup of tea?' Ken asked, going to the kettle.

'Oh yes please,' Willow said, as Kitty held a chair out for her to sit down at the table.

'And Beryl made a delicious chocolate cake this morning, would you like a slice?' Kitty said.

'I can see I'm going to get fat while living here,' Willow said as Andrew sat down opposite her. 'I had a slice of Andrew's rhubarb cake last night and it was amazing. But I've always got room for chocolate cake.'

Kitty removed the cake from the tin and cut off a big slice as Ken made a pot of tea. Andrew smiled as he watched them; they were about as far removed from royalty as you could get.

'What do you think of Sunrise Cottage?' Kitty asked, placing the plate in front of Willow as she sat back down at the table.

'It's lovely,' Willow said, taking a huge bite. 'Very cute, small but the perfect size for me and that view is incredible.'

'Andrew worked so hard on the house to get it ready for you,' Kitty said, smiling at him.

'And what do you think of the village?' Ken asked, hopefully, as he brought the tea to the table.

Willow glanced briefly at Andrew, obviously wondering what she should say. 'It… has a rustic charm.'

He smiled at her. You couldn't just walk into someone's home and start insulting their back garden and she knew that.

Although Kitty could see right through that. 'It's a bit sad and tatty right now, but it has potential.'

'Oh, it has so much potential,' Willow said, sitting straight, her eyes lighting up. 'It could be a wonderful place to live again. It just needs a bit of TLC. Well OK, a lot.'

She glanced over at Andrew again and gave him an encouraging nod.

He took a deep breath. 'That's what we wanted to talk to you about actually. We have sixteen days until the open day and we want this place to shine. I can't do everything that needs to be done on my own.'

Kitty nodded. 'Of course, we're going to be placing an ad in the local newspaper this week to get you an assistant.'

Andrew cringed inwardly. 'I'm afraid it needs more than

that.'

Kitty and Ken exchanged glances. 'How much more?'

Andrew smoothed out the list of jobs on the table and then spread the sheets out so they could see the sheer quantity of it all.

'Quite a lot.'

'But we also have some ideas to help you and the village, financially,' Willow said, excitedly.

Andrew smiled at her enthusiasm. He kind of felt like they were playing the roles of good cop, bad cop. He would upset them with the list of everything that needed doing and the expense and she would temper that with her sparkly infectious exuberance.

Ken leaned over to look at the sheets of paper. 'Come on then, let's see what we've got.'

chapter 9

'And you know someone who can do all of this?' Ken said as he glanced again at the total figure of what it was going to cost.

Willow felt bad for Kitty and Ken. It was quite obvious they had clearly underestimated how big this project was when they took it on.

'Yes, I know a good team that can take care of the bulk of it,' Andrew said. 'I can see what their availability is like. I know they've just finished one project. But they may have other jobs lined up. To complete the whole list will take several months, but if we can get Jack and his team to come in and spend a few weeks doing the surface-level stuff, at least it will help the village look good for the open day, even if the underneath isn't quite so shiny. I know a good landscape gardening team too. Oli and Tom can take care of the aesthetics on that side of things.'

Ken sighed and then nodded. 'OK, we'll let you take care of arranging all that. Let me know if you need any money up front.'

'I will.'

Ken looked utterly deflated and Willow wanted to come round the table and give him a big hug.

'Why did you buy the castle and village?' Willow asked gently, wondering if living in a castle had been the lure and the village had been this millstone around his neck.

'My dad was born and raised here, lived here until he was around twenty-five and he always used to tell me these stories of how wonderful it was, the cosy community spirit. Later, when he got older, he talked about how he wanted to move back here. We brought him down not long before he died and he was just so happy as he reminisced about his life here, but he said how everything had changed now and how it wasn't the same place any more. But I could see how much potential it had, how it could be great again.'

Kitty smiled with love for her husband. 'Ken has always had a kind heart and a soft spot for underdog projects.'

Ken smiled at her. 'Me and Kitty, well, we've been very fortunate in our life. We've made some very good business decisions over the years, made the right deals with the right people and in some cases just got very lucky. When we heard that the village and castle were for sale at a ridiculously cheap price, considering what we were actually getting, well, we wanted to help. We wanted to bring the village back to life again, to how my dad remembered it. There were a number of companies that wanted to buy the land and probably raze it to the ground and build a bunch of faceless identical red-brick houses or great big blocks of flats. We couldn't let that happen. Although it's safe to say we didn't realise the extent of the renovation project when we took it on. But I guess we'll do whatever it takes.'

Willow smiled at his determination to make it work.

'I had an idea about how you could bring some money in, maybe help cover the costs in some small way.'

Ken brightened a little. 'I'm listening.'

'I thought you could open the castle to the public.'

Ken's smile fell off his face. 'I don't think that's a viable option, it's in quite a state. Plus it has no historic significance, it didn't belong to any royalty. In fact I would be very surprised if any royalty or nobility even visited, there were no great battles or anything important that happened here. I don't think any of the historic organisations would be interested in managing it for us.'

'But it's a castle, people love castles,' Willow said, not to be deterred. 'Even the old tatty ones. Would you give me a tour?'

Ken stared at her for a moment, weighing it up, before getting to his feet. 'Come on then. I think you'll change your mind when you see it.'

He'd clearly decided that the easiest option would be to go along with Willow's suggestion, at least for now.

Willow shot to her feet, eager to explore. 'Andrew, you coming?'

'Oh yes, I haven't actually seen much of it yet. I've been too busy down in the village. I'd love to have a look.'

'You see, people will be interested in it,' Willow said.

Kitty got up too and linked hands with her husband.

'It's quite small really, despite its stature,' Ken said, pushing a door open on the other side of the kitchen and Willow followed him into a stone corridor. 'I think it was more of a folly than used for any kind of fortification purposes. As far as I can tell it's only a few hundred years old, which is very young in comparison to other castles. And this one wasn't built to last.'

'Do you know a lot about its history?'

'Not really,' Kitty said. 'The first mention of it we can find is in the mid-1700s, although it was possible it was around before that. It changed names many times over the years, almost as many times as it changed owners. The first owner, we think, was Charles Archer but we don't know anything about him and it wasn't passed down through his family.'

Ken pushed open a large wooden door. 'This is the great hall.'

Willow eagerly followed them in but felt her excitement deflate a little when she saw a gaping hole in one of the walls. In fact there were several holes and walls falling down. There was no furniture or pictures or tapestries on the walls – the room was no more than a shell. *Great* hall was a bit of an exaggeration.

'The previous owners stripped out and sold anything of value,' Ken said. 'There's not a lot left. There are also places where they tried to make renovations, very badly, and then either ran out of money or patience. That far wall with the majority of the holes in, I think the owner wanted to make the hall into a large garage for all his cars and figured he'd just knock down the outer wall so he could park in here.'

'What?' Willow said incredulously.

'Yes, the previous owners were less than respectful,' Ken shook his head, sorrowfully.

'Are all the rooms like this?' Willow asked.

'Some of them are not this bad, but yes, pretty much the whole place is in disrepair. The north tower has completely collapsed.'

'Come on, show me the rest.'

They walked from room to room with Ken reeling off some historical fact or nugget about the architecture or how the rooms were used. It was just as he had said though, the building was in a terrible state.

They walked back to the kitchen and Willow sat back down at the table again.

'Still think we can open it to the public?' Ken said.

'Yes, I still see potential here. Kids love climbing over ruins, they will enjoy running from room to room pretending they are a knight or a king or queen, regardless what state it is in. I think the first thing is to get some people in to assess how safe it is and there may be some places, like the north tower, that you have to close off to the public for safety reasons. You'll also need some public liability insurance. And a website advertising your castle, but a good website designer could come up with something snazzy. You could even run some Facebook adverts fairly cheaply. Again, someone internet savvy could set them up for you.'

Kitty and Ken stared at her with wide eyes.

'I also think, even though you don't know a lot about the castle's history, you do know quite a bit about the architecture of the place and some great general historic knowledge that you've been telling me as we've been walking around. You could spend some time writing up these little facts and putting them on display cards around the castle to provide a little historical context of each room. The stuff you told me about the still room was fascinating. While the kids are running riot around the castle, the parents might find those little snippets interesting.'

'Oh, no one is going to be interested in my waffle,' Ken tried to shrug it off.

'Of course they will,' Kitty said, defensively.

'Kitty's right, people will love it, and I bet you could do a bit more research for some of the other rooms too.'

Ken nodded. 'I could do that.'

'Bringing visitors to the castle would bring in a small amount of money to help with the restoration of the village but also it would bring life to the village and much-needed custom to the shops and the pub too. Andrew is taking care of the village for you, I think the castle could be your new underdog project.'

Kitty and Ken exchanged glances and Kitty gave her

husband an encouraging nod.

'OK, we'll look into it,' Ken said.

Willow smiled, pleased that she had done something good for the village and hopefully for Kitty and Ken too.

'Well, I better go, I need to sort out my shop,' Willow said.

'I'll give you a lift back,' Andrew said.

'Andrew, would you mind just holding on for a second?' Kitty said.

'That's OK, I can walk, it's not far,' Willow said. 'It was lovely meeting you.'

'Pop by and see us again,' Ken said. 'There's always cake here, Beryl makes sure of that.'

'I will, thank you.'

She stepped outside and started walking down the driveway. The sun was high in a cloudless turquoise sky. Something positive had been achieved today. Now she just needed to create a visually stunning window display, so the tourists would flock into her shop in their droves.

She laughed to herself; that might be a bit too optimistic.

There was a roar behind her as the quad bike came tearing down the drive. Andrew stopped by her side and she climbed on, wrapping herself around him.

'Everything OK?' Willow asked.

Andrew nodded and grinned over his shoulder at her. 'They think you're magnificent.'

Willow laughed. 'What?'

'I'd have to agree,' Andrew said, and then roared off

down the drive.

Willow smiled at that and rested her cheek on his back. Maybe coming here was the right thing for her after all.

The next day was equally as hot as the day before with the weather showing no signs of change. Willow had the door of the shop open, letting in the warm summer air as she made her candles. The radio was on softly, playing some old tunes she could sing along to. As summer was well and truly here she wanted the candles she was making to reflect that, which would be especially useful when it came to keeping her website updated and fresh.

The night before, she had cut several large oranges in half, scooped out all the flesh and then baked the peel shells in the oven overnight, making her whole cottage smell of oranges which wasn't a bad thing. She had also baked and dried orange slices, whole raspberries and strawberries cut in half too. The orange halves were now dried out and hard which meant they were unlikely to rot and go mouldy. She was going to use these as the candle holders.

Melting gently on the little camping stove was a large pot of parasoy wax. It consisted of paraffin wax and soy wax. Paraffin wax had a much better scent throw than the soy wax, but the latter was much nicer to work with, so over the years she had opted for a blend of the two.

As she danced over to the stove to take a peek, another

truck trundled past. There had been a steady stream of vehicles coming and going all morning – the renovation work was clearly starting with a vengeance. She had spent a few hours painting a few of the empty shopfronts the day before, as she had run out of freshly painted houses to add her flowers to. With only fifteen days now until the open day, she felt a bit guilty for wanting to spend a few hours making some candles. But this was her business and her regular customers were always coming back to her website to look for new candles, so she didn't want to leave it too long before she updated it. The most successful businesses were always fresh, always offering new things. And she promised herself she would squeeze in a few more hours of painting that afternoon, so she didn't feel too bad.

The wax looked like it might be ready, so she slipped on her oven glove and lifted the metal jug out of the saucepan of boiling water. She gave it a stir to check the consistency and, when she was happy that it felt OK, she started adding the orange and yellow colouring and the tangy orange-scented oils, giving it another stir to ensure the colour and scent were distributed evenly throughout the wax. She decided to leave the wax time to cool slightly as it was always better to pour if it wasn't really hot.

She turned her attention to the glass jars she was preparing for the clear gel wax. She loved working with this wax as she could get some beautiful effects, making candles that were almost too good to burn. She had already poured an inch of the blue parasoy wax in the bottom of the jars and the wick was sticking up out of that. As the wax was still cooling down and hardening, now was the perfect time to add the decorations. She sprinkled a bit of gold glitter for the sand in each of the jars and then glued some sea shells in different sizes and colours, pressing them gently into the wax so they were secure. She sprayed a clear glue over the top to set it all in place, then took the liquid gel wax off the stove and poured it on top of the shells in one jar slowly to try to decrease the amount of bubbles. She filled it almost to the top. She secured the wick between two bits of masking tape to make sure it was in the centre of the jar while the gel solidified and then she moved on to the next jar. The gel wax would harden almost completely clear but it had a shimmery quality that sparkled in the sunlight.

Once that was done, she moved back to the orange candles. She carefully glued the metal disk at the bottom of the wick inside the orange halves and then, checking the orange wax was cool enough, she poured it into the oranges. The smell was wonderful.

Next on her list was to make some candles that looked like glasses of Pimm's, champagne and other cocktails.

Willow scooped out some more gel wax and put it in the jug for melting. She opened up a box of champagne glasses and placed them on the table.

'Bit early in the day for drinking, isn't it?'

She looked up to see a paint-splattered Andrew leaning against the door frame.

She smiled, her heart leaping a little at the sight of him. OK, a lot.

'Ah, my old granddad used to say, "It's over the yardarm somewhere in the world." Although he died from liver failure in the end so probably not the best person to take drinking advice from.'

'I'm sorry,' Andrew said, moving into the shop.

'Oh, it was a very long time ago, I think I was only seven or eight. I didn't really know him that well, he just turned up at the odd family gathering and got drunk in the corner. Me and my brother used to find it hilarious.'

'Ah, you have a brother too. Older or younger?'

'Older.'

'Same. Older brothers are the worst, aren't they?' Andrew said.

Willow smiled as she thought of hers. Luke had teased her mercilessly growing up, used her as target practice when he had joined a fencing club, stole her toys, drew willies on her My Little Ponies, arranged her Care Bears into rude sexual positions and thrashed her in every single board game, card game or computer game they had ever played together. But he had also beaten up Richard Blake after he had deliberately trashed a model bridge that Willow had spent months making for a science project. He had walked her home from school every night instead of hanging around with his friends, he had cooked her dinner before Brownies every Monday when her mum had to work late. He had persuaded his best friend, David, to go on a date with her when she had confided in her brother she had a crush on him. He had held her tight when she had found her pet rabbit dead one morning. They had become very close as they grew older; it was just a shame he now lived in Australia and she rarely got to see him.

'I think I got one of the good ones,' Willow said.

'Lucky you,' Andrew said.

'Do you not get on with your brother?'

'Oh, I suppose me and Jacob get on much better now than we used to. I think he's a bit of an arse sometimes. He'll be here in a few days so you can judge for yourself. We used to fight endlessly when we were growing up, I'm sure I still have the bruises to prove it.'

'You're not supposed to get on with your older brother when you're young. There's kind of a rule against it,' Willow said.

'Ah, that's OK then.'

'Any other brothers or sisters?'

'A younger sister, Lottie,' Andrew said. 'She has a little girl called Poppy who's also deaf, although a lot more than I am. She barely speaks right now, but we all communicate with her using sign language.'

'Is Poppy the little girl in the photo in your bedroom?'

'Yes she is.'

'She looks very happy.'

He paused as if he expected her to say something else. 'She is. She's a very happy, bubbly little girl. Very bright too. Her world is almost completely silent but she doesn't know any different so it certainly doesn't get her down.'

'Kids are resilient creatures, far more so than adults. You've given her the tools to communicate, albeit in a slightly different way, but that's all she needs. Well that and a ton of pink sparkly toys.'

He stared at her for a moment. 'You know, when I tell people my niece is deaf, their first reaction, every single time, is to say, "I'm sorry." Like it's some terrible affliction or disease and they feel sorry for me and my family for having to put up with this curse. And you've picked up on the one thing that hearing people miss. Is she happy? That's the single most important thing for a child, surely. She is healthy in every way and as long as she's happy then we're happy.'

'Sounds like you have that balance exactly right.'

Andrew smiled. 'Apart from that she probably needs more pink sparkly toys?'

'A girl can never have enough.'

He paused for a moment. 'I want her to be proud of who she is. I want her to know she can do anything. Be who she wants to be. I don't want her to ever think, "I can't do this because I'm deaf."'

'It sounds to me like she has an amazing uncle who will make sure she knows that.'

He cleared his throat and frowned. 'So, are you going to tell me what you were really doing with these champagne glasses?'

He was obviously changing the subject, as if suddenly regretting going down that line of conversation with her, but she decided to let it go.

'I'm making cocktails,' Willow said, innocently, as if that explained everything. 'Would you like to watch?'

'Do I get to try them after?'

Willow wrinkled up her nose. 'You might not like these cocktails so much. Here, I'll show you the champagne ones. Will you put a small blob of glue on the bottom of those wicks for me and stick them to the bottom of the glasses?'

Willow went to check on the gel wax, which seemed to be OK, so she lifted it off the heat. She turned to watch Andrew and saw how carefully and precisely he was doing his job. She waited patiently for him to finish his six glasses.

'Is that OK?' he asked.

'That's perfect. So I'm now going to add a few drops of this honey colour. We don't want to lose the translucency of the gel wax, so we'll only add a tiny amount. I'm also going to add a few drops of this champagne scent.'

Andrew watched her avidly as she did what she said and stirred it into the gel wax. She poured a little bit into a spare glass jar so she could see the colour. 'What do you think, does it look like champagne?'

'Sure,' he said, doubtfully.

Willow laughed. 'It will.'

She put a blob of glue on the bottom of the dried raspberries and pressed them into the bottom of the glass to cover up the metal disk of the wick. She gave the yellow-tinted gel wax another stir and then poured it as fast as she could into the champagne glasses. Whereas with the seaside-themed jars she had made a short while before, the fewer bubbles she had the better, but with these candles she wanted loads of bubbles in them to look like champagne.

'Ah, now it looks like champagne,' Andrew said as she secured the wicks in place in the centre of the glass.

'Once this gel wax has cooled and set I'll add another thin milky layer of gel wax on the top which will look like the froth.'

'These are really clever.'

'Even if they aren't a valuable contribution to the village,' Willow teased.

'But they are. They're something different which will help in the long run to attract visitors to the village. And you're making a valuable contribution in other ways. Many ways in fact. The shops look great, I presume that was your doing?'

'Oh yes. I don't know what those shops will be so I didn't do any writing. I just left the signs blank but at least that part of those shops is finished.'

'Thank you. You never did tell me what your big idea was,' Andrew said.

'I haven't seen you. You're always rushing off to save the village.'

He laughed. 'Maybe I need to start wearing my underpants on the outside.'

'You'll probably need a cape too, otherwise you'll just look odd. But if you're not too busy tonight, why don't you come round for dinner and I'll explain everything. It's spaghetti bolognese, my speciality.'

He narrowed his eyes. 'Are you trying to butter me up for something?'

'I wouldn't dream of it,' Willow said, feigning innocence.

Andrew smirked, clearly not buying any of this. 'How does seven o'clock sound?'

'It's a date.' Her heart leapt. 'No, not a date, definitely not a date.'

'It's OK, I got it,' Andrew said, smiling. 'I'll see you later.'

He gave her a wave and left the shop.

She frowned. It definitely wasn't a date.

chapter 10

Willow had just finished unpacking her clothes in her bedroom that evening when there was a knock on the door. If that was Andrew he was a half hour early. She quickly went downstairs and answered the door to find Andrew standing there with bags of grocery shopping.

'Delivery,' he said, holding the bags up.

'Oh no, I forgot that was coming today. I ordered this before I came here. Did the delivery van come all the way down here?' Willow said, looking up towards the track.

'No, it can't come down this way. But not to worry, I just loaded it up on the trailer.'

'I'm so sorry, I'll make sure I'm there to meet the delivery driver next time.'

'It's no bother, just let me know in future so I can look out for it.'

'Let me give you a hand unloading the trailer,' Willow

said.

'It's OK, there's just two more bags,' Andrew said, placing the ones he was holding just inside the door and turning back to the trailer to collect the rest. He came back a few moments later.

'Are you off the clock now or do you still have work to do?' Willow asked.

'I'm never really off the clock but I'm not doing any more tonight.' He narrowed his eyes suspiciously. 'Why, what do you have planned?'

She laughed. 'No need for the shifty eyes, I don't plan on getting you back just yet for that stunt you pulled at the castle yesterday. Just the dinner is ready, it's keeping warm in the oven and I could open a bottle of wine while we wait for the pasta to cook.'

In her mind, it even sounded like a date. Good job she hadn't gone the whole hog and decided to light some candles too.

'That does sound good.' He closed the door and carried the bags through to the kitchen.

Willow followed him in with the rest of the bags. She picked up a packet of pasta shells and tipped some of it into the saucepan.

'Whoa, what are you doing? Andrew asked in shock.

'Putting the pasta on,' Willow said in confusion.

'You promised me spaghetti bolognese, that doesn't look like spaghetti.'

Willow laughed. 'I'm not really a fan of spaghetti, will

pasta shells do instead?'

'You can't go around changing the rules like that. I think the trades description people would have something to say about pasta shells in spaghetti bolognese.' Andrew shook his head in mock disappointment at her standards. 'Next you'll be telling me that you don't actually put toad in toad in the hole.'

Willow laughed. 'Wait, is that a euphemism?'

'I hope not,' Andrew protectively cupped his manhood. 'I could think of many names for it but toad isn't one of them.'

'Well,' Willow quickly decided to change the subject, 'I've never had toad before, although I did eat frogs' legs in Paris once, so I guess that counts. Normally I use sausages in my toad in the hole.'

Andrew shook his head, sadly.

'Glass of wine?'

'Well, just the one, I am driving,' he indicated the quad bike out the front, his mouth twitching in a smirk.

'Yes, of course, you don't want to be decapitating any of Dorothy's gnomes on the way back. And obviously you don't want to be caught by the police on that long drive home.'

'No, I'm a respectable member of the community.'

She poured out two glasses and sat down at the table. He joined her.

'So a successful meeting yesterday, and I see the crew have already arrived and been hard at work,' Willow said, then she held up her glass. 'Here's to bringing Happiness back to its full glory.'

Andrew chinked her glass with his own. 'Thanks to you.'

'Oh no, I was just... driving the car, you're the one that's going to do all the heavy lifting and co-ordinating. It's a big job and I've just made it bigger for you.'

'You just got me a ton of help so thanks for that. Jack and his team are here for two weeks which will take us right up to the open day. They've got other jobs to do after that but they'll come back and finish the rest off at the end of August. That will help massively in getting all the empty houses ready for potential owners, at least on the outside, and like you said, we are aiming to get at least five houses ready on the inside too. Our show houses. Oli and Tom are going to come along and help with making the place look pretty with flowers and plants. They're going to make us a load of hanging baskets and pots ready for the big day so that's good too. Hopefully people will be distracted by the flowers and not look too closely at some of the other issues.'

'We just have to grab their attention, let them see the potential of the place. A little window dressing wouldn't hurt,' Willow said. 'I'll try to paint all the houses with flowers or butterflies around the doors too. Every little helps.'

'I agree and I've also contacted a friend of mine who creates backdrop screens for plays and theatres. She's going to create one for us to put up in front of those houses near the castle entrance. There's no point really doing up those houses when no one's ever going to live in them, so I took your advice and decided to cover them up. Morgan is going to paint a screen with a medieval castle on the front, similar to Harmony Castle, with knights and jousting going on in the foreground. I thought the visitors to the castle would enjoy that.'

'That sounds like a lovely idea,' Willow agreed, getting up to give the pasta a quick stir.

'I'm feeling positive about this project for the first time since I got here,' Andrew said. 'Thank you for that.'

'Ah, I'm glad I could help.' Willow sat back down again.

'So are you going to tell me more about your bright idea that involves Dorothy and the cake?' Andrew said, taking a sip of wine.

'Well, I've been thinking about this a lot today and there was so much excitement over who had left Dorothy the cake.'

'I have to say that was the most excitement I've seen from the villagers for the last three months.'

'Exactly. They seemed so happy. From what Dorothy and a few others have told me, nothing has happened here for years and everyone seems to have withdrawn from the community. But yesterday they were all out on the street talking to one another.'

'I haven't ever seen that from them.'

'I wonder about trying to give that back to the village. Bring happiness back to Happiness.'

'OK, what do you have in mind?'

'Well if one mystery cake could bring so much happiness, I was thinking about maybe giving a few more people a mystery present.'

'Really? How many more?'

'All of them,' Willow said, quietly, suddenly realising that was a big project in itself.

'That's a lot of cake,' Andrew teased.

'It won't all be cake,' Willow laughed.

'In all seriousness, getting forty-seven presents, well forty-six since you don't need to include me, could be quite costly.'

'Forty-five now, Dorothy has already had her gift. And it doesn't necessarily need to be bought gifts – and if I do buy presents, they only need to be cheap. But maybe I can make some of the gifts or do nice things for the villagers. Like Elsie's house, have you seen that she's only painted the bottom half?'

Andrew rolled his eyes. 'Yes, she's been on at me to paint it for her and I promised her I would, but it just wasn't a priority. Getting the houses ready for the new people was more important. She clearly decided to take matters into her own hands and now it looks even worse than it did before.'

'I could do the rest for her.'

'How do you intend to do that without being seen? I'm presuming the secrecy of the gifts is going to be a big part of this plan.'

'I could do it at night,' Willow said.

He cocked his head. 'Have you really thought this through?'

'Probably not. I always rush into things without thinking about it first.'

He smiled. 'You'll need a ladder to reach the apex of the house, and probably the eaves. I know it's a bungalow but you're not going to reach much higher than she did without a ladder or some kind of extendable roller. And you'll need lights if you're going to paint in the dark. It's really a two-man job during the day, let alone at night.'

'Well fortunately for me, I'm on quite good terms with the sexy estate manager,' Willow said and immediately regretted using the word sexy.

'Oh no, you're not getting me involved in this madness and…' he paused.

Good, he hadn't noticed the compliment.

'Did you just say I was sexy?'

Crap.

'Well flattery goes a long way,' Willow tried to brazen it out. 'I could think of lots of lovely things to say about you if you agree to help me.'

He leaned his head back as if looking to a higher being for strength. He let out a theatrical groan.

She waited patiently but knew he was going to say yes.

'I'll even throw in a present for you to sweeten the deal.'

He looked back at her and shook his head with amusement. 'Fine, but it better be a bloody good present.'

She laughed. 'It will be, I promise.'

'Very well.'

'I thought we could come up with a list of everyone in the village and maybe you could tell me a little about each person, what they like and dislike, so I can start to come up with some ideas for their presents.'

'Another list.'

'I love a list,' Willow said, not taking his complaints

remotely seriously.

'Clearly.'

'But as I'm nice, I'll let you eat first.'

'So kind.'

She got up to dish up the dinner. She glanced over her shoulder to see if he was still cursing his decision to come here tonight and found he was watching her with a huge smile on his face, which he quickly swapped for a scowl when he realised she had spotted him. She turned back to the oven with a smile. This project was going to be fun and working with Andrew was going to be a huge part of that.

chapter 11

Andrew drained the last mouthful of wine from his glass.

'I think we have a good list there,' he gestured to the piece of paper between them.

'I think it stopped being a good list about half hour or so ago.' Willow picked up the empty bottle of wine and held it up to him as proof. They'd also started on a second bottle.

'You might be right there, but I think we came up with some good stuff at the beginning of the evening.'

'Let's hope so.'

It had been a good night. In between coming up with ideas to surprise the villagers, they had chatted and laughed like old friends. He really bloody liked this girl.

'Well, I better go,' Andrew said.

'No driving home, you'll probably drive straight off the cliff.'

'I'm not that drunk, it'll take a bit more than a few glasses of wine to get me in that state, but to be on the safe side, I'll walk. I've got a torch on the quad bike.'

'Just don't drop this one,' Willow said. 'I don't like the thought of you stumbling around in the dark again.'

'Anyone would think you cared about me,' he said, standing up.

'I do.'

Andrew hesitated for a moment as he stared at her, his eyes locked on hers. He was in trouble here. He felt like he needed to walk away, clear his head, before he said or did something he would likely regret.

He moved to the door and she followed him.

'Thanks for dinner.'

She opened the door for him. 'Thanks for the help with the list.'

He stepped outside feeling like he should say something but he didn't know what. Something sparked in the air between them.

'Goodnight Willow.' He bent his head to kiss her on the cheek but as she moved towards him he caught her on the very edge of her mouth. He saw desire flicker in her eyes as he pulled back. He turned towards the gate, his heart thudding in his chest. It was a beautiful night, the sea was mirror calm, the stars twinkling in the inky sky. The chill of the night seemed to wipe away any fuzziness in his head and he suddenly had this moment of clarity. He looked back to see Willow was still standing there watching him and he had never felt so sure about anything in his entire life. He walked back towards her, cupped her face and kissed her.

She immediately kissed him back, wrapping her arms around his neck. The taste of her slammed into his gut. Her lips were so soft. He moved his hands down to her waist, feeling her warmth against him. When she slid her tongue into his mouth it was the single most sexy thing he'd ever experienced. The kiss turned urgent and desperate and he knew he should stop. He pulled back slightly and she moved her lips to his throat, her hot mouth there sending all clarity and sense from his brain.

He picked her up and she wrapped her legs around his waist. He kicked the door closed behind them as he carried her back inside.

Willow landed with a thud on the sofa with Andrew on top of her. They barely stopped kissing for a second as they caught their breath at the sudden jolt on their bodies. The weight of him pinning her to the sofa was divine. This kiss was everything, this was what had been missing from her life for the last four years.

She hadn't planned for this tonight, in fact she hadn't planned for this when she came to Happiness, but right now there wasn't a single part of her that didn't want it.

She ran her hands down his back, feeling the strength

in his shoulders. He was there, surrounding her with his scent, his kiss, his touch, his warmth, it was almost too much all at once.

He must have felt the same as he pulled back slightly to look at her, his breath heavy as he took her in.

She stroked his face. 'That was one hell of a goodnight kiss.'

'It's important to do these things right.'

'Well you did that.'

'I should go,' Andrew said.

She frowned slightly at this sudden about-turn.

'Not because I want to go,' he was quick to reassure her. 'But because I really don't want to.'

'I'm glad we cleared that up,' Willow said.

He smiled and leaned his forehead against hers for a second before standing up. He held out a hand for her and helped her to her feet as well.

'Let's try this again,' he said, still holding her hand as he walked to the door and opened it. 'Goodnight Willow.' He bent his head and this time gave her a brief kiss on the lips.

He walked to his quad bike and pulled a torch from the compartment under the seat. He gave her a wave and disappeared into the darkness.

Willow went back inside and closed the door. She ran her fingers over her lips, still tasting his kiss. What the hell had just happened? And more importantly, what was she going to do about it?

Willow got up the next morning, poured herself a bowl of Cheerios, made a cup of tea and took it outside to sit on the bench so she could enjoy the spectacular view.

She hadn't been able to stop thinking about that kiss all night. She couldn't say she regretted it, because it had been incredible, but she also stood by what she'd told Ruby a few days before. It was way too soon to be getting involved with someone, she wanted time to find herself first.

She had no idea what she was going to say to Andrew either. She didn't want it to be awkward between them and she certainly didn't want to hurt him. She wondered how he felt about it this morning and whether he was now plucking up the courage to face her.

She looked down at the notepad that she and Andrew had been working on the night before. After one or two glasses of wine, they had decided to call themselves 'The Secret Society of Happiness'. She liked that. He had a wonderful silly sense of humour that was very attractive.

She picked up the pad. Andrew had drawn her a very detailed map, showing where everyone lived in the village, which was going to be a big help in delivering the presents to the right people and ticking everyone off. She looked at the list. There were some silly suggestions there, clearly they had come in the latter part of the night. She decided to circle the ones she could do now as that seemed like a good place to start.

Mary, from the pink cottage near to the pub, had recently lost her watch and had scoured the whole village looking for it. Though Willow couldn't do anything about returning the lost watch to her, she did have a replacement. She had a thing for buying things at car boot sales and she was like a magpie for anything antique-looking, unique and sparkly. Generally she bought things and then sold them on eBay for a small profit, although she hadn't got round to selling the last lot before she moved. She had been going to donate them to a charity shop rather than bring them with her but she hadn't got round to that either. Upstairs, in her bedroom, she had a small box filled with jewellery and watches. She knew just the watch she wanted to give Mary. She would put it in a gift box and deliver it under the veil of darkness later that evening.

Then there was Ginny, who constantly had fresh flowers delivered every few weeks, so Andrew had told her. Ginny would display the flowers in a big vase in her front window. There were tons of wild flowers growing alongside the track leading from the village down to Sunrise Cottage; roses, violets, sunflowers, poppies and cornflowers seemed to be growing in abundance and there was even a big forsythia bush which she could cut a few stems off. Willow was sure the bouquet that she planned to pick and arrange for Ginny wouldn't be anywhere near as good as the professional shop-bought bouquets but she hoped, as a flower lover, Ginny would still appreciate the gesture.

And she and Andrew had planned to try to paint the rest of Elsie's house that night so, with Ginny and Mary too, that felt like a really good start to the Secret Society of Happiness List.

She placed the pad down and wrapped her hands around her mug for warmth.

'Hi.'

She looked round to see Andrew hovering awkwardly at her gate and her heart went out to him.

'Hello.'

'I… just came to collect the quad bike.'

She smiled and patted the bench next to her. He sighed in relief and came and sat down next to her.

They sat in silence for a while, before eventually Andrew spoke.

'You think last night was a mistake, don't you?'

'No, I think last night was lovely. Actually it was incredible. I've never been kissed like that and there is a huge part of me that wants to explore this wonderful connection between us and say to hell with it and take you straight up to my bedroom now and test the springs on my brand-new mattress.'

He laughed. 'That sounds like a plan.'

'But I think what happened last night was too soon. At least for me. I came down here for a fresh start. I was in a relationship with my last boyfriend for four years and I kind of lost sight of who I was, of what I wanted. I drifted along in this mundane relationship and it sucked the life out of me. Since it ended, in let's say a fairly embarrassing way, six months ago, it has been such a relief to be on my own again. But I couldn't get away from feeling like a laughing stock and the looks of pity I was getting from everyone, and I needed a break from all of that. I've been part of Garry and Willow for so long that I need to find out what it's like to just be me for a while.'

'I understand,' Andrew said.

'You do?' Willow was surprised by this as she wasn't sure she totally understood it herself.

'Yeah.' He squeezed her hand and placed a kiss on her cheek. 'I've had a string of bad relationships and I swore I wasn't interested in having another, at least not for a while. And I'm not sure what came over me last night, I don't think I can even blame the alcohol. The only thing I can say in my defence is that you're really bloody lovely and I just got carried away. You have my word, it won't happen again.'

She smiled and leaned her head against his shoulder. 'I think you're pretty wonderful too.'

Which made her wonder, why was she so intent on holding back?

'How about a pact?' Willow said, suddenly feeling like she didn't want to draw a line under her relationship with Andrew completely. 'Six months from now, if I haven't annoyed you too much with all the lists I'm going to make you write, and you're still single and not married with babies on the way, we revisit that kiss and see where the night takes us when you don't have to rush off.'

He smiled. 'Have you just booked a date for us to have sex six months from now? That's a bit too organised if you ask me.'

'Is that a no?'

'Hell no.' Andrew got out his phone and she laughed as she watched him enter a new event into his calendar. *Hot sex with Willow.* 'I'll look forward to it.'

She smiled. She liked the sound of that plan.

chapter 12

Willow had decided that she needed to do some more painting in the village that day. With only two weeks now until the open day, she wanted everything to be perfect. She had spent a good deal of time the day before updating her website so that was done and until any new orders came in she had some hours to spare. It was hot already and it was still early in the morning; it promised to be another sweltering day so she didn't want to waste the good weather sitting inside her shop.

She wandered down to the far end of the village, thinking about Andrew. She just hoped that, after their kiss and their agreement that nothing should happen between them, it wouldn't be awkward for them to work in such close proximity to each other.

As she got closer she was surprised how much had changed in just a day of Jack and his team working here. But a quick head count revealed that Jack's team included at least twelve people so it was no surprise they had got so much done already. She counted at least four more houses that had been painted since she had last been down here, although she hadn't been down this end for a few days as she had been focussing her attention on painting the shops in the main part of the village.

She headed for the shed and grabbed some tins of paint and brushes. She looked around. She wanted to make sure she wouldn't be in the way of any of the work that was going on and she didn't want to start painting on a house that might still have wet paint. There was no sign of Andrew, though there was clearly work going on inside one or two of the houses.

She saw a man who looked like he might be in charge as he gave directions to two other men and she heard one of them call him Jack. He had stripped down to his shorts, as many of the men had. He had the body of someone who did a lot of manual labour. As he finished talking, she walked over to speak to him.

'Hello,' Willow called to get his attention.

He turned round and flashed her a winning smile. 'Hello,' he said, his eyes appraising her. 'Can I help?'

'Yes, I'm the one painting the flowers and designs around the doors. I just wondered—'

'Oh, you're the artist.'

'I wouldn't go so far as to say that, it's just a few simple flowers.'

'They look great. I hope he's paying you.' He jerked a thumb to one of the cottages, presumably where Andrew was busy working.

'Oh no, I live here in the village, I'm just trying to help.'

'Well, that's very kind, but don't let him take advantage of you,' Jack said.

Willow frowned. Andrew would be the last person in the world to do that. 'I was just wondering which houses I could work on, I don't want to be in your way.'

'I don't think you could ever be in my way.'

She resisted rolling her eyes. Jack was smooth and this method of flirting had probably worked very well for him in the past. She waited for him expectantly.

He eventually realised he wasn't going to get far with her. 'You can start on those two and when you've finished you'll probably be able to do that one.'

'Thanks,' Willow said and moved over to one of the houses he'd pointed at.

She started painting the curly green stem and leaves again but this time she painted bright yellow roses around the door. It looked cheery. She moved on to the next house where there was evidently work going on inside as she could hear lots of drilling and banging taking place. She peered through one of the windows just in time to see Andrew stripping off his t-shirt. God he really was glorious. Seeing his body affected her in ways that seeing Jack's didn't. Maybe it was because she had been pinned underneath that body the night before, or maybe it was because it belonged to such a wonderful man.

To her shame, Andrew saw her gawking at him through the window.

She quickly moved away but a few seconds later he came to the door.

'Are you perving at me again, Willow McKay?'

'No, I was just looking through the window to see what work was going on.'

He was smirking at her, clearly not believing a word of it.

She shrugged. She might as well be honest. 'And it came with the added bonus of this marvellous view.'

Andrew laughed. 'Well, I like to keep the workers happy. I take it you're here to do some more painting?'

'I am.'

'It's really appreciated, thank you.'

His genuine smile made her feel warm inside in ways that a simple payment for her services could never achieve.

'It's OK.'

'It really helps Happiness to look good from the outside and with our secret project maybe we can help the villagers feel better on the inside. Talking of which…' He looked around to make sure that nobody was listening. 'Are you ready for our Secret Society shenanigans tonight?'

'Yes, I can't wait. Shall we do Mary and Ginny first before we go to Elsie's house to do the painting?'

'That sounds good. We can stop at my house after we've done Mary and Ginny to pick up the paint and the ladders. Should we be wearing black with camouflage paint on our faces?'

Willow laughed. 'Wearing black might not be a bad idea but let's leave the camouflage paint for now. I think we'll certainly look suspicious if we're caught walking around looking like we've come fresh from a war zone.'

Andrew looked a bit disappointed that he couldn't go full-on commando but he soon recovered himself. 'Do you think we need a secret handshake or a special password for all those that are in the Secret Society?' he teased.

Willow smiled, she loved his silly sense of humour. 'I think we'll have to come up with one.'

'So shall we meet after dinner?' he said.

'Yes.' And then because he looked like he might be about to invite her to have dinner with him she decided to make up a prior arrangement. 'I promised my friend Ruby that I'd have pizza with her tonight.'

'She's coming here?'

'No, we're having dinner together over Skype.'

She immediately felt bad for lying to Andrew but there was no point in turning down a relationship with him in order to find herself if she was going to spend every night with him anyway. She might as well enjoy the other aspects of the relationship if that was the case. She had given herself six months to just be Willow rather than part of a couple but she honestly didn't think she would last that long. She enjoyed his company so much that it felt like a slippery slope to then spend all her time with him as well. Dinner every night could then easily lead to breakfast every morning and it would only be a matter of time before they decided to fill that gap in between.

'I was going to say that I have darts tonight down the pub so it will have to be after eight anyway,' Andrew said.

Oh god, she'd got it all wrong and the way he was looking at her suggested he knew she was lying about her plans too.

'Why not come round to my house when you're done with darts and then we can do our Secret Society business together,' Willow said, knowing that now she would have to have dinner with Ruby just to prove him wrong and would deliberately still be talking to her on Skype when he arrived.

'Sounds like a plan.'

He held his fists out as if he wanted to bump fists with her. She frowned in confusion but copied the gesture. He bumped it on the top, the bottom and either side and she laughed as she realised he was trying to do a secret handshake.

'What?' Andrew said. 'Does it need a bit more work?'

'Just a smidgen.'

'I'll keep practising,' Andrew said as he turned to go back inside the house.

'On your own?' Willow called after him.

'I have two hands, don't I?'

Willow giggled as she imagined him practising the secret handshake by himself. He waved goodbye and closed the door.

God, she really liked this man.

chapter 13

'This is not a bad idea, you know,' Ruby said, gesturing to the Chinese she had in front of her, the noodles she was eating dripping with some kind of red sauce. 'Having dinner together. It's almost like you're really here.'

When Willow had told Ruby she needed to have dinner with her that night over Skype, Ruby had leapt at the idea, although she hadn't followed the instructions to the letter when she turned up with sweet and sour chicken. But Willow had pizza so she didn't think it mattered that much.

'It's lovely to see you. It's silly, I've only been gone a few days and I'm missing you already,' Willow said.

'It's not silly at all, I am rather fabulous,' Ruby said, tonight sporting a t-shirt with Rudolph on the front with a glittery red nose. Ruby loved Christmas so much, she lived and breathed it all year long.

Willow smiled. 'Yes you are.'

'So tell me why we're doing this?' Ruby snapped a prawn cracker in half and popped one piece in her mouth.

'Because I miss you.'

Ruby let out a bark of a laugh. 'You're such a lying toad. Want to tell me the real reason?'

Willow sighed. 'Because I lied to a rather lovely man to avoid dinner plans for tonight and he wasn't even going to invite me to dinner after all. And now I feel horribly guilty and he'll be coming round shortly to help me with something and I want him to see I wasn't lying even though I was.'

Ruby laughed. 'Oh what a tangled web we weave. If the man was so lovely, why did you not want to have dinner with him?'

'Because…' Willow really didn't want to tell Ruby about the kiss because then she'd make it into a thing and it wasn't going to be a thing, definitely not. Although she knew she had to tell Ruby some of it. 'Because I like Andrew.'

'And?'

'And I'm not looking for a relationship right now.'

'Who says it has to be a relationship? Just have some fun. That's just what you need to get over your relationship with Garry.'

'I am over it,' Willow said, with a sigh.

'Yes, I didn't mean that,' Ruby said. 'I just meant passion and excitement has been missing from your life for the last four years. Why not have a bit of that again? Get out there and enjoy yourself. It doesn't have to be anything serious.'

'Andrew is too lovely for that.'

'So you're just going to avoid him in a village that's smaller than my pokey little flat.'

'I'm not going to avoid him, we're working together on a project right now. I just think that I don't need to spend every night with him too. He came round here for dinner last night, and it was… really nice.' It had been a hell of a lot more than nice. 'I just think if we end up having dinner together every night then it could so easily turn into something more.'

Ruby shook her head affectionately. 'Well at least I get to meet him.'

'Ah god,' Willow said. She hadn't thought this through. 'Don't say anything.'

Ruby crossed her heart and zipped her lips. 'I promise.'

'How's everything going with you anyway?' Willow asked, keen to change the subject.

'Oh, OK I guess,' Ruby said, with a sigh. 'I've been thinking about you and how you've just packed up everything you own and started over somewhere new. I kind of wish I could do that too. Everyone knows *everything* about me here and that's not always a good thing.'

Willow thought about Ruby and her past. Although Willow had met her when Ruby was in her early twenties, a few years after she had her heart broken in the worst possible way, Willow knew that, even ten years later, the people of St Octavia would never let Ruby forget it. But Ruby was normally so upbeat, it wasn't like her to get down. Although her elderly neighbour, Maggie, had died two months before and Willow knew that Ruby had been upset by that. She wondered if that had anything to do with Ruby's change of mood.

'Has something happened?' Willow asked.

'I don't know, life just drifts on, doesn't it. Nothing ever changes unless you make the change yourself. I sit on my little market stand every week and I see the same people come and go. Bill and Connie come into the market hall every Tuesday to get four slices of ham from the deli stand and *some of that nice cheesy bread* from the bread stall. Thomas comes and looks at the model trains on the next stand every evening after he leaves work. He never buys any of them. Sally and her son Noah come in every Saturday to get a chocolate milkshake *with extra sprinkles* and I get the impression that's the only quality time she has with him. I don't know, I just feel I need a change.'

'Is this to do with Maggie?' Willow asked.

Ruby shrugged. 'Maybe. You know she had the same job her entire life, working in the local chemist since she was sixteen, right up to when she died. I was talking to her a few weeks before she died. It was her seventieth birthday and I asked her about her life and what she had achieved, what she was most proud of – and, beyond having her kids, she couldn't think of a single thing she had achieved or done that she was proud of. She tried to laugh it off and said people would remember her for being a fantastic chemist and I just thought it was a little sad, that that was the only thing she would be remembered as. My brother is a bloody Paralympian for goodness sake and what have I done with my life? I've lived here in St Octavia almost my whole life apart from when I went to university. What will people say about me after I'm gone:

"She had great baubles"?'

Willow smiled at the unintentional euphemism. Ruby made her living selling Christmas decorations all year round. She loved it and Willow didn't think she'd ever give that up.

'So what are you going to do?'

'I don't know.'

'Go travelling?'

'I'm not sure I'm the sort of girl who would travel alone. I just feel like I need a change. I need a new routine, new faces.'

'Well what's stopping you?' Willow said. 'You could do what I did. Hell, you can even come here. Open up a Christmas shop in the village.'

'You make it sound so easy.'

'It is. You have no job to give notice to, you hate the flat where you live. Free accommodation and rent for a year. If you hate it after that, you can always move back to St Octavia. At least come and visit and see the place for a few days.'

Ruby smiled slightly as she thought about it.

'And to be honest, I could really do with your help and expertise,' Willow said, knowing Ruby couldn't say no to her little plea.

'My Christmas skills?' Ruby asked.

Willow thought about it for a moment and then found herself nodding. 'Actually yes. Christmas lights, the white ones. We need them in abundance. We have this big open day coming up in a few weeks and it needs to look magical. White lights could help with that. And you're just the person to know where to hang them.'

She hoped Andrew wouldn't mind that she had suddenly made this executive decision, but who didn't love fairy lights?

'I could do that. I have a ton of that stuff in storage, I could lend them to you for a few weeks. You know what, I will come and visit. If nothing else, I want to meet this lovely man who you've fallen in love with in person.'

'I have not fallen in love with him,' Willow protested, just as there was a knock on the door. 'Now shush.'

Ruby sat forward on the edge of her seat eagerly as Willow went to answer the door.

Andrew was standing there, dressed all in black. He looked sexy, like the Milk Tray man.

'Oh hey, Andrew,' Willow smiled. 'I won't be a moment. I'm just finishing my conversation with Ruby. Come in for a second.'

She stepped back so Andrew could come in and she watched him clock the open laptop with Ruby's grinning face on the screen. She felt like saying, 'See, I wasn't lying after all.' But she had been and this suddenly felt like a double lie.

'Ruby, this is Andrew. Andrew, this is my best friend Ruby.'

'Hi.' Ruby waved inanely.

Andrew smiled as he bent over to get closer to the camera. 'Hello.'

'Are you taking care of my friend?' Ruby said and Willow rolled her eyes.

'I'm making sure she is well looked after,' Andrew said.

'Right, I think we better go,' Willow said, before Ruby

said something too cringey. 'Lots to do tonight. I'll be right with you, Andrew.'

She ushered him back to the door and turned back to the laptop. 'Bye Ruby.'

'He's hot,' Ruby mouthed.

Willow made a noise in her throat that was a vague agreement.

'Sleeping with him would definitely put a huge smile on your face,' Ruby whispered.

'Bye Rubes.' Willow slammed down the lid of the laptop and turned back to face Andrew who was looking like he hadn't heard anything. She gave a little sigh of relief.

'How was darts?' Willow said, pulling on her boots.

'Fine, our team lost, but it was fine. Ruby seems nice, very smart.'

'She is.' Willow frowned in confusion. 'What do you mean, smart?'

'The things she said.'

Willow flushed. 'You heard her?'

'I lip-read, remember?' Andrew chuckled. 'She speaks a lot of sense.'

'Oh shush.' Willow laughed.

She picked up the gift-wrapped watch and the hand-tied bunch of flowers she had prepared earlier that day. She slipped the watch into a bag so no one would see her holding the box and put two and two together the next day. The flowers were a little harder to hide.

'These look wonderful,' Andrew said, gesturing towards

the flowers.

'They looked a lot better in my head but they'll do.'

They stepped outside together and Willow closed the door behind her.

'We'll take the coastal path I think, less likely that we'll be seen that way and Ginny's house is quite near the bottom of the village so we can do hers first,' Andrew said.

'Sounds like a plan,' Willow said.

Andrew flicked on his torch and they set off down the little path. It was completely dark here – although the moon was shining brightly above them, it wasn't giving off enough light to allow them to see where they were going. The path was slightly uneven in parts and she found herself linking arms with Andrew, but purely for safety reasons. She certainly didn't want to trip and go flying over the edge of the cliff. He didn't seem to mind.

'So can I ask you something?' Andrew said.

'Anything,' Willow said.

'Did you lie about your plans with Ruby tonight and then feel like you had to go ahead with those plans to prove to me that you weren't lying?'

Willow felt her cheeks burn red in the darkness. 'Well when I said ask me anything, I didn't mean that.'

'You don't have to answer,' Andrew said.

He was being so kind. She had lied to him and he knew it and he was still being lovely.

'Well I do now, because silence is a guilty omission and if I answer then I can at least try to defend myself.'

'Please go ahead,' Andrew said.

'I thought you were going to invite me to dinner.'

'OK.'

A rabbit leapt out of a nearby bush and darted up the hill away from them, its white tail flashing in the light of the torch.

'I enjoyed having you round for dinner last night immensely, you are wonderful company and I'm very happy to do that again. I just thought if dinner was going to become a regular thing, like every night, then…' she trailed off.

'Then we could end up testing out your bed springs a lot sooner than our prearranged six-month date,' Andrew finished for her.

She laughed. 'Something like that.'

'I understand. But if I invite you to dinner and you don't want to come, you can just say no.'

'I didn't want to hurt your feelings.'

'I'm a big boy. I can take it.'

They walked on in silence for a while and, because they were veiled in the darkness, she felt like she could say this and it wouldn't really count.

'I could fall for you Andrew Harrington. I mean I haven't, but I feel like I really could. I have a feeling that six-month embargo will come to a spectacular end a lot sooner than we think but I'd at least like to finish unpacking before I leap into bed with the first man I met.'

There was silence from him for a moment and she wondered if she had scared him with her half declaration of love. She was kind of scared of her feelings for him herself.

He pulled her to a stop, put the torch on the ground and turned to face her in the darkness. He pressed a kiss to her forehead.

Her heart erupted in her chest and she found her hands going to his waist and leaning into the warmth of his body.

'I think, sometimes, you meet someone who is worth breaking all the rules for.' He pulled back slightly to look her in the eyes. 'And sometimes you meet someone who is worth waiting for however long it takes for them to realise it too.'

Oh god. This man.

She was in trouble with him and there was nothing she could do about it.

chapter 14

'Come on,' Andrew said, breaking the moment. He picked up the torch, grabbed her hand and carried on walking across the cliff tops. He didn't know whether to kick himself or give himself a bloody medal for walking away from that. There she was, bathed in the moonlight, looking magical and breathtakingly beautiful, staring up at him like she wanted to kiss him, and instead of grabbing her and kissing her again, he'd walked away. But as much as he liked her, he wanted to respect her decision to wait. He totally understood where she was coming from, things were moving way too quickly between them.

She jogged to keep up with his long-legged stride and he forced himself to slow down. He glanced down at her and she smiled up at him.

'Stop smiling.'

This made her smile even more. It lit up her entire face.

He quickly looked away.

They reached the top of the steps to the beach and he turned off up the little path towards the village. They soon passed the stone ruins of the first houses in the village.

'They say these houses are thousands of years old.'

'Surely they can't be that old,' Willow said.

'I don't know. Apparently they had some historians digging round here many years back and they found evidence that pointed to several hundred years BC. They think it's haunted too.'

'What?' Willow said, suddenly walking a lot closer to him.

'You scared?' Andrew said.

'I wouldn't say scared but not exactly thrilled. Have you seen anything?'

'No. I don't come down this way that often. I go for a swim in the sea from time to time but I haven't seen any ghostly apparitions whenever I've walked past. But if you believe the gossip in the village – and I'd take a lot of that with a pinch of salt – some of the locals have seen something. Most people seem to think it was a story told by the older folk of the village many years ago to scare the children who grew up here from coming near the place. Although if I grew up here and heard those kinds of stories, it would be more likely to make me come down here and investigate than stay away.'

'So what kind of ghosts are we talking about?' Willow linked arms with him. 'Headless horsemen, cloaked figures, that kind of thing?'

'Vampires that suck your blood,' Andrew said, pulling her

close to him and playfully biting at her neck.

'Stop it,' Willow laughed, batting him away.

He carried on walking, wishing he hadn't done that because he could now taste her on his lips. 'I don't know really, depends who you speak to.' The lights of the village twinkled ahead of them. 'Some say it's the ghost of the woman who walks the cliff tops looking for her lost love,' he said.

Willow laughed. 'That's a bit tragic. Maybe she fell in love with the handsome estate manager but kept giving him the run-around and in the end he went off and married someone far better and she wandered the cliffs weeping. And because she had tears in her eyes, she fell over the edge and died a tragic and senseless death.'

Andrew smiled. 'Maybe. But I don't think we have any fear of history repeating itself there.'

'Me falling over the cliff in my grief?'

'Me running off with someone else.'

'Ah, you're a true gent.'

He smiled. 'Actually there is also an old wives' tale that the apparitions are really fairies.'

Willow laughed. 'I think I believe that even less than the ghosts.'

'The fairies apparently help the villagers when they are in need.'

'Well that's nice of them. They haven't done much for the village in its current state.'

'Sshhh! You don't want to anger the fairies. Maybe you have to ask for help.'

Willow stopped and turned back to face the ruins. 'OK, fairies, we could really do with your help with the village. It's looking a bit tatty and we need it to be ready for the open day in two weeks. Also we need some help with the presents we're giving to the villagers, so any help you can give us there would be great.'

She turned back to look at Andrew. 'How was that?'

'Fine. But you have to make an offering.'

'What?' Willow laughed.

'Hey, I don't make these rules.'

'It sounds to me like you're making them up on the spot. What do you suggest?'

Andrew thought about this for a moment, because while he had heard rumours of fairies, he was making up the stuff about giving the fairies an offering.

'How about a dance?'

'You want me to dance for the fairies?'

Andrew nodded. 'I think the fairies will love it.'

'On my own?'

He shrugged. 'You're the one doing the asking.'

She clearly thought about this for a moment and he honestly expected her to tell him where to shove it but after a few seconds she started to sway and swing her arms from side to side, then she started bouncing her shoulders and banging her knees together. It wasn't like any dance he'd ever seen before. He wanted to burst out laughing and he also wanted to gather her close and kiss her because this bloody woman had got right under his skin. She had captured his heart and he didn't think he would ever get over that.

He cleared his throat and she looked at him. 'That was amazing.'

'Do you think the fairies will be suitably impressed?'

'Well, I know I was.'

She smiled and linked arms with him again as they carried on walking towards the village. 'I don't believe any of this for one second.'

'You still danced though.'

'This village needs all the help it can get. If that means I have to dance naked next to a fire at midnight, under a full moon, then I'll do it.'

'Oh yes, the dancing naked part. That's what I forgot,' Andrew said, turning them back around. 'Let's do it again, this time naked.'

Willow turned them back to face the village. 'Only at a full moon.'

'Damn it.'

He smiled as they walked along in the darkness. She made him really happy.

They were approaching the first houses in the main part of the village now and luckily for them Ginny's house was one of the first they would come to. The lights were on and the noise of the TV could be heard from inside.

'OK, it's this house here,' Andrew said. He looked around to see if anyone else was around but the street was completely deserted.

He watched Willow glance around too. 'What if someone

else takes the flowers?'

'That would be a pretty heartless thing to do.'

'Maybe we should knock on the door?' she said.

'And then what, run and hide? I didn't take you for the *knock door, run* type.'

She flashed him a mischievous look and walked over to the door. She placed the flowers on the doorstep and then, to his surprise, she raised her fist to knock on the door.

'Wait,' he hissed. 'We need a plan, where are we going to hide?'

'I'll leave that to you,' she said, knocking three times loudly on the door.

Crap.

He looked around frantically as he saw the shadow of Ginny get up behind the curtains. He quickly snatched Willow's hand and yanked her into the space between two houses on the opposite side of the street. He pulled her back into the darkness just as the door was flung open. His heart was beating out of his chest as Willow stifled a giggle. He watched Ginny look up and down the street and then glance down and spot the flowers. She bent down to pick them up and he saw her whole face light up with happiness.

He felt a warm glow spread through him as she looked around once more and went back inside with a big smile on her face.

He glanced down at Willow and saw she was smiling too. They had done something wonderful tonight, well Willow had, but it felt amazing to be a part of it. This tiny gesture had just made a lonely old woman incredibly happy.

Willow looked up at him, her eyes shining in the light from the street. She was incredible.

He touched her face, grazing his thumb down her cheek. 'I think I'd wait an eternity for you Willow McKay.'

She pressed a gentle kiss to his palm. 'I don't think you'll have to. Come on, we have lots to do.'

With a quick check out on the street, she stepped out of the shadows and into the light. There was suddenly a big part of him that felt like he was doing the same. He smiled and shook his head and then followed her out on to the road.

Willow could not stop giggling. Andrew's stepladder was the squeakiest, creakiest thing she had ever heard as he carried it the short distance from his house to Elsie's. Surely everyone in the village would be able to hear it. Andrew was theatrically creeping along the little track, walking on his tiptoes, and that was making her laugh so much too.

'Could you be any louder?' she giggled.

He turned to stare at her incredulously. 'Do you want to carry this?'

'Oh no, I'm fine with carrying the paint and the brushes. I take it back, you're doing a splendid job.'

He muttered something under his breath that didn't sound too polite.

They approached Elsie's house and stood surveying it for

a moment. There was still quite a lot to do, but it was a very small house so Willow didn't think it would take them that long.

'Let's start round the back first. We can do the front last as we're more likely to be seen there, and the later we're painting that the better,' Willow said.

Andrew nodded his agreement.

They walked through the gate and crept round the back. The house was in darkness, which in some ways was worse because if Elsie was asleep then she could be woken. If she had been watching TV then she would at least be distracted by that and the noise would drown out any squeaks and creaks.

The back and front would be quite easy as even Willow could reach the top of the thatch with the paint roller. But the sides would be trickier as Andrew would have to go up the ladder to reach the apex of the house.

Andrew laid the torch down on the ground, not pointing it directly at the house probably in case the light woke Elsie up. He poured some paint into the tray; luckily Elsie had started the house in white so they didn't have to worry about matching the colours up. They both began painting the wall with their rollers, starting in the middle and working their way out to the edges of the house.

Once that was done, they picked up their paint and ladder and moved round to the side. They were just propping the ladder up against the wall when Julia walked past with her Jack Russell and, to Willow's surprise, a ginger cat on a lead. Julia didn't see them but unfortunately the Jack Russell did. He started yapping immediately as Andrew quickly pulled her to the ground.

'What is it, Colin?' Julia said. 'Did you see a rabbit or something? Oh, I bet it's that nasty fox that's been after my poor chickens.'

Frustratingly, Julia decided to try and see herself, coming right up to the fence and dragging an unwilling Colin and the angry ginger cat with her. Willow was glad for the foresight Andrew had shown in his suggestion they wear black, but she wished she'd taken his advice on the camouflage paint right now. Willow wondered if Julia could see the ladder – she was certainly taking her time with looking over Elsie's fence and Colin was still barking. Luckily the torch was still round the back but Julia could probably see the extra light coming from Elsie's back garden.

Eventually she gave up and left, taking a still yapping Colin and the angry ginger cat with her.

Willow and Andrew lay there not moving for a while longer.

Andrew sat up. 'I think she's gone.'

'She's probably creeping round the back of your house trying to spot you with a *girl*,' Willow said, clambering up. 'And are we not going to address the fact that Julia was walking a cat on a lead?'

Andrew shrugged as if it was perfectly normal. 'Rufus, apparently he likes it.'

'He didn't look very happy to me.'

'Come on. We need to be quick, she'll be back shortly,'

Andrew whispered, scrambling to his feet too.

This whole project was going to be quite stressful. If they could deliver the presents to all the villagers over the next few weeks without getting caught it was going to be a bloody miracle.

Andrew followed Willow through her gate, which he still needed to fix, and she let them into her house. He was bone-tired. After spending most of the night before lying awake thinking about that incredible kiss and then getting up early to help with the renovations in the village, and now spending the last few hours painting Elsie's house, he was exhausted. Julia had been back along the road three times, either because she suspected something was going on or she just wanted to give Colin and Rufus a good walk, but it held them up considerably. Julia wasn't the only one on a late-night walk either. They'd seen Connor from the pub walking his Labrador and Dorothy out for a random stroll too. Who knew that Happiness village was such a social hub for late-night activity?

He flopped down on Willow's sofa for a moment.

'I'll make you a coffee,' Willow said, disappearing off to the kitchen.

He felt his eyes droop closed and leaned his head on the back of the sofa. He wondered what the rule book said about him spending the night on Willow's sofa because right then he didn't have the energy to make it back home. He didn't want her to feel uncomfortable with him staying but maybe she'd let him have a kip for a half hour or so. He felt himself dropping off as he heard her move around in the kitchen. After a few minutes, he heard her come back in and place the coffee cup on the table. He couldn't even open his eyes. He felt a blanket being draped over him but the next thing he felt her snuggling in by his side, resting her head on his shoulder and wrapping an arm round his stomach. He opened one eye to look at her but her eyes were closed now too.

'I really like you Andrew Harrington,' she whispered.

He put an arm around her and kissed her head. 'I really like you too.'

She looked up at him. 'Are you planning on staying here tonight?'

'Just for a little while,' Andrew said, closing his eyes again.

She got up out of his arms and he felt a bit bereft. 'Then let's go to bed.'

Both eyes snapped open to see that she was holding out a hand for him. Good god. Of course he wanted that but he also respected her decision to not get involved in a relationship right now. He didn't want her to do something she would later regret. He must have looked like a startled rabbit because she laughed.

'To sleep, you pervert.'

He smiled with relief because he wasn't sure sex would be a good idea for two people who didn't want to get involved. Although sleeping in a bed with her probably wasn't a good idea either, it would make things very complicated. But the thought of going to sleep with her in his arms… well, there was no way he could walk away from that. He was respectful but he wasn't a saint.

He stood up and took her hand. 'I can think of nothing I'd like more.'

'Oh, I'm sure you could think of something,' Willow said, a mischievous glint in her eyes.

'I'm not sure I'm up to anything else.'

He followed her up the stairs and sat down on her bed to take off his boots. He stripped down to his boxer shorts and got into bed, closing his eyes so Willow could get changed in private. He felt her slip into bed and cuddle up to him again, with her head on his chest. Yep, definitely complicated. He slid an arm round her shoulders.

'Thank you for helping me tonight,' Willow said.

'It was my pleasure,' Andrew said, honestly. 'I really enjoyed it. Seeing Ginny's face when she saw those flowers, that was pretty special wasn't it?'

'It really was. There'll be lots of talk in the village tomorrow. We should get our stories straight about what we were doing.'

'I'm going to tell everyone that I spent the night in bed with an incredible woman,' Andrew said and she laughed.

They fell silent for a while and he knew she was dozing off. Normally he would wait for the woman he was with to fall asleep before taking out his hearing aids, he hated drawing attention to his deafness, but he didn't have to do that with Willow. She already knew and he liked that. He still felt a little self-conscious about it but he felt so at ease with her, nothing seemed to faze her.

'I'm going to take my hearing aids out now,' Andrew said. 'So don't talk to me if you want an answer or at least make sure you're facing me. And if there's a fire in the middle of the night, you'll have to give me a big nudge.'

'What do you do in your house to protect yourself from a fire?'

'I have my smoke alarm linked to a strobe light and a vibration pad under my pillow.'

'Oh, OK. Well, I promise not to let you die.'

He smiled and took his hearing aids out, his world going almost completely silent, so he couldn't hear her breathing any more and that bothered him more than anything else. She lay on his chest, her head propped up on her hands, just watching him, a smile on her face. He popped the hearing aids on top of her bedside drawers. He looked back at her to see she was still staring at him, a big smile on her face. He stroked her hair, needing to be connected to her in some way now he wouldn't be able to hear her.

She started to talk and he focussed on her lips so he could see what she was saying.

'So lip-reading, how accurate is it?' she said.

'Not very accurate, a lot of it is guesswork based on the context, plus other facial features, body language and the expression in someone's eyes. Even the best lip-readers in the world can only read about thirty to forty percent of what is being said. And that's only if the person talking is well lit and looking face on. Facial hair is also a bit of a problem. So don't grow a moustache. There are also many words that look very similar or identical on the lips, like "I love you" looks the exact same as "olive juice" and "elephant shoes".'

She laughed and he hated that he couldn't hear that either. It was just an echoey noise, like being underwater.

She looked back at him. 'OK, just so there's no confusion, I'm going to stop talking and do this instead.'

And with that, she leaned forward and kissed him.

Christ, there could be no misunderstanding this. He stroked down her hair, tasting her lips, inhaling her scent, all of his other senses coming alive. She was magnificent and she made him feel utterly spectacular. He had kissed quite a few women in his life, but it had never felt like this. This was different, better in so many ways, and he had no idea why.

She pulled back slightly and smiled.

'Well thanks for clearing that up,' he said.

Her smile grew and she gave him another brief kiss on the lips. 'Goodnight Andrew.'

She reached up and turned off the light but the moon outside poured through the windows, bathing everything in silver. She lay back down and snuggled into his chest where he knew she would feel his heart hammering against his ribs. Sleep would be very far away again tonight.

chapter 15

Willow woke the next morning to an empty bed and, judging by the silence in the rest of the house, Andrew wasn't there either. She sat up and looked around. Next to her on the pillow was a note and a yellow rose. She picked it up and stroked the soft petals as she read the note.

My lovely Willow,

You are quite honestly the most incredible woman I have ever met and I could quite easily have stayed in your bed for the rest of the day, holding you in my arms and maybe even enjoying more of those glorious kisses. But I'm not sure where we are, whether that wonderful kiss last night was just a temporary reprieve or a step forward, and I thought if you woke up this morning and regretted the kiss, I would save you the awkwardness of having that conversation again. If you still don't want a relationship just yet, then I'm happy to wait until you do. But if last night was you throwing caution to the wind and you'd like to do this thing properly, then I'd like to ask you round to dinner tonight as our first official date. I make a mean chicken tikka masala and there will be candles and flowers and definitely more kisses. If you don't want that just yet, you don't need to worry. I can freeze the extra curry and I promise you it won't be awkward if you say no. But if it's a yes, then I look forward to seeing you at seven.

Yours hopefully
Andrew x

Oh god. She couldn't help but smile at this wonderfully sweet note. This man, it was ridiculous how much she felt for him already. And while there was a part of her that still wasn't sure whether running head first into a relationship mere days after arriving in Happiness was a good idea, there was a part of her that wanted to see where this incredible connection would lead.

She wondered what her mum would say if she knew Willow was falling in love just a few days after she had arrived in her new home. She didn't really have a close relationship with her mum. After her parents divorced several years before, her mum had moved to Scotland rather than stay near her dad and Willow had moved to St Octavia, where Ruby lived. But Willow had never been close to her mum. The overriding sense she got from her mum was disappointment. '*Oh Willow*' was one of her mum's favourite phrases, followed by a sad shake of the head every time she heard what Willow had done or said.

When Willow had announced she was moving to Happiness, '*Oh Willow*' must have been used three or four times in the same conversation. Willow certainly didn't need her mum's approval or most likely disapproval when it came to matters of the heart.

Ruby, however, would probably go to completely the opposite end of the spectrum and tell Willow to stop messing around and go for it. They had known each other since going to university together and had shared a room in their halls of residence. Ruby was definitely more the throw-caution-to-the-wind type.

No, if she was going to make a decision like this, she would have to do it on her own. And what she really wanted to do and what she *should* do were probably two very different things. But when she next saw Andrew, she would simply listen to her heart and then she'd know what she should do.

Willow got down to her shop just before nine and the street was almost deserted. She waved at Tabitha who was opening the pub for breakfast. Maybe news hadn't spread about the Secret Society's deliveries the night before.

Just as Willow pushed open the door she saw Mary running down the street, waving at Tabitha.

'I got one, Tabby, I got one.'

'Mum, are you OK?' Tabitha asked. 'What did you get?'

'A secret gift!' Mary said excitedly as Willow watched

from inside her shop.

'Really? What was it?' Tabitha asked as she put the menu board outside the door.

Willow watched Roger walk out of his cheese shop with Dorothy and his sister Liz.

'What's going on?' Roger said.

'Mary got a present too,' Tabitha said.

Willow wanted to wander over and join in the chat but she was a terrible liar and she wasn't sure she'd be able to withstand the inquisition, should any questions come her way.

She decided she would clean the windows so she could at least listen. She quickly filled a bowl with soapy water, grabbed a cloth and stepped back outside.

Mary was showing off her new antique watch to anyone who was passing and there was quite the gathering now.

'There was a knock on the door late last night and when I went to answer it, no one was there,' she said. 'But there was this beautifully wrapped box there instead and this watch was inside.'

Willow glanced around as she started scrubbing. Dorothy looked a little put out that Mary had received a mystery gift too. Of course, if Mary had received a gift too, then Dorothy's gift was less likely to be from Joseph.

'Who do you think it's from?' Tabitha asked. She'd now been joined by her husband Connor, Julia and several other villagers Willow hadn't met yet.

'I don't know, maybe Kitty and Ken,' Mary said.

'Lord, I think they've done enough for us,' Julia said, her

pink candyfloss hair styled in a beehive today, wibbling like jelly on top of her head. 'This whole village could probably be a contender for some best-looking village award by the time all the renovations and improvements have been made. I don't think they're roaming the streets late at night giving presents to us all as well.'

'Well who is it then?' Dorothy asked.

'Well you thought your gift was from Joseph. Maybe he's giving presents to everyone,' Liz said.

'It's not Joseph,' Dorothy said, protectively, as if Liz was trying to steal Joseph from her.

'Well who is it?' Connor asked, admiring the watch.

'Are you sure it's not that lovely Andrew?' Liz asked.

'I don't think it's Andrew,' Julia said, quite proudly, as if about to impart some great pearl of wisdom to exonerate him. 'I was walking Colin and Rufus past Sunrise Cottage early this morning and who should walk out of there but the man himself. His hair was all dishevelled and he hadn't shaved. He had the biggest grin on his face. I think it's safe to say he stayed the night at our young Willow's house last night, which meant he had other things to occupy himself than giving out secret gifts in the middle of the night.'

Everyone turned to stare at Willow and she found her cheeks flushing bright red. Here was the perfect alibi for both of them – but at what cost? By the way they were all looking at her with excitement in their eyes, this was probably the biggest piece of gossip the villagers had heard since the invention of sliced bread.

Oh god, what should she say? If she lied and said that he'd just popped round that morning then they would know instantly that she wasn't telling the truth and then their alibi would go straight out the window.

Fortunately, she was saved from any more embarrassment or questions by Ginny's arrival.

'What's going on?' Ginny asked the happy throng. 'Did you all get a present too?'

'Did you get one?' Dorothy asked, incredulously.

'Yes,' Ginny beamed. 'Someone left a beautiful bouquet of flowers on my doorstep. They knocked on my door and—'

'When you answered, there was no one there,' Roger said. 'Yes, we got the picture.'

Another man joined the group then. 'Are you talking about last night's activities?'

'Did you get a present too, Pete?' Liz asked.

'No, but Elsie's house was painted.'

The little crowd collectively *ooohed.*

'Oh, it's definitely Andrew then,' Liz said, knowingly.

All eyes swivelled in Willow's direction to see if she would say otherwise.

'He came to my house straight after he'd finished playing darts,' Willow said honestly. Telling the truth was far easier. 'And we spent the rest of the night together.'

Good lord, now it sounded like something far more wonderful than what had actually happened.

Everyone looked so delighted by this piece of news, it was as if they had just won the lottery. They all leaned forward eagerly to hear the next bit of gossip. Oh to hell with it, there was no going back now.

'And let me tell you, he was definitely far too *busy* with me to go out painting houses in the middle of the night.'

There were gasps and squeals of excitement and Willow wanted the ground to swallow her up. She'd just practically declared to the whole village that she and Andrew had had sex the night before.

'Well, must get on, lots of work to do.' Willow quickly scuttled into her shop and closed the door.

She sat down and let her head fall into her hands. It was safe to say that when Andrew heard that piece of gossip, their date would be well and truly off the table, and she didn't blame him at all.

Willow had been busy working in her shop all morning, keeping her head down, not getting involved in the gossip that continued to be bandied about outside on the street. She was so embarrassed that she'd said that about her and Andrew. Of all the things to say to preserve their alibi, why did she have to come out with that? And what would Andrew think when he heard? He seemed like a private person, he wouldn't want that kind of gossip spread around the village even if it was true, let alone when it was false.

She busied herself with the ice candles she was making. She draped the wick inside the paper cup and attached the other end to a lollipop stick which she rested on the top of the cup. She grabbed the jug of small ice cubes she had just taken from the freezer and started pouring it out into the paper cup, either side of the lollipop stick, until the cup was half filled with ice. She took the jug of melted bright yellow wax off the heat and gave it a stir.

There was a noise at the door and she looked up to see the silhouette of Andrew leaning against the door frame. The sun was blazing behind him so she couldn't see his face and whether he was angry or not.

She quickly ran over to him and wrapped her arms around him, burying her face in his chest in embarrassment. God, she needed to apologise, to explain why she did it. She realised he wasn't hugging her back. He really was pissed off.

'Well this is a lovely greeting, although I don't think my brother would be too impressed,' Andrew said, sarcastically, except it didn't actually sound like Andrew at all.

She frowned in confusion and looked up. This was a man who looked like Andrew but was definitely not. It looked like someone had tried to copy Andrew's face but not got it exactly right. It was the eyes that were so different. There was no warmth or kindness there.

She yelped in fright and stumbled back, tripping over a box of wax on the floor. She would have fallen over if the doppelganger hadn't reached out and grabbed her arm.

She stepped back out of his touch to look at him some more and suddenly what he'd said made sense.

'You're Andrew's brother, Jacob?'

'Yes, good to meet you, although I wasn't expecting a welcome as warm as that.'

'God, I'm so sorry. I thought you were Andrew. I don't normally go hugging strange men.'

'No, just kissing them and sleeping in the same bed as them.'

She frowned; she didn't like his tone. 'If you're talking about me and Andrew then that's absolutely none of your business.'

'He's my little brother, it comes with the territory,' Jacob said.

'Sticking your nose in?'

'Looking out for him. You're all he's been talking about all morning. And I wanted to come and meet the woman my brother has fallen in love with.'

Willow swallowed. 'He said he's fallen in love with me?'

'No, but the huge grin on his face speaks volumes.' He cocked his head to look at her. 'So what's your story, Willow McKay?'

He'd come here to see if she was good enough for his brother. She didn't know whether to be incensed by that or find the whole thing hilarious.

She turned her attention back to the yellow wax, gave it another stir and slowly poured it into one of the paper cups covering the ice cubes, then moved on to the next cup and did the same.

'What would you like to know?' Willow said, her eyes on the wax the whole time.

'Well, Andrew said you're not interested in a relationship after not long coming out of a crap one. Yet you've kissed him, slept in the same bed as him and, he says, he's asked you out on a date tonight and he has no idea if you're going to turn up. So what I'd like to know is, are you just playing some weird little game with my brother?'

Holy shit. Put it like that and she did sound like a complete bitch. God, she didn't want to play games with Andrew. That wasn't what this was. But in trying to decide whether it was best to avoid having a relationship or just to go for it, she was messing him around and she hated that. He was so utterly lovely and he deserved better than that. He was being so sweet and patient but she *had* kissed him and slept in the same bed as him. No wonder the poor guy was so confused. And just because she wasn't ready to have these feelings didn't mean they would go away. Working with Andrew on the Secret Society business, spending time with him, those feelings were only going to intensify. It was crazy to try to deny how she felt any more and it wasn't fair on him either.

She carefully filled another cup with wax, listening to the ice crack and hiss a little as it came in contact with the hot liquid. 'You're right. I had no intention of coming here and falling straight into a relationship. And then I met your brother with his kind eyes and his beautiful smile and his silly sense of humour. I love how easy he is to talk to and his patience and warmth. I really like your brother. And yes, I have been overly cautious because it scares me how much I like him, but it was never my intention to hurt him, that was the very last thing I wanted. Truth be told, I think I've fallen a little bit in love with Andrew Harrington and that terrifies me.'

Jacob was completely silent and she looked up at him to find he was staring at her like she was a complicated puzzle he was trying to work out.

She carried on pouring the wax into the remaining cups, wondering if he was waiting for more from her.

Jacob moved to the table and picked up the first paper cup she had filled which had probably gone hard already. He carried it over to the towel she had laid out on the other side of the table and started ripping the paper cup carefully away from the wax. 'I made these with my niece a few weeks ago, she loved doing them.'

Willow watched him. 'Poppy?'

He looked up. 'Yes, did Andrew tell you about her?'

'Yes he did. She sounds like a lovely little girl.'

A smile appeared on his face, the first one Willow had seen. 'Yes she is.'

Willow watched him remove the candle carefully, letting the water drain out onto the towel. She wasn't sure what was going on. He seemed to have completely moved on from the subject of her and Andrew already.

'You'll have to bring her here one day, she can help me make some candles.'

His smile grew. 'This place would be like heaven for her, she loves making candles.'

'Then I'd definitely like to meet her. Although I don't know any sign language so maybe you could stay and help her.'

'I could do that. Although Andrew knows sign language too and I'm sure you'd rather spend the day with him than his grumpy older brother.'

Willow smiled. 'I don't think you're half bad.'

He smiled at this, then he frowned.

'He told you Poppy was deaf?'

'Yes.'

She could see he was mulling this over.

'I know he's deaf too, if that's what you're wondering.'

His eyebrows shot up. 'That does surprise me. He doesn't tell anyone that, especially not so soon into a relationship.'

'I sort of caught him out and he explained he was deaf.'

He picked up another candle and started tearing the paper away.

'He's really sensitive about it, I wouldn't expect him to go into too much detail about it.'

She nodded. 'He told me a bit about his childhood, how your mum made him have therapy.'

'Wow, you really have got under his skin. He never discusses that. In my mum's defence she was trying to do the best for him. My aunt had a tough time growing up deaf in the sixties, there just wasn't the support that we have now. There wasn't that much support when Andrew was growing up, but there was a lot more understanding and awareness of it. My aunt didn't even learn sign language until much later on in her life as it wasn't something that was encouraged and I think Mum felt so useless in not being able to help her. Mum decided that Andrew's upbringing would be different. The whole family learned sign language so we could communicate. She was determined he would be treated the same as any other children, but sometimes I think she went too far in trying to prove to him and to everyone else that he wasn't different.'

Willow was quiet, wondering if there would be more.

He sighed. 'As we grew up, Andrew always thought he had to show that he was as good as everyone else, because my mum was always fighting to prove it. She had to fight to put him into a mainstream school because it was thought he should go to a special school that could cope with his needs, whatever they were. So he worked hard, studied long hours, made sure he always did his homework on time to prove he deserved to be there. It wasn't easy for him.'

Willow thought about this; she knew Andrew had only shared the tip of the iceberg when it came to that side of him. She wondered if she could get him to open up some more, rather than keeping it bottled up inside.

'You're not what I expected, Willow McKay. When Andrew told me all about you, well I was expecting…'

'A manipulative bitch?' Willow supplied.

'I don't know if I would go that far but I didn't exactly have high hopes. Andrew has had his fair share of crappy girlfriends and I think it's put him off anything serious. Over the last few years every girl he has been with has been very casual and I suppose it's safer that way for him. Don't fall in love, don't get hurt. He certainly hasn't been in love for a very long time. To see him floating around on cloud nine this morning, well I wanted to make sure he wasn't falling for someone crappy again.'

Willow picked up one of the other cups and started tearing the cardboard away. 'And do I meet with your approval?'

'I wouldn't go so far as to say that,' Jacob said, a mischievous smile on his lips. 'But you'll do.'

Willow laughed.

Jacob walked to the door and then turned back. 'Are you going on this date tonight?'

Willow hesitated for just a second before nodding. 'Yes I am.'

Jacob nodded. 'Good. I'll be here for a few days so I'm sure I'll hear all about it tomorrow, so keep it clean for my sake.'

'I can't promise that.'

Jacob rolled his eyes and walked away.

Willow smiled. Andrew was right, his brother was an arse, but she liked Jacob nonetheless.

She turned her attention back to the candles and then her heart leapt. Shit. She had a date that night.

chapter 16

Willow went to the pub at lunch, deciding she couldn't hide away from the villagers forever. It was nice to see that it was a bit busier today than it had been on her first day. There were several tables or large groups all talking in excited tones. She had no idea whether it was the Secret Society business that was keeping them entertained, or her non-existent sex life with Andrew, or something else entirely, but it was still good to see.

She went up to the bar and Tabitha greeted her with a smile.

'What do you recommend for lunch today?' Willow asked.

'The fish and chips are good. The fish was fresh off the boat this morning and Connor makes all his own batter.'

'That will do,' Willow said. 'And can I have a glass of lemonade too?'

Tabitha picked a glass from under the counter and half

filled it with ice. 'So the mystery presents have been the talk of the village all morning. Would you happen to know anything about it?'

'Me? No,' Willow said, the lie coming that little bit more easily.

'It just seems a little convenient that the first gift appeared after you arrived here.'

'As you heard, I was with Andrew last night,' Willow said.

'Well he was here earlier and he seemed very surprised by the news that you two had slept together.'

Willow cringed. 'I never said that.'

'You implied it,' Tabitha said.

'I just said we were busy all night.'

'Doing what?'

Willow blushed.

'Aha, so you are sleeping with him?' Tabitha seemed even more excited by this than the prospect that Willow was the secret gift-giver.

'We're… getting to know each other,' Willow said.

'Ah, is that what the kids are calling it these days?'

Willow smiled to herself. Tabitha couldn't be more than ten years older than Willow. She decided to change the subject slightly. 'So if it wasn't me and Andrew that delivered the presents, as we were both *getting to know each other* all night, who is the most likely suspect?'

'Well, there's lots of ideas. Dorothy is still insisting that Joseph gave her the cake, so maybe he's trying to woo all the ladies in the village,' Tabitha said, handing over her glass of lemonade.

'Ha, maybe he is.'

'My money is still on Kitty and Ken,' Tabitha gestured to the other side of the room. Willow looked round to see the couple in question tucking into their fish and chips in one of the booths. 'What would anyone else have to gain from it?'

Willow frowned slightly. 'Why do you think it's being done for some kind of gain?'

'People don't just give presents to other people for no reason.'

'Of course they do, sometimes people do things for other people just to be nice.'

Tabitha shook her head. 'Maybe you're right but my gut says there's some other reason for this.'

Willow didn't like that. When it inevitably got out that it was her and Andrew who were giving the gifts, would the other villagers think she was doing it for some ulterior motive too?

'I'll be over there with Kitty and Ken,' Willow said, taking her drink. She walked over to their table and they looked up. 'Do you mind if I join you?'

'Not at all, dear,' Ken said, patting the seat next to him.

She slid onto the bench. 'Beryl not cooking for you today?'

'Ah, it's her day off. Besides, Connor's fish and chips are the best for miles around,' Kitty said.

'Well, if we get any visitors to the castle, if you decide to go down that path, maybe we can encourage people to go to the pub after. We could print the pub name on the back of the castle tickets, "Try the best fish and chips in the world, five percent off with this ticket", or something like that.'

Ken nodded as he chewed his fish. 'That's not a bad idea.' He looked around and lowered his voice. 'Though personally, as much as I love Connor's fish and chips, I think he could do so much more with fresh fish, different sauces, different dishes. I think he could attract more visitors to the village if he offered something a bit more than great pub grub.'

'Oh shush, the food is lovely.' Kitty waved her hands at her husband, protectively.

'It is, I'm not saying it isn't, Connor is a great cook,' Ken said. 'I just think he could up his game slightly.'

'Well, if we start to get more outside visitors maybe that's something we can gently encourage with him,' Willow said.

'Oh, I wouldn't want to interfere,' Ken said.

Willow smiled. 'I look at it more like positive suggestions or constructive feedback. And as they are renting the property off you, albeit for free, you are technically their boss.'

Ken clearly thought about this. 'Maybe you're right.'

'For now, the locals seem happy enough and we don't get too many outside visitors, and probably won't unless we give them something to come here for,' Willow said, carefully. She tapped her chin thoughtfully as if thinking about ways to bring people to the village. She didn't want to push them into opening the castle to the public – having people traipsing all over their home was not going to be everyone's idea of fun.

Kitty smiled, seeing right through Willow's attempt to be vague.

'We've been seriously thinking about your idea actually,' Ken said. 'There's a man that's coming out tomorrow to see whether it's safe or which areas we can open to the public. I've looked into getting a website designed and spoken to someone I know about marketing. I've looked into insurance too. But everything hinges on tomorrow. We have to make sure it's safe for the tourists above everything else. It might be that we need to do a few repairs here and there, or it might mean we can't open it to the public at all. *But* if the man gives us the OK, at least for parts of it, we thought we'd try to coincide the big opening of the castle with the open day of the village. There's a nearby battle re-enactors group, and we've asked them if they would come along on the day and teach the children how to be knights. We might even get a jousting group in. I mean, the castle isn't medieval, not even close, but I don't suppose the little kids will care too much about historical accuracy when they have a wooden sword and a shield in their hands.'

'I think that sounds like a wonderful idea,' Willow said, excitedly.

'Try to rein in that excitement for a bit longer,' Kitty said, practically. 'I think we've all been getting carried away with the idea but the castle is in a bad way. And although I agree with you about the children loving the ruins, we won't be able to open at all unless we're given the all-clear tomorrow.'

Willow nodded. 'OK, no excitement. I'm not really that bothered at all.'

Kitty laughed. 'You're a terrible liar. Anyway, do you know anything about these gifts that everyone has been receiving? It's quite exciting actually to think someone is doing this for all the villagers.'

Kitty and Ken were the last people she wanted to lie to, and it was their village, so maybe they should be kept apprised of what was happening inside it. Although she didn't know if she could trust them to keep the secret if she told them, and the secrecy of the gifts was key to making them a success.

However, by the looks on Kitty and Ken's faces, they'd already guessed it had something to do with her.

'I… may know something,' Willow said, quietly.

The smile on Kitty's face grew.

'We think it's a wonderful idea. Do you know if the plan is for everyone to get a gift?'

'Yes, that's the idea. I believe,' Willow quickly added.

'Well, if you think whoever is responsible might need any help with it, then let us know,' Ken said.

'I'll… pass that on, thank you,' Willow said.

Kitty finished her lunch, wiping her lips with her napkin. 'Now, more importantly, we want to hear all about you and Andrew.'

Tabitha walked over at that point with Willow's fish and chips and she deliberately hovered for a few minutes, laying out the napkins and the knife and forks then getting salt and pepper and sauce for the table. It was quite clear she was hoping to hear more gossip. Willow busied herself with eating and waited patiently for Tabitha to go away. Eventually she did, but only because she had to serve someone.

'Andrew is such a lovely boy,' Kitty gently pushed.

'He is. I really like him. I'm not sure what you've heard but we haven't… we're not… We've kissed a few times and we've got our first official date tonight. So we'll see how it goes,' Willow said, wanting to be honest with Kitty and Ken, at least about that. 'It's very early, and really I've only just met him.'

Ken nodded. 'I think in life, you can meet people who you like and you can meet people you fall in love with and sometimes, very occasionally, you meet someone who is your soulmate. It was like that for me and Kitty. We knew, from the very first moment we met, that we were going to spend the rest of our lives together. I asked her to marry me after one week and everyone thought she was crazy for saying yes. We've been together forty-six years now. I'm not saying that's going to happen for you and Andrew but don't let the time you've known him put you off. When you know, you know.'

Willow stared at him. That was very wise advice. There was no right time to fall in love, the heart decided that and there was no point in fighting it. She wasn't sure if she believed in the whole soulmate thing but it was definitely time to see where this connection between them would lead.

Andrew dipped his roller in the tray of paint and then spread it across the wall, smiling to himself at how much fun it had been the night before doing this with Willow. He had been exhausted, they had nearly got caught too many times, but they had been giggling and laughing the whole time about the ridiculousness of painting a house in the dark. He had been by the house earlier and they hadn't done the best of jobs, although it certainly looked better than it had before.

'Are you thinking about Willow again?' Jacob said, dipping his roller in the tray and painting his section of the wall.

Andrew grinned. 'What gives the game away?'

'You have that big stupid smile on your face again,' Jacob said. 'I haven't seen you like this about a woman in… well, forever. It's kind of a bit creepy, like my brother has been possessed by something.'

'Ah shut your face, you're just jealous.'

'I met her earlier. When I went into the village, I kind of…bumped into her.'

'You met her, why didn't you say?'

'We only chatted for a few seconds, I just forgot. She seems nice. Not my type, but nice.'

'What does "not my type" mean?' Andrew said, feeling suddenly very protective of Willow.

Jacob smiled. 'She's… soft and sweet and lovely. Definitely not my type.'

Andrew liked that description of her, Jacob had summed her up perfectly.

'Look, I know she's important to you and quite honestly I can see why,' Jacob said, in a rare moment of seriousness. 'Just… try not to fall in love with her, not yet anyway. Tread carefully.'

Andrew stared at him. 'Are you seriously trying to give me advice about matters of the heart?'

'I know. Trust me, I hear myself and it sounds ridiculous even to my own ears, but… I don't want you to get hurt.' Jacob said the last bit so quickly, Andrew wasn't sure he had even heard him correctly.

'Christ, are we going to start hugging soon? I'm not sure we're ready for that,' Andrew said.

'Let's not go that far,' Jacob muttered. 'And remind me again why I'm here helping you paint when I'm supposed to be on holiday?'

Andrew noted the change of subject and decided to let it go. Jacob could be an arse sometimes but he had always looked out for him. It seemed that habit had never gone away, despite them both being grown-ass men now. 'Because you have nothing better to do with your time.'

'I could go on long coastal walks, look for inspiration for my sculptures,' Jacob said.

Andrew laughed. 'You're not really the outdoorsy, coastal-walk sort of person. You're more the sitting-in-the pub, faffing-about-on-your-phone type.'

'Wow, you make me sound such a catch,' Jacob said, dryly.

'I'm simply saying, living in a tiny village by the sea isn't really your thing. You're a townie through and through.'

Jacob carried on painting for a moment. 'I don't know about that. This place has a certain… charm.'

'Could you really see yourself living in a place like this?'

Andrew said. He wasn't sure he actually wanted his little haven taken over by his brother.

Jacob shrugged. 'I lived in London for several years and hated it. And living in Penzance now is… it's nice but it doesn't feel like home. This would be a good place to settle down and raise a family one day.'

Andrew stared at him in shock, paint dripping from his roller. 'What the hell is going on with you? You suddenly care about me getting hurt, you want to get married and have kids. This is not the Jacob I know. You've never had a serious relationship in your life.'

'Maybe it's time that changed.'

Andrew resumed his painting. He wasn't sure if he was ready for that change, especially not on his own doorstep.

chapter 17

Willow looked down at her black dress despondently. It had taken her over an hour to decide what to wear for her date with Andrew. She had no idea what people wore on dates any more. In fact, it had been way too long since she'd been on one. She'd never even been on a date with Garry. He had been her flatmate and it had slowly turned into something more. By that time she'd already been to the pub with him as a friend on several occasions with other friends or just the two of them. So there had never been a time when he'd actually asked her out on a date.

She had tried on multiple outfits for tonight and nothing seemed to be right. In the end she had settled for her trusty black dress, but now she was standing on Andrew's doorstep she was doubting that decision. Black wasn't her colour at all. She liked sparkles and bright patterns. Maybe she had time to go home and change. But she didn't want to be late for the date, she hadn't seen Andrew all day to confirm she was coming and she hated the thought that he would be sitting there feeling disappointed that she wasn't.

She spotted a sunshine-yellow rose growing near the front door. She quickly snapped it off the branch and threaded it into the thin braid she'd done at the side of her head. There, that was a little bit of colour at least.

The door was suddenly flung open and Andrew was standing there, dressed smartly in a pale blue shirt that was open at the collar and had the sleeves rolled up to show his strong, tanned forearms. He was smiling at her.

'You thinking of coming in or running away? I've been watching you hovering for the last five minutes.'

'Oh no, I was just thinking I'd go home and change.'

'Why? You look lovely,' Andrew said, stepping back to let her in.

'I look like I'm going to a funeral. Or an interview. Or an interview at a funeral parlour.' Willow pulled at her dress as she stepped up in front of him.

'Willow, you're beautiful,' Andrew said, softly. He stroked one hand down her cheek and kissed her.

All doubts and fears disappeared from her head instantly. She was on a date with a wonderful man. That was the only thing that mattered.

'Thank you for coming,' Andrew whispered against her lips before kissing her again.

'I'm happy to be here.' She held his face, staring into his eyes which were filled with so much warmth for her.

He took her hand and started leading her off to the kitchen. 'Come through, dinner's nearly ready.'

'Hang on a minute.'

He turned back to face her.

'I'm sorry for messing you around.'

He frowned. 'Are you going already?'

'No, I just meant, over the last few days, kissing you, putting that ridiculous six-month hold on our relationship, lying to you, kissing you again, inviting you to share a bed with me. I've been sending you some very mixed messages and I'm sorry.'

'You don't need to apologise.'

'I do. I was with Garry for four years and, even after we split up, he stayed in the flat for a while until he found somewhere else. Which was hard given… given how we broke up. After that humiliation, I just wanted a break, just some time for me. But then there was you and I quite honestly have never felt this way about anyone before. I would be crazy to walk away from what we have. I want to explore this connection with you and even if it all fizzles out to nothing after a few weeks, I don't want to regret not giving this a chance.'

He stared at her for a moment and she realised she'd gone too far with her apologies.

'I'm sorry. I haven't had a first date for a very long time. I turn up here in this hideous funeral dress and practically declare my undying love for you. I bet you're desperately trying to come up with some excuse to cancel the whole evening.'

He smiled and came back to her. Sliding his large hands

round her back, he kissed her again.

'I don't do dates either, not really and not for a very long time. But I can tell you that this is shaping up to be one of the best dates I've ever been on.'

Willow frowned in confusion and her heart melted a little when Andrew kissed her frown away.

'Why is this a good date?'

His eyes were locked on hers. 'Because it's you.'

Oh god, it was crazy to feel this way about him so quickly. She leaned up and kissed him, cupping his lovely face between her hands. He ran his hands up her back and she suddenly liked this dress a whole lot more when his fingers grazed her bare skin. The dress had a deep V cut into the back which always left her feeling a little chilly but right then she was red hot. His fingers danced gently across her skin, tracing her spine all the way up to the top of her neck.

'I really do like this dress,' Andrew said against her lips.

She smiled. 'I do too.'

'Now, as much as I'd like to stand here all night and kiss you, dinner will be ruined if we don't dish it up soon and I'd hate for you to miss out on the world's best curry,' Andrew said.

'The world's best? Now that's a bold claim.'

'Well, certainly the best in Happiness.'

'I think Connor might have something to say about that. You better lead the way then and I can judge for myself,' Willow said.

Andrew took her hand and she followed him into the

kitchen. The table was laid with a beautiful silver candelabra that looked like it was made entirely from forks. Three tall white candles were burning happily away in the middle of it.

'That's an interesting piece,' Willow said.

'It's one of Jacob's. That's his thing, he makes sculptures from old bits of metal. He buys forks and spoons and things like that from charity shops and makes them into the most incredible things. Although don't tell him I was singing his praises, it will go to his head.'

Willow laughed. 'I met him today.'

'Yes, he said he bumped into you.'

Willow thought about that for a moment. 'Bumped into you' made it sound so much simpler than it was. Jacob had specifically come looking for her to warn her off his brother, something he had clearly not told Andrew. But despite that, they had parted on good terms and she certainly didn't want to stir up any bad feelings between the two of them. So if Jacob hadn't mentioned the true reason for his visit then she wasn't going to either.

'Did he tell you I hugged him? I thought it was you and I threw my arms around him and hugged him before I realised it wasn't.'

'He didn't mention that,' Andrew said, as he retrieved a big dish from the oven.

'I think he found the whole thing a bit embarrassing, I know I did,' Willow said. 'Oh, talking of embarrassing, I'm so sorry for letting people assume we'd had sex last night. Everyone was talking about who had given the mystery gifts and because Elsie's house was painted they all thought it must be you. So I tried to cover for you and said we'd spent the night together and everyone just assumed that meant we'd had mad passionate sex. And to be honest, the alibi was such a good one I might have played up to it a bit.'

Andrew grinned as he dished up white fluffy rice onto two plates. 'I kind of liked it, everyone I met today was clapping me on the back as if I was some kind of stud. I've never had that reputation before. Jacob has always been the one who had women falling over themselves to go out with him. When we were teenagers, Jacob had a different girlfriend every week. I didn't even lose my virginity until I was eighteen. Besides, the villagers will find out about us sooner or later. The village is so tiny, everyone knows everyone else's business. I wouldn't be surprised if they have this place bugged. And Julia saw me leaving your house very early this morning, so word would have got around anyway. We did need an alibi. A lot of people will think it's you as it all started happening after you arrived.'

'Kitty and Ken have already guessed. And though I didn't admit it to them, I didn't lie to them either. It didn't feel right, it is their village.'

Andrew scooped out some of the amazing-smelling curry on top of the rice. 'I was going to suggest telling them, they should know what's going on down here.'

'We'll have to induct them into the Secret Society,' Willow said.

'Only if they're prepared to learn the secret handshake.'

Willow laughed as she watched Andrew bend down to retrieve the nan breads, admiring his gorgeous bum as he did so.

'You checking out my bum Willow McKay?'

She laughed loudly. 'You caught me. Would you like any help?'

'You can open a bottle of wine, I have one chilling in the fridge.'

Willow retrieved a bottle of sparkling wine and unwound the cage around the cork. She tried to ease the cork out but it seemed to be stuck fast. She grabbed a tea towel and wrapped it round the cork and tried to wiggle it from side to side. She felt it give slightly, rising up out of the bottle, but when she tried to ease it out some more it seemed to be stuck again. She took the tea towel off so she could prise it out of the bottle. Just as she did so, the cork shot out, up in the air like a missile, and took out the light bulb with a smash, plunging them into semi-darkness, the only light coming from the flickering candles.

Andrew stood there in shock with the two plates in his hands. Fortunately, the light bulb was far enough away from him that none of the glass could have gone into the food.

'I'm so sorry. I can't even open a bottle of wine.'

'It's OK, makes the room more romantic.'

'Where's your dustpan and brush, I'll clear it up.'

'Honestly, don't worry about it,' Andrew said, putting the plates on the table.

'Please, I feel awful about it.'

'Well, we can't have you feeling awful. It's under the sink but leave it until after we've eaten.'

Willow retrieved the dustpan and brush anyway and bent to sweep it up, while Andrew poured out two glasses of wine. Luckily, the bulb seemed to have smashed into several big chunks rather than tiny smithereens and she was able to clear it all up relatively quickly.

She sat back down with Andrew who was patiently waiting for her.

'I'm really sorry.' She took her seat and Andrew sat down opposite her.

'It's just a light bulb, no big deal. Here's your wine, shall we make a toast?'

'OK.' She let out a deep breath, as she tried to refocus on their date. She rose her glass in the air. 'To us.'

He smiled. 'To… getting to know each other, to lots of wonderful kisses, to cuddling in bed and to making love under the stars.'

'That's much better than my toast,' Willow said. 'I like the sound of that very much, especially that last bit.'

'Well the beach is very secluded, no one ever goes down there because of the number of steps. I often swim naked down there. We could make love down there in broad daylight and no one would ever see us. But there's something magical about going down there at night.'

Now that was a wonderfully delicious thought. She was half tempted to suggest they go down to the beach for their *dessert*, but there was still a cautious part of her that wanted to go slow with him.

He must have read her mind because he linked hands with her. 'There's no rush though. I'm very happy to just spend some time getting to know you.'

She smiled and decided to change the subject slightly.

'You swim naked?'

He grinned. 'Yeah. There's something very liberating about that.'

The image of him naked, his glistening wet body powering through the water, was not something she was going to be able to erase from her mind very easily. And this wasn't helping her forget the idea of making love on the beach either.

She cleared her throat and took a bite of the curry. It was wonderfully tangy, creamy, the spices dancing on her tongue.

'This is amazing,' Willow said.

'Told you, the best curry in all the lands,' Andrew said.

'So tell me, what brought you to Happiness?' Willow asked.

Andrew focussed his attention on dipping his nan bread into the sauce for a moment, clearly giving himself time to answer. He looked up and frowned.

'It's OK, you don't need to answer,' Willow said. He was clearly uncomfortable with the question.

'No, it's not that. You, erm… have a caterpillar on your forehead.'

Willow let out a little squeal as she felt around her head, found the offending critter and flicked it off. It landed with a splat in Andrew's curry.

Andrew looked down as the caterpillar struggled against the sauce and burst out laughing. He grabbed a piece of kitchen towel, carefully scooped it out and then gently wiped the curry sauce off before taking the bug to the back door and probably releasing it with a pat on the head.

Urgh, what if there were other creepy crawlies in that rose, which was where the caterpillar had evidently come from? She grabbed the rose and yanked it from her head, but the braid was wrapped around one of the thorns and it got stuck in her hair. No amount of pulling would free it, in fact she was pretty sure it was getting more tangled and knotted the more she tried to yank it out.

Andrew came back from releasing the beast and watched her struggle for a moment.

'Here let me help,' he said.

He gently tried to untangle the rose.

'God this date is turning out to be—'

'Memorable,' Andrew said, fondly. 'If we get married one day, this is the story I'll tell in my wedding speech.'

'You'll do no such thing,' Willow laughed. 'You'll tell everyone how you fell in love with my magnificence.'

'Well that too. But they also need to know the dark and murky truth. I'm sorry, I can't get this out. I think I'm going to have to cut it, it's knotted up pretty bad.'

'This is what I get for stressing too much over what I was wearing, a bloody caterpillar on my face and a massive knot in my hair.'

Andrew pulled out a pair of scissors from the drawer and

carefully cut the rose out of her hair.

'There, all done.'

'Well now you have a lock of my hair, you can keep it in a box by the side of your bed,' Willow said, as Andrew sat back down.

'Creepy. Although I could use it to clone you.'

'And that isn't creepy?'

Andrew laughed.

'Sorry about throwing a caterpillar into your food.'

He shrugged and carried on eating, seemingly not bothered at all.

She watched him with a smile. 'Nothing really fazes you, does it?'

He thought about this for a moment. 'I think there are quite a few things that faze me but the big stuff, not any of this. I'm enjoying spending time with you and caterpillars and smashed light bulbs aren't going to change that.'

She smiled as she watched him. She could really fall in love with this man.

chapter 18

As Willow lay on the sofa with Andrew kissing her, she knew she couldn't be happier. There were no longer any doubts and fears about whether she should or shouldn't be doing this, or whether this was moving too fast. She had never been so sure in her life that she was doing the right thing.

'What are you smiling about?' Andrew said, pulling back slightly to look at her.

'You. Us.' She stroked his face. 'This is…'

'I know…' His eyes were soft as he looked at her.

'And the crazy thing is, if I'd stuck to my silly rules, we wouldn't be doing this for another six months.'

'I'd have waited,' Andrew said, rolling onto his back and bringing her onto his chest. 'And I don't want to rush anything with you. We'll go as slow as you want. And if you think it's going too fast, we'll stop and we'll just go back to being friends again – well, friends who kiss. I'm not sure I could give this up.'

She smiled and rested her head on his chest as he stroked her hair.

'So what was so awful about your last relationship?' Andrew asked. 'I want to make sure we don't make the same mistakes.'

'It wasn't awful, but we didn't love each other, never did. We were flatmates and we got on well. We had the same friends, and all our friends assumed we were a couple long before we were. He was nice, good-looking and my friends couldn't understand why we weren't together. Even his friends were egging him on. I guess in the end I thought, are they all seeing something that I'm not. Before Garry, I had two boyfriends that cheated on me and I knew I could trust Garry. But you need more than that in a relationship. We had zero chemistry. Sex was nice, he was a nice kisser. I don't know. So many of my friends were desperately trying to find a man and the men they did date, well, a lot of them would turn out to be arseholes. My friends all said that I was so lucky to be going out with Garry that I started to think maybe they were right. He was nice, he used to cook for me, he always took the bins out.'

God, even to her own ears it sounded so dull.

'I started to think maybe this is what being in a relationship was like. That maybe the books and films over-romanticised everything and that as long as you got on with the man you were with, he didn't cheat or treat you badly, maybe it was better than being alone. When actually, being single for the last four years would have been far better. We just drifted along, never rowed because we simply didn't care enough to get angry or upset. We had sex once a week, always on a Saturday morning, before he'd bring me breakfast in bed. It was boring and neither of us could be bothered to do anything about it. Well, that was until I asked him to marry me.'

'What? You've just described the most mundane relationship ever, where you clearly weren't happy, and you decided marriage would fix that?'

'I don't know what I was thinking actually. I was desperate for change and I wasn't entirely sure breaking up was the answer. I guess I wanted to see if he did love me, whether we had anything worth fighting for. I think I was kind of hoping he'd say no, just so I knew it was really over.'

'And did he?'

'No, he said yes and for a few hours I got swept away with the excitement of a wedding, of wearing that dress, the champagne, the special day. I'd already picked out the bridesmaid dresses in my head. I announced it on Facebook and texted all my friends and family. All the ones that were married said it was about time, Ruby went mad at me and said I'd be a fool to marry him and I did start to panic and wonder if she was right. Next day, he told me that he'd changed his mind, that although he loved me, he wasn't in love with me and that he didn't want to spend the rest of his life with me. It was a bit of a kick in the teeth but I was relieved more than anything. Except that I then had to tell all my friends and family that the wedding was off not even twenty-four hours after it had been on. Slightly embarrassing.'

'And what was everyone's reactions?'

'"Oh no, I'm so sorry, this is so sad." I tried to tell them that actually it was a good thing but no one really believed that. They just thought I was putting on a brave face. Anyway, after we broke up, I felt like I was stepping out into the light. I vowed then that I didn't need a man to make me happy, I was just fine on my own.'

'And now?'

'Well, I still don't *need* a man to make me happy, I'm perfectly fine without one, but I'm also very very over the moon with one too,' Willow giggled, knowing she wasn't really making a lot of sense. 'I think in reality swearing off all men was a bit ridiculous. What I should have said was that I didn't want a relationship with a man unless he set my world on fire.'

Andrew chuckled. 'And I tick that box for you?'

'Oh god yes.'

'Well that's good to know.'

'What about you, why were you not interested in a relationship? You said you'd had some crappy ones.'

Andrew sighed and he didn't speak for a while. 'I think my biggest issue with being deaf is people's reactions to it. It's something different to what they know and some are scared of it.'

Willow frowned. 'Really?'

'I had one girlfriend, thankfully we hadn't been going out that long, maybe a month, she was horrified when she found out I was deaf, saying I should have told her because she could catch it.'

'I don't know whether to laugh or cry at that,' Willow said.

'You can laugh, I did.'

'People can't seriously be that stupid,' she said.

'Don't forget we live in a world where thousands of people still believe the earth is flat. Trust me, there are lots of stupid people in the world.'

'That's depressing.'

'I know. I've had quite a few similar issues over the years. I think a lot of hearing people don't understand what it really means to be deaf.'

Willow thought about this for a moment. She could never really comprehend what it was like to be deaf. She could stick earplugs in and walk around like that all day but that was very different from living with that for the whole of her life. And dealing with people's prejudices and opinions on it would be something else entirely too. She'd never had to cope with being labelled as different. Would this lack of understanding on her part eventually be a sticking point for them as it had been for his other girlfriends?

'When one girlfriend found out I was deaf, she said things like, "But you look just like a normal person, you talk like a normal person," without realising how offensive that was. It was a big novelty to her, she'd ask me to lip-read what people were saying, she'd ask me to teach her sign language, but only the swear words. It didn't last long.'

'I think I'd rather know how to sign cake or biscuit or the

kinds of things that we are most likely to say in bed when you've taken your hearing aids out. Things like "Kiss me" or "Make love to me."

He grinned. 'Trust me, you're never going to have to ask for those things.'

She smiled and then reached up and stroked his cheek. From what Jacob had said, Andrew had his heart broken in the past. And though these women he'd dated didn't sound like they were the best, it didn't seem like any of them had broken his heart.

'Did you love any of these women?' she asked carefully.

He nodded. 'None of the ones I've mentioned, but there was one woman, Sophie. I loved her. Looking back, I'm not sure why. She had this perfect image of what her life was going to be. I don't think she was over the moon when she found out I was deaf, it didn't fit in with her perfect ideals, and I thought for a while we might break up but we didn't. We were together for about two years and I thought we were happy. We talked about marriage, kids, buying a house together. When my niece, Poppy, was born, it was clear from very early on that she was deaf. And Sophie just couldn't get her head around that. She asked me if we were to have children would our kids be deaf too. I told her that statistically more deaf children were born to hearing parents than to deaf parents but yes there was a chance, especially as there seemed to be a gene in our family. She said she didn't want to have deaf children and we broke up. I was… heartbroken.'

'Oh Andrew, that's horrible.'

'I think that was the first time in my life that I didn't feel good enough. It was even worse that I was made to feel that way by someone I loved.'

'No, don't ever think like that. That was more her issue than it ever was yours.'

'I know, I do realise that. And in many ways I do feel like we'd had a lucky break.'

'What kind of person doesn't love their child unconditionally regardless of whether they can hear, see, talk, read, write, or even walk as well as their peers? I understand having a child who is deaf or blind could be a challenge, but having children *is* a challenge. Those sleepless nights, potty training, settling a child at night, is the car seat fitted properly, are they getting enough milk, is the bath water hot or cool enough for them. As they get older the responsibility of teaching them right from wrong, teaching them about different cultures and beliefs, how many sweets is too many, how much screen time is too much, their friends, their boyfriends and girlfriends, are they happy, are they safe. All of that is bloody hard work. But I would love my child, completely and utterly, regardless of any condition they might have.'

Andrew smiled, giving her a kiss on the forehead. 'I think that is the right answer.'

'Please, please don't take that on your shoulders. You are an incredible man and any woman would be very lucky to raise their child with you,' Willow said.

He stared at her for a moment and then bent his head and kissed her. But this was very different to their other kisses. This was sweeter, more tender, filled with love.

He pulled back slightly. 'I think I better take you home now.'

'Oh.' Willow felt a little disappointed that their date had come to an end already but a quick glance at the clock showed that it was approaching midnight.

'Not because I want to, but because I really want to take you upstairs and spend the rest of the night making love to you—'

Willow opened her mouth to speak but Andrew quickly carried on talking.

'And before you say that's a good idea, I'm going to remind you that we're supposed to be taking this slow.'

'I'm not sure I agreed to that.'

Andrew groaned and stood up. 'Come on, let's get you home.'

He pulled his boots on as Willow tied up her own shoes and then he quickly bundled her out of the house.

Willow giggled at his haste. She couldn't help feeling a little disappointed that his plan for the rest of the night wasn't going to happen but there was a large part of her that was quite relieved. A few days earlier she hadn't even wanted a relationship; it made sense to take things slow, at least for now. She'd never slept with a man on a first date before and, although it felt like she'd known Andrew for a lifetime already, she still thought it was probably a good idea for her to go home.

He linked hands with her as he switched on his torch. The

path wound away from them, disappearing into the trees, the bushes either side of them casting odd shadows in the torchlight.

'You can give Jacob a call now and tell him the coast is clear,' Willow said.

'He's staying in the pub actually, they have a few rooms there. There really isn't enough room in my house for the two of us. There really isn't enough room in this village for the two of us, but he's thinking of moving here.'

'Really? Is that so he can keep an eye on you?'

'I hope not. But he can be a bit overprotective at times, he's been like it all his life. He says he wants somewhere quiet to settle down and raise a family. Those are honestly words I never thought I'd hear coming out of his mouth. I mean, it'll be nice that I get to see him a bit more often but I kind of wish his settling down wasn't happening right on my doorstep.'

'Do Lottie and Poppy live nearby?'

'Not too far away so I guess it'll be nice for Jacob to be closer to them too. He adores Poppy. We all do.'

'I can't wait to meet her.'

He looked down at her. 'She will love you. You pretty much have her dream job.'

Willow smiled. 'It's my dream job too.'

There was a screech of an owl nearby which made her jump, though Andrew didn't seem bothered by it at all.

'Did you always want to be a candlemaker when you were growing up?'

'Oh no, I changed my mind weekly about what I wanted

to be. A vet, a dancer, an astronaut, a scientist – which I thought would involve dealing with lots of potions – an actor, an archaeologist… I've always been very crafty though, and when I got older I knew I wanted to run my own business. I took business studies at university which is where I met Ruby. Making candles was something I enjoyed and it just sort of turned into my job while I was looking for something practical to do with my degree. What about you, what did you want to be when you grew up?'

'Batman.'

Willow laughed. 'Now that's a great goal.'

'I think the anonymity appealed, no one knowing who he was. Everyone knew who I was at school. I could have had my own persona, "Deaf Kid". Except I'm not sure what my superpowers would have been. I was pretty crap at most things.'

Willow frowned. His childhood would have been very different from hers in many ways.

'What was it like growing up with that label over your head?'

He was silent for the longest time. 'It was fine really. All kids have issues growing up, don't they? Anyway, I heard there was a lot of interest in the mystery gifts today.'

He had changed the subject again. Every time he started opening up to her, he slammed that door closed before she could see inside. She didn't know whether to push it, but if he wasn't comfortable talking to her about that, what could she do? It did hurt a little that he didn't want to share that with her.

If they were going to be in a proper relationship they needed to be able to talk to each other about the good, the bad and the ugly. Still, it was very early days for them, maybe that level of trust would come later. She decided to let it pass for now.

'Oh yes, the whole village was talking about it, who it could be, who is going to be next, why they are doing it. Everyone is very excited.'

'So who's next on our list of Secret Society gifts?' Andrew asked.

'Well, a lot of people think it's Kitty and Ken giving the presents so I wondered if we should give them one so people would stop thinking it was them.'

Andrew clearly thought about this for a moment. 'If people think it's them, let them carry on thinking it for a while. It takes the attention off us.'

'That's a good point. What about Joseph? That way, if Dorothy still thinks the cake is from him, Joseph getting a gift will make it clear that it wasn't before she embarrasses herself with her declarations of undying love for him.'

'Good idea,' Andrew said. 'Any ideas what you're going to give him? I can't remember much from the night we compiled that list, other than that was the first time we kissed and that was pretty bloody memorable.'

'Mmm, most heated first kiss ever,' Willow said. 'I do have an idea for him, but I think it's something that will need to be made.'

She looked up at him with hopeful puppy dog eyes.

Andrew laughed. 'Don't look at me like that. I have a

whole village to renovate.'

'How is that coming along?' Willow asked as they walked past Joseph's house and into the trees.

'It is actually coming along a lot faster than I thought it would. Jack and his team are doing a great job and, although there will still be a lot of work that will need to be done at the end of August, there are now twelve houses that are painted on the outside and four that are ready to move in.'

'That's good.'

'Yeah, I'd done a few before they started and they've been working on the ones that didn't need too much doing to them. Some of the houses that need a lot more work we are just going to paint the outside so it at least it looks good for when we have the open day. If a lot of people suddenly want to move in, we will have to stagger their arrival so all the houses are finished in time. I'm not sure how much interest we will have but hopefully we'll get a few more people who want to move here.'

'We just need to make sure the open day goes off with a bang. Oh, talking of which, I was thinking—'

'Here we go again,' Andrew teased. 'More bright ideas.'

'Hey!' Willow laughed. 'You love my ideas.'

'Go on then, tell me your idea.'

'I think we need to have stuff going on in the village that will encourage people to stay for most of the day. The longer people are here, the more likely it is they will fall in love with the place. If the castle opens, that could take care of entertainment during the day, but I wonder if we should do something on the night, a firework display perhaps, maybe over the castle or at the end of the village overlooking the sea. We could do a lantern parade where everyone will carry a lantern down to the cliff tops, show everyone who visits this thriving community spirit. I could make the lanterns very easily. We could make it a big family day.'

'It's not a bad idea,' Andrew said. 'Although firework displays can be very expensive. I have a friend, Leo, who runs his own firework display company. He owes me a massive favour actually, maybe he'd do it on the cheap. I'll speak to Kitty and Ken about it tomorrow and then I'll give Leo a call. Anyway, back to Joseph. This thing you want making for him, is it big, small, metal, wood?'

'I'm not sure,' Willow said. 'He loves gardening and I saw him on his knees the other day, doing some weeding, and it was a real struggle for him to get up. I kind of thought we could make him some kind of knee cushion that had a frame around the outside so he could use that to help him get back up.'

'That sounds like it should be made from metal. If it's wood, it could rot if it gets wet and muddy. Jacob would be your best bet for something like that. He's a whizz with any kind of metalwork. I'll ask him tomorrow.'

'OK.'

They cleared the trees and Sunrise Cottage gleamed in the moonlight that sparkled over the sea.

'If Joseph's gift is going to take a few days, I'll have to think of someone else to give the gift to tomorrow,' Willow said as they walked up the path to her house. 'Maybe even a few people like we did last night.'

'Why don't we meet for lunch tomorrow, in the pub and you can tell me what the plan is for tomorrow night,' Andrew said.

'OK. Is lunch going to be our second date?'

Andrew grinned. 'Yes, why not.'

'OK, I'll see you tomorrow.' Willow leaned up and kissed him and he wrapped his arms around her back, holding her tight.

He pulled back. 'Goodnight Willow McKay. Sweet dreams.'

She smiled. 'Oh, I'm sure they will be.'

He gave her a sweet kiss on the nose and then walked off into the darkness.

She watched him go and then went inside. Her dreams were going to be very nice indeed that night.

chapter 19

Andrew woke up with a huge smile on his face. The night before had been wonderful and it was safe to say he was completely smitten with Willow McKay. He was going to see her again at lunch and he couldn't wait.

Also his friend Morgan was coming today with the screens for the backdrop to cover the houses at the entrance to the village. She'd be here for a few days painting the screens and erecting them.

He got up and quickly washed and dressed. He made himself some toast, wrapped it in a piece of kitchen towel and left the house.

He automatically looked down towards Sunrise Cottage in the hope he might see Willow, and was surprised to see Jacob walking up from that direction.

'I'm guessing I'm not who you were hoping to see,' his brother said.

'Your ugly mug versus Willow's lovely face, hmm tough choice,' Andrew said, as Jacob fell in at his side and they started walking towards the village.

'I've just seen her,' Jacob gestured over his shoulder.

'You did?' Andrew looked back towards Willow's house but sadly couldn't spot her.

'She was sitting on the bench in her front garden with a big happy grin on her face. I didn't talk to her, I didn't want to interrupt whatever daydream she was in. She didn't see me anyway. I'm sure she was too busy thinking about you.'

Andrew smiled at that, although the smile fell off his face when Jacob swiped a slice of toast from the paper towel.

'Hey!'

'I'm hungry.'

'Then go to the pub for breakfast.'

'Oh I'll do that too, this is my starter.' Jacob took a big bite.

Andrew rolled his eyes. 'What were you doing down there anyway?'

'I was just out for a walk.'

'Really?' Andrew asked, dryly.

Jacob laughed. 'Genuinely. I thought I'd explore a little. It's a nice place.'

'Don't start that again. This place is too small for you and your ego.'

'My ego would fit in perfectly here, thank you very much.'

Jacob munched on his toast. 'OK, maybe the walk had the added bonus of seeing if you spent the night at Willow's house again.'

'Ha. I knew it. Actually I was the perfect gentleman.'

Jacob snorted. 'You mean she turned you down.'

'No, we're taking things slow.'

'And I bet that's killing you.'

'Like you wouldn't believe,' Andrew said and his brother laughed.

Jacob finished his slice of toast and then went to take another but Andrew held it out of reach.

Jacob shrugged. 'So it went well, last night?'

'Yes, it was wonderful. I know you're going to give me hell over this but I don't care. I honestly think I'm going to marry this girl.'

'Christ!' Jacob muttered. 'I told you not to fall in love with her.'

'I haven't. Yet.'

'I thought you were taking it slow.'

'We are but… she's pretty bloody special.'

'You've been on one date; do you know how ridiculous you sound?' Jacob said.

Andrew couldn't help smiling as he nodded. 'I'm well aware how it sounds, there's just something different about this girl. We even talked about having children last night.'

Jacob groaned and Andrew laughed, having only added that little titbit to wind his brother up.

'In the general sense, not "Let's make a baby now."

Just… I told her about Sophie and she was horrified.'

'Well, most decent human beings would be. I never knew what you saw in Sophie anyway. In fact, most of your girlfriends have been questionable. Remember that one, the over-enunciator?'

'Tammy, yes that did get annoying,' Andrew said as he remembered how she would carefully pronounce each word for him and overexaggerate all of her lip movements to help with his lip-reading. He did try to explain that with his hearing aids in it was unnecessary, and that when he had them out her excessive lip movements actually made it a lot harder, but she didn't seem to comprehend.

'And the one that shared her bed with hundreds of cuddly toys,' Jacob said.

Andrew laughed as he remembered Beatrice. The cuddly toys had gotten everywhere which always made having sex a bit of a challenge. She had been a sweet girl but not someone he could hold a decent conversation with.

'And Saskia, she was into all that kinky stuff, wasn't she?' Jacob said.

'Trust you to remember *her* name.'

'Why did you let her go?'

'If I'm honest, she was more than a little scary,' Andrew said.

'You couldn't handle her, you mean?'

'Something like that.'

They approached the crossroads with the pub and he smiled to see Willow's shop window filled with all manner of candles in different colours. She certainly brightened up the place.

'And then there was Morgan,' Jacob said, scathingly.

'Morgan was never my girlfriend. Not really.'

He'd known Morgan for a long time. Her brother was deaf and Andrew had been friends with him. Morgan sort of came with the package. They'd kind of grown up together and then lost touch over the years. They'd bumped into each other a couple of years before and somehow ended up in bed together. Neither of them had wanted something serious, although they had slept together four or five times over the next few months. But it had never been more than just sex between two friends. He hadn't seen her for nearly a year now and last he'd heard she had been dating a pilot. She had seemed delighted to hear from him when he'd called her a few days before to ask her to do the screens. He just hoped she wasn't coming here in the hope of rekindling their *friendly* arrangement.

'And why do you say her name like that?' Andrew asked.

'I always felt she used sign language around hearing people because she loved being in this secret club they weren't privy to.'

Andrew didn't agree with that. Sign language had always been such a big part of Morgan's life. With her mum and her brother being deaf, sign language had been Morgan's first language so she would often lean towards that in a conversation.

'Morgan doesn't switch to sign language to annoy or exclude hearing people. She constantly flicks between the two in the same way that a person who is raised in a bilingual family might switch between the two languages in a conversation,' Andrew said, feeling the need to defend her.

'No, I get that,' Jacob said. 'But I always got the feeling that wasn't what it was for her. She had a bit of a nasty side sometimes. I never liked how she would use sign language to take the piss out of hearing people, knowing full well they wouldn't understand what she was saying. There was something a bit cowardly about that. And I've never liked bullies.'

Andrew suppressed a smile. Jacob had been like a bodyguard when they were at school, standing up for him against anyone who would dare say anything derogatory about him. Jacob had landed himself in detention many times after getting into fights. He wasn't the only person his brother had stuck up for, it was safe to say he was champion of the underdog. But Jacob was right, Andrew hadn't really liked that side of Morgan either. After being on the wrong side of insults and jokes growing up, he didn't like to see other people being exposed to that, whether they knew it or not. But whenever Andrew stopped her from doing it she always insisted she was only joking. And Morgan did have a lot of good qualities; she raised a lot of money for charity, spent a lot of time fighting for more accessibility for deaf people, and Poppy adored her. Morgan was great with his niece, she always had a lot of time for her.

'She's coming here today actually, so try to be nice,' Andrew said.

'Whoa, why is she coming here?'

'She's doing a big backdrop for the entrance to the village.'

'Your old girlfriend and your new girlfriend together, is that wise?'

'Morgan was never my girlfriend. She dated other people while she occasionally came to me for no-strings-attached sex. We're friends. I'm sure it's going to be fine.'

Jacob didn't look so sure. 'Does Willow know?'

'Yes. Well, no. She knows Morgan is coming here to do the backdrop. She doesn't know that we…'

'Were friends with benefits?' Jacob helpfully supplied.

'Yes, if you like. She doesn't need a detailed rundown of all the women I've been with just like I don't need to know a potted history of all her ex-boyfriends.'

'OK, you keep telling yourself that. Personally I think if you want this to work with Willow then you need to be honest with her.'

'OK, OK. I'll tell her. Jeez, I just hadn't given it any thought. It's been a year since I've seen Morgan, she's not exactly been uppermost in my thoughts.'

'Just tell Willow. I'm going for breakfast, I'll catch you later.'

Andrew nodded and watched Jacob disappear inside the

pub. Well that was a conversation he wasn't really looking forward to. Suddenly his day looked a little bit duller.

Willow was busy working in her shop when Liz and Roger came in.

'Hello,' Willow said in surprise. Apart from Andrew and Jacob, they were the first visitors in her shop. Although something told her they weren't there to buy anything. 'Are you here to buy or…'

'There were more presents delivered last night,' Liz said, almost bursting at the seams with the exciting news.

'What?' Willow asked in confusion.

'Kitty came down to the village this morning to buy some milk and she said she had been left a parcel last night, a beautiful hand-knitted pink scarf. Kitty loves scarfs and this one had lovely little flowers all over it,' Liz said.

'Well who left that for her?' Willow asked. Were there secret members of the Secret Society that she didn't know about? Seeing that her and Andrew were the only members, that was unlikely.

'Well that's the question, isn't it?' Roger said, bouncing on his toes and fixing Willow with a look.

'It wasn't me,' Willow laughed and for the first time she could be completely honest about it.

'Julia did say she saw you and Andrew eating in his kitchen when she walked Colin and Rufus past the back of his house early evening,' Liz said.

Willow made a mental note to close the curtains whenever they were in Andrew's house or hers from now on, especially at night time.

'Well there you go, we were busy. It was actually our first date,' Willow said, trying to deflect the conversation away from their possible guilt.

'Talk about shutting the stable door after the horse has bolted,' Roger muttered.

'I'm sorry?' Willow said.

'Well, you've already slept with him, seems a bit late now to have a first date.'

'We haven't slept together. We've been—'

'*Getting to know each other*,' Liz and Roger echoed.

'Umm yes, exactly. Anyway, it wasn't us, we were together all night and then Andrew walked me home.'

'Aha, so you could have delivered the scarf then. Or Andrew could have done it after he dropped you off,' Liz said.

'It was very late and we were both very tired. Andrew has been so busy helping with the renovation of the village. I doubt he went home after dropping me off, hand-knitted a scarf and then walked all the way up to the castle to deliver it.'

Liz and Roger looked at each other as if they might actually believe her.

'There was another present too,' Roger said.

'Oh my god, who?' This was getting more and more bizarre.

'Joseph. He found a book about roses this morning on

his doorstep. It was gift-wrapped.'

At least Willow had a good idea who that might be from. Dorothy had probably left it there to thank him for the cake she was so convinced he had left. But did that mean that she had left the present for Kitty too?

'Well this is getting a bit mysterious,' Willow said. She certainly needed to talk with Andrew about it over lunch. What did this mean for her list if Joseph and Kitty had already received a present? 'Maybe it's the fairies.'

'Hmm, we've got our eye on you, young lady,' Roger said, which sounded a bit too stern considering her only crime was to give presents to people.

Willow smiled. 'I'll keep that in mind and if I see the fairies, shall I give them a message?'

'Yes, tell them we don't like it,' Liz said.

'Aw Liz, I bet the fairies will give you a present too, I'm sure they will make sure everyone gets one,' Willow said.

Liz snorted her disapproval and left the shop. Roger watched her go and then turned back to Willow with a glint of excitement in his eyes.

'Chocolates, she loves chocolate,' Roger said. 'Just in case you are in contact with the fairies. Or tea. Liz loves flavoured tea. She has hundreds of different flavours in our kitchen. I gave her some cheese-flavoured tea once, she wasn't so keen on that but most flavours she loves.'

Willow grinned. 'I'll be sure to pass that along… if I see them. And is there anything in particular that I should tell the fairies that you would like? No guarantees of course.'

'Ah no, I'm fine. A calendar with half-naked men or that Chris Hemsworth, or a half-naked Chris Hemsworth. Something like that would go down a treat.' He winked at her and left the shop.

She smiled. Well this was getting interesting.

chapter 20

Andrew leaned against the door frame of Willow's shop as he watched her engrossed with her work. She looked like she was doing a very weird version of KerPlunk with this latest candle, sticking kebab sticks into a large paper cup at different angles so their ends came out the other side.

He approached her from behind and slid his hands round her waist, placing a little kiss on her neck. She immediately turned round and wrapped her arms around his neck, kissing him deeply. He gathered her close as the kiss continued. God, he could keep kissing this woman all day.

'Hello,' she whispered against his lips as she pulled back slightly.

'Well that's the nicest greeting I've had in a very long time,' Andrew said.

'Let me just finish this and I'm all yours,' Willow said, turning round in his arms to face her candle. His hands, which had been at her hips, were now resting on her bum. He didn't move them away and she didn't seem bothered by it either. In fact as he stroked his thumbs down her bum, she gave a little wiggle against him that drove all sense and any coherent thought from his mind.

He cleared his throat and tried to focus on something else instead.

'What are you doing?' he asked.

'It's a bit of an experiment really. I kind of wanted a Swiss cheese effect with these holes all the way through the candle. Once it's hard, I'll take the sticks out and the holes should still be intact. If it works, I'll try thicker sticks to make the hole bigger. The only problem I have is the wax might seep out of the holes in the cup so I'm going to use this melted wax which has been cooling for a while and I'll pour a little bit into the cup first to try to seal the holes around the sticks.'

His hands were still on her bum and he was having trouble concentrating on anything she was saying. He decided to step away so he could listen to her properly. She flashed him a smile.

He watched as she poured a bit of the wax into the cup and rotated the cup in her hands so the wax sloshed around its sides. Once she was happy, she poured the rest of the wax inside and filled the cup to the top.

'There, that should do it. We'll see how it turns out later,' Willow said, turning back to him. 'Now I'm all yours.'

'Well, would you like to accompany me to lunch?' Andrew said, offering out his arm.

'I'd be delighted. Are you taking me some place grand?' Willow said, locking the door behind her and linking her arm through his as they left the shop.

'Yes, the finest eating establishment in the whole of the village.'

Willow giggled. 'Oh, I have some interesting news. There were two more presents delivered last night.'

'What?'

'I know, that was pretty much my reaction. Have you been sharing that secret handshake with other people?'

He laughed. 'No, I promise, you're the only one I'm… shaking hands with.'

She grinned up at him. 'Glad to hear it.'

'So go on then, spill. Who got the gifts?'

'Kitty got a scarf and Joseph got a book about roses.'

'Well, that is interesting.'

'That's what I thought.'

'People who have received the gifts are trying to pay back the people who they think gave the presents to them,' Andrew said.

'Yeah, maybe. Or, they are paying it forward: "I've received a nice gift, I want someone else to have a nice gift too."'

'Yeah, it could be that.'

'Although personally I think Joseph's gift was from Dorothy,' Willow said.

He nodded. 'I was thinking that.'

'Great minds.'

He pushed open the door of the pub which was a lot busier than normal. There was a steady hum of happy noise as people sat and talked. Andrew and Willow walked up to the bar where both Tabitha and Connor were busy serving.

'What's going on?' Andrew asked Connor.

'I don't know, but it's been like this ever since those gifts have started to appear. They all want to come here and catch up on the latest news surrounding the gifts. Of course the two of you getting together has also added to the excitement. So for god's sake, don't break up,' Connor said.

'We'll try not to,' Willow said, looking up at Andrew with a smile.

Andrew gave her a kiss on the forehead and to his surprise there was a little cheer of appreciation from behind him. He looked around to see that almost the whole pub was watching them. Small communities were not all they were cracked up to be.

'What do you have on the menu today?' Andrew asked.

'We have lasagne.'

'That sounds great.'

They ordered their drinks and took them over to a small booth.

Willow looked around to see if anyone was listening to them, but they were all too busy with their own conversations to bother with them any more.

'So what do we do about Joseph and Kitty now?' Willow asked quietly. 'Do we go ahead and give them a present anyway, which will mean they get two presents, when everyone else will get one? Or do we cross them off the list now they have received a gift, regardless that it wasn't from the Secret Society?'

Andrew thought about this carefully. It didn't seem right that some people in the village didn't get a present from the Secret Society, but they had at least received a present, even if it wasn't from them. 'I think, for now at least, we cross them off the list. It will look suspicious if they get two, like you said, and lots of people haven't even had one yet.'

Willow nodded. 'OK. So who should we do next?'

Andrew looked around. 'How about Tabitha and Connor?'

'Excellent idea. And I have just the thing for Connor too.'

'Oh yes?'

Willow leaned across the table. 'Ken was saying the other day that he wished that Connor was a bit more adventurous with his cooking, especially with his fish. I have a huge fish cookery book my brother bought for me when I was on a bit of a fish health kick a while back. I never made any of the dishes, it pretty much sat untouched on the shelf in my kitchen for the last few years, but I brought it with me as it was from Luke and it seemed wrong to throw it out. Now I think it would be much more appreciated by someone else.'

'Great idea,' Andrew said, taking a sip from his drink. He watched her pull the list out from her pocket and flatten it on the table.

'What should we give Tabitha?' she asked.

'What did we put down on the list?'

Willow pulled a face. 'I think hers was one of the ones we filled in towards the end of the night. We put chocolates, but that's a bit lame.'

That *was* a bit rubbish. 'The Secret Society can do better than that.'

'Well, you know her better than I do. What kind of things does she like?' Willow asked.

'Cliff Richard.'

'Really?'

'She loves him,' Andrew said.

'Yeah, I can't see us getting Sir Cliff to come down here for a pint,' Willow said.

'No.' Andrew thought about this for a moment. 'But there's a young lad who lives in the next town. He does a tribute act of Cliff Richard. Apparently he's really good. Looks like him too, in his younger years. He used to do all the local pub gigs over the last few years. I think he's stopped lately because he's at university, but he did a gig a few weeks ago for charity. Maybe we could convince him to come here and do a small set in return for free fish and chips.'

Willow broke into a smile. 'That's a great idea.'

'OK, let me see if I can make a few phone calls, see if he's willing and what his availability is like.'

Tabitha came over then with their food. She didn't linger though, they were a bit too busy for that, which was nice to see. Their hard work was already starting to pay off in terms of getting the community to socialise more and that filled Andrew with a warm buzz of encouragement.

'A live act would also be great business for this place too. And if it does well maybe Tabitha and Connor might be persuaded to do it more often.'

Andrew nodded as he tucked into his food.

'Have you seen Kitty and Ken today?' Willow asked, waving her fork around. A bit of lasagne flew off and landed on his plate. 'Oh god, sorry.'

Andrew pierced the errant piece of pasta with his fork and ate it. She giggled. She had the most wonderful-sounding laugh.

'No I haven't, why?' he said, bypassing her faux pas.

'Ah, I'm desperate to know what the surveyors think of the castle. They're coming today to see if it's safe to open up to the public. But I don't want to go up there and ask, it would be too pushy.'

'They know you're pushy, I don't think there's any point pretending you're not.'

Willow laughed in mock outrage. 'I'm not pushy.'

He cocked his head. 'What would you call it?'

She smiled as she chewed on a piece of garlic bread, clearly thinking it over. 'Passionate.'

He laughed. 'OK, I'll give you that. And I have to say, I do love your passion.'

He watched her carry on eating, smiling to herself.

He stared at her. This really wasn't like any date he'd ever been on before, this was two people who got on really well, just chatting as if they'd known each other for several years. There was this ease between them that he'd never had with any of his previous girlfriends. There was no need to try to impress the other because it seemed both of them were already sold.

She looked back up at him. 'I've just realised we've spent the whole time talking about the gifts and the castle, we haven't talked about anything… dateish.'

'What counts as dateish topics?' Andrew said.

She grinned. 'I don't know, what was the name of your first pet? Who was your favourite teacher? That kind of stuff.'

'It kind of feels like we've bypassed all of that. But in the interest of keeping this dateish, first pet was a rabbit called Muffin, favourite teacher was Mrs Gillespie.'

'Why was she your favourite?' Willow asked.

Andrew didn't want to tell her that Mrs Gillespie understood what it meant to be deaf more than any other teacher, that she always discreetly sat him at the front so he could lip-read more easily, made sure she was always facing him when she spoke to the class, used visual aids wherever possible and gave him handouts at the end of each lesson to go over what had been taught. He had found it hard to concentrate in class, his hearing aids picking up a lot of background noise, but for some reason her class was quieter, which made listening so much easier. He didn't want Willow to know any of this. He didn't want to appear less in her eyes.

He shrugged. 'She gave me sweets.'

For a second he saw a flash of hurt in her eyes. She knew he was lying.

'My favourite teacher was Mr Ray,' Willow said after a while. 'He loved drama and always had us dressing up to play different historical characters.'

She was going to let him off the hook. She knew he didn't want to talk about it and she was just going to let it go. He felt a bit bad but mostly he just felt relief that he wasn't going to have to talk about that side of his life with her. Well, not now anyway.

She looked up at him and he leaned over the table and kissed her briefly on the lips, something that was met with a resounding cheer from the other villagers. He didn't even care.

'What was that for?' Willow asked.

'Just because, I really like you.'

'Well I really like you too but you know you're just stoking the fire here,' she gestured to their little impromptu fan club and he shrugged.

'They'll get used to it soon enough.'

'I suppose it is a bit surprising for them. We are moving quite quickly.'

He frowned slightly. 'Are you having doubts?'

'No, god no. This thing between us, it feels so right and maybe we don't need to follow proper conventions. We need to do what feels right for us and to hell with anyone else. Did you know Ken proposed to Kitty after only a week?'

He cleared his throat. Was that how Willow saw their relationship? If so, that was suddenly moving a lot quicker than he imagined.

Willow laughed. 'I'm not expecting a proposal from you. Hell, if you did propose now, I honestly don't know what I'd say but I don't think I'd be booking the church just yet. My point is, I'm very happy with how things are going right now, we don't need to speed things up but I certainly don't want to slow down either. In fact, I would love it if you came for dinner tonight. If three dates in twenty-four hours is not too fast for you.'

He smiled. 'That would be perfect.'

'And we can deliver Connor's gift after dinner and maybe we can give a gift to someone else if there's something easy we can do tonight.'

'Good idea.'

'I've ordered a few things online for a few of the other presents, so that might take a few days to arrive,' Willow said.

'Well keep checking at the post office, you won't get post delivered to your door here. Julia keeps a good log of everything that comes in so it won't take her long to check if you have any deliveries.'

'Yes she showed me the log, she was quite proud of it.'

Andrew smiled; Julia was definitely proud of her post office.

Willow finished her lunch and stacked her plate on Andrew's already empty one. Then she took his hand.

'Thank you for lunch, but I better be getting back, I have a number of orders I need to package up and take to the post office this afternoon. Come round about seven?'

Ah crap. The date was over and he hadn't mentioned Morgan. Although was a date really the right time to bring up an ex in the first place? But he knew he needed to tell her. He wanted to be nothing but honest with Willow.

'Listen, I wanted to talk to you about something for a moment. I mean it's not something, I mean it was. Well I wouldn't exactly call it something even back then,' Andrew started.

Willow looked at him in confusion. 'Are you going to spit it out or shall we play charades and I can guess it?'

He smiled, slightly. He watched her across the table, this funny, brilliant, dazzling woman. He was enjoying himself way too much with her to want to throw a spanner in the works so early on. His semi-relationship with Morgan was in his past and there was no reason to bring it up now. To draw attention to what he'd had with Morgan would make it seem like her coming to the village was a much bigger deal than it was. She was here to do a job, there wasn't anything more to it than that, so why did he need to upset Willow with something that was nothing?

'Do you know what, it can keep.'

'Are you sure?' Willow said.

'It's not important.' And it really wasn't.

'OK, I'll see you later.' She stood up, kissed him on the cheek and then left him alone.

He watched her go but he couldn't help the uneasy feeling in his gut that he'd just made a terrible mistake.

He pushed that thought away. Jacob was making him doubt himself, a man who had never had a serious relationship. Why would Andrew take advice from him?

It was going to be absolutely fine, he was sure of it.

chapter 21

Andrew rode his quad bike up towards the entrance to the village so he could meet Morgan. He'd left it to the last possible minute to go up there. He certainly didn't want to be waiting for her to arrive as that would seem like he was keen to see her, but he also didn't want to keep her waiting as that would be rude. Morgan was his friend and, although he had no intention of picking up where they had left off, he didn't want to be horrible about it.

He shook his head as he drove along. She probably didn't have any interest in him in that way at all. After all, she had stopped calling him, she had been dating a pilot for several months. It was rather arrogant of him to assume she was coming here to have sex with him. Just because she had sounded delighted that he had called, it didn't mean anything. It could simply be because she was looking forward to catching up with an old friend. Although it had been a long time since they'd had that kind of relationship.

He left the main high street and manoeuvred round the slopes leading up to the castle. He could see Morgan's little van parked outside the four houses, where she was unloading her stuff, and he pulled up behind it.

She straightened from unpacking a large bag and her face broke into a huge smile when she saw him.

He climbed off the quad bike but the next thing she ran towards him, slamming into him and wrapping him in a huge hug.

He hesitated. He wouldn't think twice about hugging any of his female friends but this somehow felt different because Morgan *was* different to his friends. He had history with her. He had seen her naked, made her scream in the throes of passion. There was a reason why men and women couldn't really stay friends after they'd slept together because it was awkward as hell. Although was it only awkward because he was with Willow now? Would it be this awkward if he wasn't thinking of her the whole time? But, not wanting to hurt Morgan's feelings, he gave her the quickest of hugs in return.

'Andrew, how are you?' Morgan stepped back to look at him, her hands still on his arms.

'I'm good, really good actually. I live here now and I love it. I have a lovely girlfriend, Willow, I'm sure you'll meet her later, but yes things are great.'

He cringed a little at mentioning Willow. He knew it would seem as if he had deliberately shoehorned her into the conversation to make his status clear, which in many ways he had.

'A girlfriend?' Morgan seemed surprised at this, although she didn't relinquish her hold on him. 'I thought you didn't really do girlfriends.'

'Willow's different. I *really* like her.'

'So it's serious?'

'Yes it is.'

'And she knows that you're…' she trailed off but signed the word '*deaf*'. She knew he didn't really like to tell anyone.

'Yes she does,' Andrew said.

'Wow, that is serious.'

'Ah, things change. I suppose we grow up. I'm thirty-two next month. Maybe it's time I settle down.' He refrained from saying that when you met the right person then it was worth giving a proper relationship a chance, because he didn't want it to sound like Morgan wasn't the right person for him. He didn't want to be mean. 'You must feel the same, you're with that pilot bloke, aren't you? What's his name, Jim is it?'

'Yes. We broke up. He was sleeping with one of the air hostesses.' She shrugged as if she didn't care but he could tell that she did. 'I guess not all men are ready to grow up.'

'I'm sorry to hear that,' Andrew said.

She suddenly switched to sign language but he was used to the change with her.

'*Oh, I'm not the settling-down type*,' Morgan signed, trying to pull off an air of nonchalance she didn't quite achieve. '*I'm much more the having-fun, no-strings-attached type. That way no one can get hurt. You used to be so much fun, Andrew.*' She ran her hand down his chest in a gesture that didn't need any sign language to understand. 'Are you still fun?'

Andrew stepped back slightly out of her reach. Her question was crystal clear and he wanted to be as direct with his answer so he didn't reply with sign language as he normally would.

'I'm very very happy with Willow. This is something serious for me and I can't imagine being with anyone else but her. So if your question is am I still up for no-strings-attached sex then I'm afraid my answer is no.'

Morgan stared at him for a moment. 'Jesus Andrew, I was only joking. I'm happy for you, really I am.'

She moved back to the van and grabbed a few more things and he could tell that he'd hurt her by his rejection. He felt horrible. But he knew she hadn't been joking either.

He cleared his throat and decided to move on to safer subjects. 'So, what are your thoughts about the screens?'

She paused for a moment as if she hadn't been expecting the sudden change of direction in conversation, then she turned back to face him. 'Well I'm going to use four separate screens, I simply can't get screens that big to cover all four of the houses. But the picture will run across the screens so it will be continuous. I've ordered screens with a hilly background and I'll paint the picture on top of that.'

He nodded. 'How can I help?'

'Well I need to peg the screens open next to each other on the ground so I can ensure the continuity of the paintings and drawings across all four of them.'

'OK, I can help with that.'

'I'm only going to draw the castle and characters today and then I'll start painting each screen separately tomorrow. Fortunately the weather is lovely and warm so I can leave the paint to dry in the late afternoons, early evenings, before putting the screens away overnight. The whole thing will take me a few days but we're not in any great rush, are we?'

'Not really. But the open day is in twelve days so it needs to be finished and erected by then.'

'That's no problem. It shouldn't take me longer than a week.'

'That's great,' Andrew said, but inwardly cursed that she would be here that long. This whole thing was uncomfortable and he didn't know what Willow was going to make of it either.

Willow closed the shop door and locked it. She glanced down the high street towards where she knew Andrew was working, but there was no sign of him.

She looked up the high street and saw Kitty coming towards her. She waved and headed over to meet her.

'I hear you got a present last night,' Willow said.

'Yes, a beautiful scarf, thank you.'

'Ah, I can't even take credit for that. It seems there really are mystery gift-givers in the village.'

Kitty looked confused. 'So who was it?'

'I have no idea,' Willow said. 'Maybe it was the fairies.'

Kitty laughed. 'Anyway, enough of that for now. I came down as soon as we heard. The surveyors have approved the castle to be opened to the public. Two of the towers are out of action – well we knew that one of them certainly would be, and in actual fact we need to block off part of the gardens immediately surrounding that tower – but other than that we are free to let people in.'

'Oh my god, that's great news,' Willow said. 'I really think this will help the village.'

'There's loads to do, paperwork and websites and advertising, but we might just be ready for the open day.'

'Well I'm not sure what use I will be on that side of things but whatever I can do to help, just let me know.'

'Thank you. I better go, I feel like we have a mountain to climb, but I just wanted to let you know as all this was your idea,' Kitty said.

'I hope it makes a difference, I really do.'

Willow waved Kitty off and then did a little excited bounce on the spot. This would make such an impact on the village in a good way. She decided she would go and find Andrew and tell him the good news.

She moved off down the road, heading in the direction of where all the work was taking place. She saw Jacob coming towards her and she waved to say hello.

'Have you seen Andrew?'

'He said he was going for a swim before your hot date tonight.'

Willow smiled and then a thought occurred to her. Andrew said he swam naked.

'Thanks Jacob. I think a swim sounds a lovely idea.'

'I bet it does,' Jacob grinned and sauntered off to the pub.

Willow made her way down through the village until the houses fell away and she was left with only fields and the old ruins. It was a gloriously warm summer's day and the sea was a gorgeous turquoise green as it sparkled in the sunlight.

She reached the top of the steps to the beach and quickly went down them, although there were a lot more steps than she'd thought. The beach was completely deserted, beautiful golden sands stretching right around the cove. It seemed such a waste that no one from the village came down here.

She spotted Andrew out in the sea straight away. He wasn't too far from the shore but, as she had hoped, he was completely naked. She could see his strong arms powering through the waves, the water glistening off his back and his bum, the occasional glimpse of that spectacular tattoo. For a few minutes she just stood and watched him; it was a dazzling sight.

She noticed his pile of clothes and walked over to them, wondering whether she should wait there for him to come out or take off her clothes and go out and join him.

Suddenly she had an idea. She had sworn revenge on him for making her curtsey to Kitty and Ken and this seemed like the perfect opportunity.

She started picking up his clothes and then hesitated for a second. He wouldn't be swimming with his hearing aids in and she didn't want to take them away from him. They would probably be in his clothes somewhere. Unless they were in his boots. She grabbed the boots and put her hands inside. Sure enough, she found a handkerchief inside one with the hearing aids wrapped up carefully inside. Putting them back inside the boot, she scooped up the rest of his clothes and his towel and quickly ran back to the steps.

'Oi!' Andrew yelled as he started wading out the water.

She gave him a little wave and ran as fast as she could up the stairs. Sadly she wasn't that fit and reached the top panting and heaving. She stopped for a few seconds to catch her breath before moving off towards her cottage, not running – she was too worn out for that – but walking quickly.

She turned round to see if Andrew was in hot pursuit and saw him reach the top of the steps and start chasing after her. Finding a new lease of life, she broke into a run and raced back to the cottage, giggling so hard she could hardly catch her breath.

She got back to the house and shoved his clothes in a cupboard, knowing it wouldn't be long before he arrived to claim them back.

She couldn't stop giggling as she imagined him dashing stark naked along the cliff tops wearing only his boots. He was going to be furious.

It only took a few moments before he was bursting into her lounge in all his magnificent naked glory. It was clear he had been running as his chest was heaving slightly and he was still wet from his swim, little water droplets pouring down his chest.

'You took my clothes,' Andrew said, incredulously.

'Consider it payback for the curtsey debacle.'

He arched an eyebrow in amusement. 'Oh I see. You want to play that game?'

'I think we're even. There is no need for you to get me back for this.'

'You think one little curtsey is equal to making me walk naked along the cliff path?'

'I left you your boots. I'm not completely heartless.'

He clearly thought about this for a moment as he caught his breath and she used the moment to enjoy the view some more. He really was spectacular… in every way.

'See something you like?'

'Oh yes, very much,' Willow said.

'I think you better give me my clothes back.'

'Or what?' Willow said, unable to keep the smug smirk from her face.

'Or… I'll take all of yours.'

It was a nothing comment, a threat plucked straight from the air. But the thought of him stripping her out of her clothes was suddenly all she could think of. And clearly he was suddenly thinking of that too as all amusement faded from his eyes.

Right then, there wasn't a single fear or doubt that this next step for them wasn't the right thing to do.

She swallowed and stepped up to him, feeling bold. 'I'm not going to give your clothes back.'

He stared at her, not moving, not saying a word. He was barely even breathing.

'So you better take my clothes,' Willow said, raising her arms in the air so he could take her dress off more easily.

His fingers twitched at his side and then he stepped forward and pulled at the hem of her dress. Sliding it slowly upwards and over her head, he let the dress slide to the floor.

He stared down at her standing in just her bra and knickers. 'You did say you'd take *all* of them,' Willow said.

'I'm working on it,' he muttered.

His hands moved around her back, gently stroking up her spine until he reached the clip of her bra. He slowly unhooked it and then slid the straps down her arms, until her bra landed neatly on top of her dress. He ran his fingers down her sides until they reached the waistband of her knickers. She quickly toed off her sandals as he started sliding her knickers down her legs, kneeling down on the floor to help her out of them. He stood back up, tossing her knickers onto her small pile of clothes.

'I think you better take your boots off too,' Willow said and Andrew practically kicked them across the room. 'What are you going to do now you have all my clothes?'

He cleared his throat. 'Well my first thought was to run away with them, but now I'm having other ideas.'

'Want to show me what those ideas look like?'

He hesitated for the longest moment and she wondered if he was going to talk himself out of it.

'Or I could show you my ideas,' Willow said, placing a

gentle kiss on his chest and then another on his tattoo.

'I think our ideas are very similar,' Andrew said.

He cupped her face and kissed her hard. Her heart exploded in her chest, this desperate need for him bubbling through her.

He hauled her close to him and she could feel he wanted this as much as she did. Without taking his lips off hers, he bent and scooped her up into his arms. She giggled against his lips as the kiss continued and he carried her upstairs.

He laid her down on the bed and he was right there over her, kissing her, stroking, touching everywhere. He tore his mouth from hers to kiss her throat, her chest, before kissing her breast, making her shout out a whole load of noises she had never heard herself use before. His mouth dipped lower, trailing his tongue across her stomach and then even lower still until he was kissing right at the top of her thighs. She ran her fingers through his hair as every coherent thought went straight out of her brain. This man knew exactly what he was doing. That wonderful tingling sensation spread out through her whole body before she was screaming and shouting and writhing with the most glorious orgasm she'd ever had.

He moved back over her body, pinning her to the mattress with his weight as he kissed her again.

'Please tell me you have a condom,' he said.

She smiled. 'I do have condoms. Lots of them in fact.'

'Thank god for being prepared,' Andrew said.

'They're in the bedside drawer. I would get them myself, but I seem to be trapped under this big, beautiful man.'

He grinned and leaned over to grab one. He gave her a brief kiss on the lips before sitting back on his knees to put it on. She sat up too, kneeling up on all fours, leaning over to kiss him as he dealt with the condom. He kissed her, running his hands down her back. Then suddenly he hauled her on top of him so she was sitting on his lap, her legs wrapped around his back. With his hands tight on her hips, he pushed inside of her.

'Oh god Andrew.' Willow let her head fall back as he kissed her throat, moving inside her harder, deeper, holding her tight against him with his large hands around her back.

He kissed her breast, taking her nipple into his mouth, and she clung onto his shoulders, feeling the strength in his back.

That feeling was building in her already and she looked back at him, lifting his chin so she could kiss him again.

This man, this wonderful, kind, glorious man, it was ridiculous to have these feelings for him so soon. She wanted to tell him, to shout it out, but she wouldn't do that. She pulled back slightly so he might see what was in her heart as she fell over the edge, clinging to him. His eyes were locked on hers as he watched her fall completely and utterly in love with him. Did he know? Did he feel it too? But before she could catch her breath, he kissed her hard, gasping against her lips, holding her tight as he lost all control too.

chapter 22

Andrew stared at the ceiling as the pink glow of the sunset danced across the waves. Willow was lying snuggled up against his side, peppering soft kisses across his chest. They had dozed a little and kissed a lot. But they hadn't really spoken since they'd made love. Quite honestly he had no idea what to say to her and now it was getting a little awkward.

Because what do you say to someone you've fallen in love with? Should he tell her? But that felt way too soon. They were supposed to be taking it slow and, although they had broken that rule by jumping into bed with each other, to suddenly declare his love for her felt like he'd be smashing that rule into smithereens.

But then not telling her felt like a lie. It was as if the next words out of his mouth would be deceitful somehow if he didn't tell her the truth.

He honestly hadn't expected this. Yes he'd really bloody

liked Willow and he'd told Jacob that he might even marry her one day. That day had felt very far away but now…

He hadn't been in love with anyone for many years. Every woman he'd been with he'd kept it casual, something fun. And while he knew that being involved with Willow was always going to be something much more than that, he hadn't expected to fall so hard so quickly.

No, this was lust, pure and simple. No one falls in love during sex. Sure he was very fond of her, she made him smile a lot and he cared about her deeply, and he was definitely attracted to her, but it wasn't love. He simply wasn't ready for that yet.

She stroked a hand down his stomach and then pressed a gentle kiss right over his heart.

Christ, he was in trouble.

She looked up at him, her eyes so filled with tenderness and affection, and the words nearly fell from his mouth right then and there.

He ran his hand through her hair, stroked his thumb down her cheek.

'Are you OK?' Willow asked.

He nodded, swallowing down the lump in his throat.

'You're very quiet.'

'I'm just… that was… I didn't expect… I've never felt…' He trailed off because he couldn't find the right words to even begin to describe what was going on in his head, to explain what had just happened for him.

She smiled as if she understood but he didn't think she

did. Not really.

She kissed his heart again and then slid her hand lower. As it slipped beneath the sheet that was covering his hips, his body responded to her touch instantly. God, he needed her again.

She looked back up at him with that beautiful mischievous smile. 'Want to do it again?'

He quickly rolled her, pinning her to the mattress and she let out a little shriek of surprise.

'Hell yes,' he said, kissing her hard.

This was easy, he could do this. Amazing, uncomplicated sex. He ignored the little voice at the back of his head that told him it was way more than that.

She gasped against his lips as his hand moved between her legs. She clung to him as she let out a groan of pure ecstasy. He kissed her again, capturing it on his lips.

He leaned over and grabbed a condom, he slid it on and moved inside her, barely taking his lips from hers for a second. Passion and need for her drove him beyond insanity. This was lust, that's all it was. He moved against her faster and harder, desire sending him close to the edge.

It was her gentle touch that made him pause, a caress over his shoulders, a hand sliding up round the back of his neck and cupping his head. He pulled back slightly to look at her and it was her expression that floored him: trust, happiness, this complete blissful serenity like this was where she belonged and amongst all of that was this look of complete adoration.

He started moving against her slower, gentler, taking his

time. She wrapped her arms and legs around him, holding him close, and the whole time he just watched her, their eyes locked together. He felt the change in her body, heard the hitch in her breath as he drove her closer and she reached up and held his face.

And just before she tumbled over the edge, he heard her whisper, 'I think I'm falling for you Andrew Harrington.'

Then she was shouting out all manner of words and noises that didn't seem remotely recognisable but it was those first words that made him lose control, kissing her hard as he trembled in her arms. He collapsed down on top of her, his heart thundering against his chest.

Christ, she was falling in love with him and, even worse than that, he knew he was falling in love with her too – if he hadn't already fallen. He could deny it all he wanted but this was so much more than lust.

Willow looked across the table at Andrew and smiled. She had relented and given him his clothes back. Well, some of them. Well, his tight black boxer shorts. Everything else was still in the cupboard. There was not a finer sight in the world than Andrew Harrington sitting across from her wearing next to nothing as he finished his very late dinner or in reality a very early breakfast.

Willow would have been more than content to spend the rest of the night in her bed with this wonderful man but their rumbling stomachs had driven them to go in search of food, even if the planned meal of chilli con carne had gone out of the window. They had settled instead for a chicken sandwich and a bowl of chips which Andrew seemed equally happy with.

They still hadn't spoken a great deal, other than to discuss food options. She frowned as she ate the last chip from her plate. Was he regretting what had happened? She didn't believe that. Not after the way he had looked at her while they'd been making love.

But something had changed between them. She just wasn't sure what.

'So are we just doing Connor's present tonight?' Andrew said, carrying on as normal as if they hadn't just spent the last few hours having the best sex of her life.

'Yes, I think so. We need to have a think about some of the others and come up with some ideas. Right now, I'm a little bit too exhausted to have to think about that list too much. I kind of want to just climb back into bed again.'

He flashed her a mischievous grin.

'To sleep,' Willow laughed. 'God, I've created a monster. No more sex for you.'

He smirked. 'That seems a bit harsh. You seemed to be enjoying yourself.'

'I absolutely enjoyed myself. I'm not saying no sex ever, but no more sex until… tomorrow morning.'

He looked outside at the twilight sky of the dawn. The sun hadn't risen yet but it wouldn't be long before it arrived.

'I can wait that long,' Andrew said, with a grin.

She shook her head. 'You're an animal.'

He smiled, then leaned over and took her hand, circling his thumb around her palm in soft sweeps. It was such a gentle gesture, he was barely touching her, but it did things inside her that made her breath hitch. He must have realised what he was doing because his smile grew.

'So no regrets?' he said.

'No, definitely not,' Willow said, without hesitation.

'Good.'

'Do you have any regrets? You've been fairly quiet since we…' she gestured to upstairs.

He copied the gesture with a smirk. 'Since we?'

'Since we… had sex,' Willow said.

'Since we made love, you mean,' Andrew said.

Her heart filled with love for him because he was right, *having sex* just didn't seem to cover what had happened between them.

'Look, I know you didn't come here looking for a relationship but this thing between us…' he shook his head as if he didn't quite believe it. 'I have never had a relationship that has felt so completely and utterly right. I don't regret it for one second. Tonight was incredible and I just wasn't expecting that.'

She smiled with relief. 'I thought so too.'

She wasn't sure what was going on here but she really liked it. Maybe it was moving too fast, maybe she was a fool for letting herself fall for him so soon, but she really wanted to see where this was going to go.

'Come on, we should go and deliver Connor's present before the village wakes up,' Willow said, changing the subject because with the way he was looking at her right then, she wanted to take him straight back to bed. 'And then maybe we can squeeze in a few more hours' sleep before morning.'

'OK, sounds good. Just one little problem.'

'What's that?'

'I'm going to need my clothes.'

The sun was merely a whisper on the hazy pink horizon when they left Sunrise Cottage to deliver Connor's present. It was ridiculously early and not even the birds had woken up but it was light enough for them to see.

Andrew slipped his hand into Willow's as they walked up the track towards the village. She looked up at him and smiled. There was this peace between them now, like they both knew they were unbreakable. Maybe it was too early to think stuff like that, but he meant what he'd said earlier: this felt so right.

'My friend Ruby is coming tomorrow,' Willow said. 'Well, later on today.'

'Ah wonderful, we can tell her we took her advice.'

Willow laughed.

'Where is she staying?' he asked.

'At the pub. She can keep Jacob company.' She paused. 'I'd really like her to meet you.'

'I'd love to meet her. I'll be a bit busy during the day but we could all do dinner tomorrow night in the pub. I have arranged for the Cliff Richard man to come so that will be entertainment for us all.'

'Ah, that will be brilliant. Ruby will love that and hopefully Tabitha will too. And thank you for wanting to meet her. She's important to me and so are you, so…'

'It will be my pleasure,' Andrew said.

'And I'd like to meet your friends too. Morgan, for instance, I must pop along and meet her.'

'Ah, Morgan isn't really a friend…' Andrew trailed off because that felt mean. Morgan was a nice girl and they had been friends in the past when they had been much younger, before it had become more than friendly. Even the day before, after her offer of sex had been turned down, they had worked alongside each other for a few hours to get the screens ready. And actually it had been easy between them, as if that moment had never happened. 'I mean, we haven't seen each other for so long now that we've kind of drifted apart. Of course she's still my friend but I wouldn't say we were close any more.'

'Oh, I see.'

'But you'll meet Leo at the open day, he's agreed to do the fireworks for us in the evening.'

'Oh, that's going to be fantastic, such a great celebration of our open day. And it'll be great to meet Leo too,' Willow said.

'He'll be bringing his wife and son along. Well, technically his stepson… well actually it's a bit more complicated than that, but yes he'll be bringing his family with him so you can meet Isla too.'

'I look forward to it.'

They arrived at the pub and Andrew checked up and down the high street to make sure there was no one around. He gave Willow the nod and she took the gift-wrapped book for Connor from her bag and left it on the doorstep.

'Come on, let's go,' Willow said. 'Before anyone sees us.'

They were making their way back down the lane when they saw Mary come out from a little alleyway that led from the main part of the village. Andrew grabbed Willow and they ducked behind a large bush to watch her. What was she doing out this time of the morning? Over the last few months he'd gotten to know the villagers pretty well, and they were mostly creatures of habit. Julia was a night owl, walking her Colin and Rufus around the village at very odd times of the night, but Mary stayed up late watching TV and was rarely seen out and about before nine in the morning.

She was carrying some kind of large box or tin as she made her way up the lane towards them.

'What's she doing?' Willow whispered.

'I'm not sure,' Andrew said.

They watched her walk up the little path to Eileen's house, look around to make sure no one was watching and then leave the tin on the doorstep, before hurrying back the way she had come and disappearing up the alleyway again.

Willow looked up at Andrew with excitement. 'She just left a mystery gift. Do you think she had anything to do with

Kitty and Joseph's presents last night?'

'I don't know, but shall we go and see what she left?' Andrew said, more curious about that than anything else.

Willow looked around and then nodded. 'But let's be quick.'

They quickly moved over to Eileen's doorstep, giving another look over their shoulders, and then Andrew carefully lifted the lid. It was a cake tin and inside was the most amazing-smelling apple pie.

Willow smiled at him, clearly bubbling over with excitement.

He carefully placed the lid back on and they hurried off back down the lane towards Willow's cottage.

The sun was well and truly up now, this glittering golden orb in the cloudless sky blanketing the sea with ribbons of fire.

They walked into the lounge and Willow closed the door behind them and then turned to face him.

'I love this, I love that the villagers have taken our lead and are now leaving each other gifts as well,' she said.

'I do too, we've inadvertently created something amazing,' Andrew said, then gathered her in his arms. 'This is all you, you know, this was your idea. You've given something wonderful to the village.'

She smiled and he kissed her and then the kiss quickly developed into something more.

'No more sex,' Willow said, pulling his t-shirt over his head.

'But it's morning,' Andrew said, not really feeling the conviction of her words as she was already busily undressing him.

She smiled. 'OK, fair point.'

He lifted her and carried her to the sofa where they fell in a tangle of kisses and arms and legs and discarded clothes. They didn't move from there for a very long time after that.

chapter 23

Willow made her way up to the village entrance the next morning with a huge smile on her face. Everything seemed so completely perfect at the moment, nothing was going to ruin her mood today. She had spent the entire night with Andrew, kissing, cuddling, making love, sleeping in each other's arms. It was safe to say she was completely smitten by him.

She couldn't wait to see Ruby today and tell her all about him. Ruby had stayed in a hotel a few hours away the night before, halfway between St Octavia and Happiness, but she had phoned Willow not long before to say she was only half hour away now. It hadn't been that long since Willow had seen her but she couldn't wait to catch up with her again. She was up to speed with everything she needed to do in the shop so she could take the day off and spend it with Ruby. The sun was out so Willow thought they could spend a few hours down on the beach.

As she approached the village entrance Willow spotted a woman on her hands and knees as she painted a large screen just in front of the four old houses. This must be Morgan.

She hurried over to say hello to Andrew's friend.

Although the screen was still in the initial stages of being completed, she could see how brilliant it was going to be when it was finished.

'This looks amazing,' Willow said and Morgan looked round and smiled.

'Thanks, it will be. It's not there yet, but thank you.'

Morgan turned back to her work but Willow wanted to introduce herself properly. 'I'm Willow.'

'Oh, Andrew's girlfriend,' Morgan said.

'Yes.'

Morgan stood up, wiping her hands down her denim shorts. 'It's lovely to meet you.'

'I wanted to come and say hello,' Willow said. 'I know you and Andrew are friends.'

'Oh, you don't need to worry about me and Andrew.'

'Sorry?' Willow was confused.

'It's fine, I get it.' Morgan smiled as she waved her hand dismissively.

'No, I'm not—'

'We go way back,' Morgan interrupted her. 'We were friends growing up. I think for him, I was always someone he could talk to about being deaf because I understood. My brother is deaf too. I know how hard it was for Andrew sometimes and I was the only one who didn't treat him differently. I think you're naturally drawn to someone who understands the significant things in your life, that's why work colleagues always end up together. Andrew has always had a bit of a soft spot for me, I get him like no else can.'

Willow found herself chewing on her lip. She hadn't been worried about Andrew and Morgan before but she certainly was now. It sounded like Morgan was staking a claim on him, which was odd. They were just friends, weren't they?

'Andrew's talked a lot about you, he says it's something serious?' Morgan went on.

'You sound surprised.'

'No, I mean… a little,' Morgan laughed. 'He doesn't really do serious relationships.'

'Yeah, I know he was hurt in the past,' Willow said.

'He was? I mean, yes he was. I'm surprised he told you about… *that*,' Morgan said.

'Well… yes, we've told each other everything,' Willow said.

'Oh, he just doesn't really talk about that… Wait, are we talking about the same thing here?' Morgan said.

'I don't know, I was talking about… Sophie.'

'Oh that,' Morgan waved her hands dismissively. 'I thought you meant the other thing.'

'What other thing?' Willow asked.

'Oh, nothing, I probably shouldn't say. Andrew should probably tell you about the time he really had his heart broken.'

Willow frowned. Why hadn't Andrew told her that when he'd told her about Sophie?

'So things are going well between you?' Morgan asked.

Willow smiled slightly to herself. Things were going very well between them for two people who had only known each other for around a week. 'Yes they are. I don't think either of us were looking for a relationship but when we met we just sort of clicked.'

Morgan nodded. 'I've always thought Andrew would make a great boyfriend, he has all those wonderful qualities you would look for in a husband. That's if he can stay with one woman longer than a few weeks, he has a very small attention span when it comes to women, he gets bored easily. But I'm sure that's not the case for you two. How long have you been together?'

'Umm, about a week.'

'A week?!' Morgan was incredulous. 'From the way he was talking I thought you two had been together for a lifetime. Ah, you're still in that lovely honeymoon period where you both think the other person is completely perfect. Soon enough you'll start to get annoyed about him leaving his boots everywhere or that he never takes the rubbish out.'

Willow cleared her throat uncomfortably. 'I'm sure there will be things we both do that will piss the other person off but I suppose as long as the good outweighs the bad that's all that matters.'

'Oh yes, totally. No one ends a relationship over smelly socks and bad breath.'

'Andrew doesn't have bad breath,' Willow said.

'Oh, I didn't mean Andrew.'

Willow was mortified. Did Morgan mean she had bad breath?

'I didn't mean you either,' Morgan quickly said. 'I was just talking generally, you know. That's not why people break up. There are much more serious reasons to break up with someone. Why am I talking about breaking up? You two are clearly head over heels for each other.'

'Right,' Willow said. This whole conversation was making her feel just a little uneasy.

'Why would you break up with him over boots or socks when he is that amazing in bed, who would ever walk away from that?' Morgan nudged her with a wink. 'I mean, I have never had multiple orgasms with anyone else, but Andrew… that man has a gift for them.'

Willow's heart sank. 'You and Andrew used to be a thing?'

'Yes. Oh god!' Morgan's hands went to her mouth. 'You didn't know. I'm so sorry. I just assumed he would have told you, as you've told each other everything.'

Willow wondered why Andrew hadn't told her.

'It was nothing, just a casual fling,' Morgan went on. 'I mean, it didn't last longer than six months, nine months tops, so it wasn't anything serious.'

Willow stared at her. Nine months sounded pretty bloody serious to her.

'It was just sex really,' Morgan tried to rectify the situation but only succeeded in making it worse. 'I guess you could say we're friends with benefits.'

And why the hell was Morgan using the present tense?

Willow swallowed. 'You mean you were?'

'Yes, yes, that's what I meant,' Morgan quickly reassured her. 'I'm making a right balls-up of this. Andrew really likes you, please don't pay any attention to my inane ramblings.'

Willow had no idea what to say. Knowing Andrew had kissed Morgan, touched her where he had touched Willow, whispered things in Morgan's ear as they made love made her insanely jealous. Which was ridiculous, Andrew was thirty-one. Of course he had a history, they both did. But why hadn't he told her that Morgan was one of his exes?

Fortunately Willow was saved from having to think of something to say by the arrival of Ruby's custard-yellow Mini and Ruby tooting cheerfully on the horn as she spotted Willow.

'That's my friend, she's here to stay for a few days so, umm… I'll guess I'll see you later.'

'Yes, look forward to it,' Morgan said, smiling before returning her attention to her painting.

Willow moved away from her to greet Ruby, a million thoughts swirling through her mind. She tried to push them all away to concentrate on her friend.

Ruby scrambled out of the car and threw herself at Willow, wrapping her in a big hug. Willow felt the lump in her throat as she held her friend tight.

'I've missed you,' Willow said.

'You daft lump, it's only been a week,' Ruby said.

'I know, but I've got so much to tell you.'

Not least that she had stupidly fallen for someone who she probably didn't know at all.

'Well, let's get all this stuff stowed at the pub and then you can tell me all about it,' Ruby said.

'This Morgan sounds like a complete bitch if you ask me,' Ruby said after Willow had told her everything about her and Andrew and her conversation with Morgan.

Willow wiggled her toes in the sand as she stared out over the gold-crested waves.

'I don't think that Morgan was saying those things to be mean. We were just chatting about Andrew and of course it would come up in conversation that she used to date him or whatever kind of arrangement they had that involved him giving her multiple orgasms.'

Willow swallowed the bitter taste in her mouth.

'You're right, it would come up in conversation that they dated, but not that she had amazing sex with him. Who would say that to their ex's current partner? Morgan was deliberately trying to stir up trouble,' Ruby said.

Willow knew Ruby was right. That was not a normal conversation topic.

'And what about all that other stuff about you having bad breath?' Ruby said, slathering sun cream onto her shoulders.

'She didn't say *I* had bad breath.'

'You were just chatting about people in general having

bad breath?' Ruby said, sceptically.

'Yes,' Willow said, although now she was starting to doubt herself. She cupped her hand in front of her mouth and breathed into it.

'Oh my god, you do not have bad breath,' Ruby said. 'Believe me, I would tell you if you had.'

Willow sighed. Why was she suddenly doubting everything?

'And what about that stuff about Andrew having a short attention span when it comes to women? It was almost like she was telling you this thing between you two wouldn't last.'

Ruby was right, about everything. The whole conversation had made Willow feel uneasy. She had wanted so much to like Andrew's friend that she had tried not to see what was staring her in the face. Morgan was a bitch and for reasons Willow wasn't entirely sure about, Morgan wanted to cause trouble between her and Andrew.

But Willow wasn't only angry at Morgan.

'I just feel a bit let down by Andrew more than anything else,' Willow said. 'Why did he invite his ex here in the first place? I wouldn't want to invite any of my exes to come and do a job for me. That's a little weird, right?'

Ruby shrugged. 'I suppose it depends how well you get on with them.'

'Is it wrong that I don't want him to get on well with someone he gave multiple orgasms to?'

'I think there would be something wrong with you if you weren't bothered by that.'

'I think the thing that bothers me the most is that he didn't tell me that he and Morgan had history. I mean, it's not something you can forget.'

'No, quite.'

'So did he deliberately hide that from me? And what is the big thing that broke his heart if it wasn't Sophie? We lay together and talked about our life and he told me how devastated he was over what happened with Sophie but Morgan said there was something far bigger than that, so why didn't he tell me about it? I mean, I don't need to know all of his romantic history, just like he doesn't know all of mine, but if it was as significant as Morgan says, do you not think he would have mentioned it to me then?'

'I think you need to talk to Andrew about all of this,' Ruby said.

'I'm such an idiot Rubes, I've fallen for this man after one week and I really don't know him at all.'

'You're not an idiot, you're just… rose-tinted. There's nothing wrong with seeing or hoping for the good in this world.'

'But then there's always the disappointment when you're wrong.'

'I think I'd much rather hope for the good than expect the bad, it's a much nicer way to live your life,' Ruby said.

Willow sat up and took a swig from her water bottle. She decided to change the subject as this whole conversation was making her a little bit fed up.

'Tell me something about St Octavia to cheer me up,'

Willow said.

'Why, are you missing us?'

Willow thought about that for a moment as she lay back down. She had only moved there after she had left university and her parents had split up and moved to opposite ends of the country, but for a while St Octavia had been her home. Although beyond Ruby she hadn't made any lasting connections. Many of her friends had been Garry's friends and, when they broke up, their mutual friends hadn't really known how to act around her. She didn't really miss any of them.

'Not really. I know I rushed into this decision to move here, but I don't regret it. Regardless of what happens with Andrew, I do love it here.'

Ruby paused for the longest time before she spoke. 'There is something. I didn't know whether to tell you or not.'

'Just tell me.'

'St Octavia is such a small town and I know you're still Facebook friends with a lot of people there, and many of them would take great pleasure in telling you all the gory details. And I kind of wanted you to hear it from me first.'

'God Ruby, what is it?'

'Do you want the bullet points or the unabridged version?'

'I guess the unabridged.'

'Garry's engaged.'

'What?' It was safe to say Willow hadn't been expecting that.

'To that new girl who moved into the town six months ago.'

'Imogen?' Willow asked.

'Yes. Apparently they've been seeing each other for around four or five months now, not long after you two broke up. Garry wanted to keep it quiet out of respect for you. He said he didn't want to rub it in your face after he'd broken your heart by turning down your proposal—'

'Wait, he didn't break my heart,' Willow said. 'I was more relieved than anything.'

'I did try to say that to everyone, but as you did propose to him, no one believes me.'

Willow rolled her eyes in defeat. 'I can't believe he's engaged.'

'He's really excited, I've never seen him excited about anything. I didn't even know he had that emotion as part of his repertoire. He's head over heels for her too. He's giddy. Now you're gone he wants to tell everyone he meets how much he's in love. He's even been caught a few times around town having sex outdoors. He can't keep his hands off her.'

Willow thought about this for a moment. Garry didn't do excited and giddy, or at least he never did with her. They'd never had sex anywhere but the bedroom and he certainly hadn't been the touchy-feely tactile type. God that was depressing. When they had broken up, she had felt like she had escaped from four years of mundane hell, but had he been bored out of his mind too? He had never proposed to her, never wanted to, she hadn't been enough for him, but four months of going out with Imogen had made him a changed man. The kind of man who wanted to shout his love from the rooftops.

Ruby watched her for a moment. 'Ah Willow, I should have done the bullet-points version. Are you OK? What are you thinking?'

'Just feeling a little bit inadequate. Garry never did any of that for me.'

'Would you have wanted him to? Would you really want to be married to him?'

'No of course not, but clearly I wasn't the sort of person that invoked those kinds of feelings in a person.'

'Not in Garry maybe, because you two were completely wrong for each other in every way, but when you meet the right person you will. And even if Andrew isn't that person, it sounds like things got pretty passionate between the two of you, that Andrew got *pretty excited* about being with you.'

Willow laughed as she blushed.

'What's going on with you anyway?' she asked, changing the subject again.

'Would it surprise you to know I've put my flat on the market?'

Willow sat bolt upright. 'Oh my god, that's amazing. What are you going to do?'

'I don't know. Maybe travel for a little while. Maybe I could move here for a year and save up some money if I don't have to pay any rent, then use that money to travel the world. I just need a break, to do something different.'

'I would love it if you moved here,' Willow said, delighted. 'Even if it is only for a year. And Happiness needs more unusual shops to attract different visitors so I'm sure Kitty and Ken would be thrilled to have you. And who knows, you might even be tempted to stay after you've been here a few months.'

Ruby smiled. 'I don't think I could live here for the rest of my life, but it would be lovely to live here for a short while. Especially if that hot bit of stuff we saw in the pub lives here too, he would be just the sort of distraction I need.'

Willow laughed. 'That guy you spoke to for all of five seconds at the bottom of the stairs?'

'Yes, he was yummy.'

'That was Jacob, he's Andrew's brother. And he doesn't live here so I wouldn't go getting your hopes up of falling in love and having a happy ever after.'

Ruby laughed. 'You know me, Willow, I'm not really the happy-ever-after and sunshine-and-sparkles kind of girl. I'll leave that up to you. And if I intend to go travelling in a year's time, I hardly want to put down roots with anyone, even if it is with Hottie McHotFace.'

Willow laughed. She had really missed this, and although it was all very much pie in the sky, she couldn't think of anything nicer than living in the same place as Ruby again.

chapter 24

Andrew had just finished repairing a fence when he saw Willow coming towards him with what must be her friend Ruby. Willow looked sun-kissed, her hair damp probably from a swim in the sea, her face clean and a little shiny from where she'd overdone it slightly with the sun cream. She was beautiful. He caught Jacob looking at him and rolling his eyes. Andrew knew he probably had a loved-up grin on his face.

He threw down his hammer and stood up to greet them but, as he moved to wrap his arms around Willow, she put a hand out to stop him.

He frowned in confusion.

'I spoke to Morgan this morning,' Willow said, with no preamble.

'Morgan?'

'Yes, the girl you gave multiple orgasms to, does that ring a bell?'

Ah crap.

Jacob cleared his throat awkwardly. 'I think I might go and see what the pub has on for lunch.' He put his tools down.

'I'll think I'll join you,' Ruby said and they both walked off up the hill together.

Andrew stepped back and shoved his hands in his pockets. 'I should have told you.'

'Yes you should have. All morning, I've been thinking, why wouldn't you tell me? We've told each other so much.'

He sighed. 'I didn't want you reading something into me inviting her here. Why upset you over something that doesn't mean anything to me? It wasn't anything serious.'

'She says you were seeing each other for nine months, that's sounds fairly serious in my book.'

He shook his head. 'It wasn't like that. It was just sex. I suppose from the first time we slept together up to the last time it might have been a nine-month period, but we had sex probably no more than five times in those nine months. It was a very casual arrangement. She'd ring me occasionally and we'd meet up. We haven't seen each other for a year. We're friends on Facebook but, other than the odd comment on each other's posts now and again, we've not been in touch either. As I said to you before, we're not close any more. We were friends growing up and then we drifted apart. We met up again years later, had sex a few times. She's a nice girl but we didn't date or have any kind of relationship.'

'Yet you've shared things with her,' Willow said.

'What have I shared with her?' Andrew asked. Other than

his bed.

'You told her about Sophie and—'

'She does not know about Sophie. I don't talk about that with anyone.'

Willow seemed to stall at this but then she carried on. 'And what about the other time you had your heart broken?'

Andrew stared at her in confusion. 'What other time?'

'She said there was a time that was much worse than Sophie.'

He shook his head. What had Morgan been telling Willow? Had she deliberately been trying to stir up trouble between them by making up these lies or had Morgan got him confused with someone else? Or had Willow got the wrong end of the stick completely?

'Willow, I'm not sure what Morgan told you but before I came here there was only one person that I had been in love with, one person who broke my heart, and that was Sophie. There has been no one else before or after. I have not shared anything personal with Morgan. We were friends who had sex, nothing more. There is no reason to be jealous.'

'I'm not jealous,' Willow said.

He resisted arguing with her on that. He had to pick his battles.

Willow let out a huff of breath.

'OK, when she talked about how amazing in bed you were, how you gave her multiple orgasms…' she trailed off.

He could feel himself getting angry. Why the hell would Morgan discuss that with Willow?

'Yes. I was jealous that you had touched her in the same way you had touched me, that you made love to her—' Willow went on.

'Sex,' Andrew corrected her. 'Willow, me and Morgan had sex. There's a big difference between sex and making love and what me and you shared was something I've not shared with anyone before, not even Sophie.'

She stared at him with wide eyes, then she let out a big sigh.

'I know we both have pasts, boyfriends, girlfriends, things we've done or said, good and bad. Those experiences are what shape us, make us who we are now. Sure, I wouldn't exactly invite my past to come and hang out with me. Garry would be the last person I'd want to see now, despite the fact that we parted on fairly good terms. Yes, I'm not exactly thrilled that you want to hang out with your ex but she's your friend and I don't want you to stop seeing your friends because of me. But you should have told me.'

'I don't… that's not… she was just the best person for the job, I didn't think of anything beyond that. You were the one who suggested covering the houses up.'

'And your first thought was Morgan?'

'Because that's her job. It's quite a specialised thing we're asking for here, it's not like looking for a plumber or a painter.'

Willow nodded. 'No, I get that.'

'I don't have feelings for her,' Andrew said, quick to reassure her. But by mentioning that, he felt like he was drawing attention to something that hadn't even been considered. 'I've barely given her any thought at all since the last time we met up.'

Now he was making it worse.

'Then we don't have a problem, do we?' Willow said.

Although by the tone of her voice he guessed it was a bit more of a problem for Willow than she was letting on.

'You should catch up with her properly while she's here. Go to dinner tonight with her, rather than me and Ruby,' Willow said.

He smiled at that. He could imagine how well that would go down if he decided to spend the night with his ex rather than Willow. And quite honestly, if Morgan was trying to cause trouble between him and Willow, she was the very last person he wanted to hang out with. Furthermore, faced with a choice of spending time with Willow or Morgan, there was absolutely no contest.

He reached out and took her hand. 'There is no place in the world I would rather be tonight than with you. This thing between us, I'm enjoying it way too much to want to stop.'

She smiled slightly.

'Morgan is… an acquaintance. I don't need to catch up with her. She is here to do a job. That's it.'

She was quiet for a moment. 'OK.'

'OK?' He dipped his head to look her in the eyes. He could see the affection for him return and the anger fade.

She nodded. 'I'm being an idiot.'

'No, not at all. If one of your male friends turned up here, someone you'd had *amazing sex* with, I wouldn't exactly be over the moon either. But for the record…' he lowered his voice. 'Sex with her wasn't amazing, not like it is with you.'

She smiled and shook her head. 'You're too smooth Andrew Harrington.'

'It's true.' He gingerly pulled her into his arms and after a few seconds she wrapped her arms around him and leaned into him. He breathed a sigh of relief into the top of her head.

She pulled back to look up at him. 'So no more secrets?'

'None at all,' Andrew said. 'I promise.'

'OK. What time does Cliff arrive tonight?'

'I think about seven.'

'Is he bringing loads of gear with him? That kind of thing is hard to keep hidden.'

'No, just him and his guitar,' Andrew said.

'OK, cool. Are you coming for lunch?'

'No, I really must finish here.'

She nodded and then reached up and kissed him. She leaned her forehead against his, holding his face between her hands, then she looked up at him, frowning slightly.

'What did you mean when you said, *before* you came here you had only been in love with one person?'

He thought about the words he had chosen to use. He had said that, which implied that there had been someone he had been in love with since he had moved here. Whereas before he'd just *thought* he might be falling for Willow, it now seemed his brain had already made the decision for him. But he certainly wasn't going to say those words now. If he was going to tell her he loved her then it wouldn't be in the aftermath of an argument. Those words were important and he wasn't going to use them to win opportune brownie points.

He smiled and kissed her on the forehead. 'Maybe that's a conversation for another day.'

She grinned. 'No secrets, remember.'

He laughed. 'In that case you should know, I adore you Willow, I think what we have could be something amazing.'

She smiled. 'I'll take that.'

She kissed him briefly on the lips and gave him a little wave as she walked up the hill.

He watched her go, unable to take the smile off his face. He really was in trouble with this one.

chapter 25

Willow sat in the pub watching Ruby and Jacob flirt with each other as they got the drinks at the bar. It was quite an interesting thing to watch, two people who obviously liked each other a lot go through the motions of attracting the other. Ruby twisted a strand of hair round her finger, Jacob touched her hand, Ruby laughed at all of Jacob's jokes, Jacob licked his bottom lip. Willow had watched a nature documentary a few weeks before on mating rituals and this was like watching that. The only thing was that after mating with Jacob, Ruby was likely to eat him for breakfast just like the praying mantis.

She wondered what people would make of her and Andrew's mating ritual. Whether outsiders looking in would see a couple that were going to stand the test of time or just survive a few weeks. Her relationship with Garry had lasted four years and that had been a disaster. None of her other relationships had lasted longer than a few months. Maybe she wasn't long-term relationship material. Maybe she *was* boring or just wasn't enough for people to want a long-term commitment from her. After all, the thought of marrying her had been so horrifying to Garry he had turned her down the day after he'd said yes. Would Andrew get bored of her too? In terms of the nature documentary she had watched, would they be like swans and mate for life, or be like dolphins who quite often mated for pleasure and then moved on to another willing partner?

'Hey!' Andrew said, sliding into the booth next to her and placing a kiss on her forehead. 'What are you thinking?'

Willow leaned into him; he smelt clean and zesty like limes. 'Whether we'd be swans or dolphins.'

'Oh, swans definitely,' Andrew said, without missing a beat. 'Have you ordered food yet?'

She sat up and looked at him in surprise. 'Did you just get my obscure nature reference?'

'Swans mate for life, right?' Andrew shrugged as if it was obvious.

She smiled with love for this man and she cupped his face and kissed him.

'Oi! None of that,' Jacob said, sitting down opposite them and placing the tray of drinks for them all on the table. 'This is a respectable family establishment. We don't want any canoodling going on here.'

'No, that should be kept for behind bedroom doors,' Ruby said, eyeing Jacob as she sat down too.

'Agreed,' Jacob said.

Willow suppressed a smile.

'Ruby, we haven't properly met. I'm Andrew and I see you've already met my no-good brother.'

Ruby smiled as she looked at Jacob. 'He doesn't seem all that bad.' She turned her attention back to Andrew. 'It's nice to meet you, Willow hasn't stopped talking about you since I arrived. She's obviously completely smitten.'

'The feeling is very mutual,' Andrew said.

Willow smiled.

'Just don't hurt her or you'll have me to answer to,' Ruby said.

Andrew clearly wasn't fazed at all. 'Duly noted.'

'So there were more presents delivered last night,' Willow said, trying to be as vague as possible in case there were ears flapping nearby. The pub was packed so anyone could be listening. There were several groups of people in the pub that Willow hadn't seen before – maybe the young Sir Cliff had spread the word about his performance that night. 'Eileen was delighted to receive an apple pie, and Connor received something too, but he has been out all day so Tabitha doesn't know what his present was. I've just seen him come in about half hour or so ago so I guess we'll soon find out what he got.' Or, more to the point, what he thought of it.

Andrew looked at his watch and Willow knew he was looking to see what time Tabitha's present would arrive.

She looked at him expectantly.

'About ten minutes,' he said, quietly.

'What is going on with all these presents?' Ruby asked.

Willow hadn't told her about her involvement in the Secret Society of Happiness. Although her friend could be trusted to keep big secrets, she wasn't so good at keeping the smaller ones. But Ruby had already been there while Willow picked up some of the presents she had ordered from the post office earlier and when she'd opened them back at her cottage, Ruby had been intrigued over why Willow had bought such an array of things. She had especially loved the calendar of half-naked men holding up bits of cheese to preserve their modesty. It had taken Willow ages to find that but she was hopeful that Roger would love it. She was sure Ruby had put two and two together after seeing the presents and hearing the rumours. She wasn't sure how much Andrew had told Jacob either and what Jacob had told Ruby.

'People in Happiness have been receiving mystery presents and no one has any idea who is delivering them,' Andrew said.

'Oooh, that's interesting. I wonder who it could be,' Ruby said, giving Willow a look that said she knew exactly who it was. 'Have you two had any presents yet?'

'Not yet,' Willow said, suddenly realising that if she was going to go undetected as the present-giver she would have to give herself one too.

Willow spotted Connor up at the bar and decided to change the subject. 'Shall I go and order the pizzas? There's three different kinds, shall I just get one of each?'

There were nods around the table and Willow hurried up to the bar.

Connor came over to take her order.

'Can we get one of each pizza for our table please.'

'Sure,' Connor said, ringing it through the till.

'So I hear you had a mystery gift last night? Everyone is dying to know what it is,' Willow said.

Connor made a noise of disapproval. 'A fish cookery book.'

Willow hesitated. 'You don't sound too pleased?'

'My fish is good, everyone loves my fish. But someone clearly doesn't think so. It's offensive is what it is.'

Her heart sank. 'I'm sure it wasn't supposed to be offensive.'

'And how would you know how it was intended?'

'I… I don't. I just think all the gifts so far have been… thoughtful, nice gifts. I'm sure the mystery gift-giver just thought about what kinds of things you liked and knew cooking was one of them.'

'Someone is trying to tell me how to do my job. How would you like it?' Connor said as he gathered together cutlery for her.

Willow thought about it for a moment. 'I love making candles, I love playing with wax and creating different results. If someone got me a candlemaking book, I'd be over the moon. Even if most of the candles in the book I'd already made before, I'm sure there would be one or two ideas in there that I hadn't tried or at least could adapt, put my own spin on. I wouldn't be offended, I'd be thrilled that someone had taken the time to give me a book about something I loved.'

Connor grunted. 'That's a very rose-tinted outlook.'

Willow shrugged. 'It's normally better to see the good in things than to try to find the bad.'

She took cutlery and napkins back to the table and then flopped down next to Andrew.

'What's up?' Andrew said.

'Connor didn't like his present.'

'Why? What did you get him?' Ruby asked and Willow smiled and rolled her eyes.

'*He was given* a fish cookery book. He thinks it's offensive.'

'That's a bit small-minded,' Jacob said. 'I don't think you ever stop learning, in any profession.'

'And most people are gracious enough to say thank you for a gift whether they like it or not,' Ruby said.

'I hate the thought of upsetting anyone though,' Willow said, quietly.

The door of the pub opened and Willow sat up as a man with a guitar walked in.

She nudged Andrew. 'Is that him?'

Andrew looked over. 'Yes.'

'Tabitha Butler?' the man called out, addressing the bar at large. Willow was actually really impressed, he really did look like a younger Cliff Richard.

Tabitha looked up from where she was serving a customer and gave an uncertain wave.

Cliff smiled. 'I'm your mystery gift.'

And with that he launched into 'Summer Holiday', strumming away on his guitar. He sounded so similar to Cliff too.

'Oh wow,' Tabitha said, running round the bar and pulling up a stool in front of him. Cliff sat down next to her and carried on singing, seemingly just for her, not aware of all the other villagers and guests staring in their direction. Tabitha looked ridiculously happy as she stared at him, bobbing along with the music.

Other people started joining in, singing and clapping along. 'Summer Holiday' finished and Cliff launched into 'Devil Woman' and Tabitha laughed and started joining in too.

At least Tabitha was happy with her gift.

Connor came over with the pizzas just as Cliff started 'Living Doll'.

'Great,' he said, sarcastically. 'The mystery gift-giver has given my wife a hot young man to drool over. This day keeps getting better and better.'

Willow sighed. There really was no pleasing some people.

chapter 26

'I hope Connor isn't too upset,' Willow said, as she wrapped one of the gifts they were going to deliver that night in tissue paper.

'I still think that Connor sounds like an ungrateful sod,' Ruby said, sticking ribbon on one of the wrapped gifts now that she and Jacob had been enrolled into the Secret Society of Happiness.

Willow chewed on her lip. She kind of agreed with Ruby a little but then Ruby didn't have to live alongside Connor. At some point it was sure to come out who the mystery gift-givers were and what would happen then?

'Do you think we should get him another gift?' Willow asked.

'Absolutely not,' Andrew said, as he pulled Sellotape off the table to wrap his present. 'This is not a shop where you can take the gifts back if you don't like them. This is something nice we are doing for the whole village and it's Connor's problem if he doesn't like his present.'

'Remind me again why you are doing this?' Jacob said, curling the ribbon expertly with a pair of scissors.

Willow blushed. It sounded saccharine even to her own ears. 'To bring happiness back to the village,' she said, quietly.

'Wow you really are sweet, aren't you?' Jacob said, but not like it was a bad thing. 'Although, I can understand why this is bothering you. You want everyone to be happy and you can't tick that box in Connor's case. But I have to agree with the others, a fish cookery book was really thoughtful and I think he's been a bit of an arsehole about it. If it's any consolation, I did see him singing along to some of Cliff's songs tonight, so maybe Cliff could be considered a gift for both of them.'

Willow smiled slightly at that thought. Cliff had been brilliant that night. It seemed he had worked his way through almost the entire repertoire of Cliff Richard's back catalogue, even singing songs that Willow had never heard before, although Tabitha had sung along to every one. The whole pub had loved the live music and she had seen Connor take Cliff's card at the end of the night with a view to booking him again. Maybe he wouldn't take the fish cookery ideas on board, but it seemed he liked the idea of having live music, so something good had come out of that night.

'So if the goal is to make everyone happy by giving them presents—' Jacob started.

'It's not just trying to make them happy by giving them presents, but by providing them with a mystery to get excited about,' Willow said. 'It's all everyone is talking about at the moment, it's pulled them all together.'

'Yes I can see that, but what happens when it ends? What happens when all the villagers have received a present? What happens when the mystery has been solved and they all know it's you and Andrew?'

Willow hadn't thought about that.

It would be really sad if the village reverted to their old ways, keeping to themselves with none of the lovely community spirit that had started to blossom over the last few days.

'Do you have to be so negative about everything?' Andrew said.

'I'm not being negative, I think what Willow is doing is lovely. I'm just not sure that you're going to get out of it what you want. These villagers are set in their ways and, while this is all new and exciting for them now, what will they have to keep them happy and excited once the presents stop?'

Jacob had a point.

'I suppose that I was hoping the presents and the excitement would bring them together and that camaraderie would last. But I guess you're right, when all this is done, it may just fade away,' Willow said. If that was the case was there really any point in carrying on?

'You need to do something that will make this community spirit continue and you can't keep giving presents away to people for the rest of your life,' Jacob said.

'You need to get the rest of the villagers involved too,'

Ruby said.

'Some of the villagers have been giving gifts as well, I think either to say thank you to the person they believe gave them their gift or in some attempt to pay it forward to someone else. That's been one of the lovely unexpected side effects of this mystery gift-giving: some of the villagers have really embraced it,' Willow said.

'Maybe we can get the villagers to embrace the whole spirit of the gift-giving going forward. Mowing lawns for each other, taking neighbours' dogs for walks, doing nice things for each other. That's what all of this has been about, just generally being nice to our neighbours,' Jacob said.

Willow thought about this for a moment. 'How do we get people to want to mow each other's lawns?'

'I don't know but surely everyone in the village will see the benefits of helping each other out. This is just the catalyst, but they are going to have to want to continue with this frame of mind if it's going to work,' Jacob said.

Andrew passed his present to Ruby to add the ribbon. 'I suppose for me, I really want all the people that visit us on the open day to see this wonderful village spirit, the kindness and our big hearts, and then people are going to be more likely to want to move in here. Hopefully seeing that generosity as the baseline will make them want to be part of that too.'

Willow finished wrapping the last present. 'Andrew's right, it's not enough that people will see nicely painted houses or that the shower has lovely new tiles and the gardens look pretty. The village has to feel like a home. It's going to be the villagers themselves that are going to be the big selling point on the open day, it's the villagers who are going to be the neighbours of the new people, the newcomers need to see them in the best light. Maybe we can show the visitors our generosity by getting the villagers to give little presents to anyone who comes to the village that day. We can have cakes, knitted toys, wooden ornaments, plants, candles, and each visitor can go away with a little gift of happiness to remind them of their day and of the wonderful village which might be their new home.'

Andrew smiled at her. 'I like that idea.'

She wondered how the villagers would take to the idea. She had only been here just over a week and it didn't seem right that she should start dictating to the villagers what they should be doing or coming in here with her bright ideas about how to change the place. The villagers might be really happy with how the village was now. Besides, announcing her idea of how to extend the mystery gift-giving to the village would be outing her and Andrew as the gift-givers and she wasn't sure if she was ready for that yet, especially not after Connor's reaction to his gift that night.

'OK, are we all done with the presents?' Willow asked and everyone nodded. 'Shall we go out and deliver them?'

'Why don't me and Ruby take the ones nearest to the pub? I'm knackered and I'd like to get into my own bed sometime before midnight,' Jacob said.

'Me too,' Ruby said. 'My bed that is, not yours.' She laughed nervously. 'I feel like I spent the whole day yesterday driving, I could do with a good night's sleep as well.'

Willow eyed the two of them. There was definitely something going on between them.

'Good idea, these three are the nearest to the pub,' Andrew said, handing them over. 'Stephen has a red front door, Suzanne has the big hanging basket and Coral has a gnome in a red hat sitting on her doorstep.'

Willow smirked at the fact that he knew all that.

Jacob took the presents and then practically bundled Ruby out of the house.

'God, the chemistry is almost tangible between those two,' Willow said, slipping on her jacket.

'I know. I hate to say bad things about my brother, but he's not the settling-down-and-happy-ever-after type. I hope he doesn't break Ruby's heart.'

'She's not the settling-down type either, not any more. She had her heart broken many years ago and hasn't looked for a serious relationship since. Maybe they'll be well suited to each other,' Willow said. She opened the door, grabbed her bag of presents and stepped outside. Andrew closed the door behind them.

'So, I heard you talking to Ruby earlier in the pub about Garry's engagement. You don't exactly seem happy about it,' Andrew said, slipping his hand into hers as they walked along the darkened lane, lit only by Andrew's torch.

Willow had brought it up again with Ruby. It had been niggling away at her, but she hadn't meant for Andrew to overhear.

'I'm not unhappy because I'm jealous if that's what you're thinking,' Willow said.

Although there was an element of that, not because she wanted to be married to Garry, nothing could be further from the truth. But because he had never made love to her out in the open, he had never told anyone how much he loved her, he had never been giddy with excitement over being with her and he had never wanted to marry her. She had to ask herself if there was something wrong with her.

'Well I wasn't thinking that, but now I am,' Andrew said.

'Oh no, don't feel like that. If Garry turned up here now and asked me to marry him the answer would be an immediate and emphatic no. I just feel like…' She had no idea how to describe it without sounding jealous. 'I feel like, I wasn't enough for him. By all accounts he is a completely changed man now, he's happy and head over heels in love, but I didn't give him that. He was as miserable with me as I was with him. And I just feel a little bit sad that I didn't give him what he needed or what he wanted.'

'He didn't give you what you wanted or needed either. It takes two people to fail at a relationship.'

'I know.'

'By the sounds of it you two were completely wrong for each other.'

'We were, we drifted together because it was easy. We knew each other, I liked him and that felt like enough. I trusted him. I suppose I knew I could never get hurt with Garry probably because I just didn't love him enough to be hurt if it ended.'

That was an awful thing to say. Poor Garry deserved more than that and now he'd found it.

'So why are you letting this get to you?' Andrew asked, shining his torch on an owl that suddenly took flight from a nearby tree.

Willow thought about it for a moment. 'What I have with you is different. It's something I've never had with anyone before. I suppose I'm just scared that…' she trailed off. 'I don't want to lose you.'

'You're scared because you think you weren't enough for Garry and that maybe you won't be enough for me?'

He'd hit the nail right on the head.

'You have no idea how completely and utterly you've captured my heart, Willow McKay. What we have is something incredible. I'm not going anywhere.'

She smiled and leaned against him, he wrapped an arm around her shoulders.

'Sorry for being an idiot.'

'Don't apologise. I'd rather you tell me your feelings and worries and then we can talk about them together. I want us to be completely honest with each other, I think that's the only way we will work. I had this huge feeling of inadequacy too after it ended with Sophie, that I clearly wasn't enough for her. I think I did exactly the same as you when I dated after that: I chose people who were uncomplicated choices, people who I knew I wouldn't get hurt by. I'd known Morgan for a long time before we got together. We grew up together. Her brother is deaf and he was a good friend of mine so I knew her very well, we had a lot in common. We drifted apart but when we bumped into each other years later, it just felt so easy and like the natural progression in our friendship.'

If this little pep talk had been designed to make her feel better, it was having the complete opposite effect. She didn't want to hear how easy and uncomplicated it was with Morgan when Willow seemed to come with a lot of baggage.

'Why do you think it didn't work out between you?' she asked.

'That wasn't what it was for Morgan. She wanted no-strings-attached casual sex, she made that very clear. Let's cut through here,' Andrew indicated the little alleyway they'd seen Mary use the night before to deliver her apple pie to Eileen.

They followed the darkened lane, the moonlight barely penetrating through the trees above them.

'And if she'd wanted more, do you think things would have been different?'

Andrew was silent for a moment as if really considering that option. 'I suppose if she wanted more we would have dated, but we never really did that. We never talked about our past or our hopes for the future. It was never that kind of relationship.'

'Did you want it to be?'

Willow knew she was opening up a whole can of worms here. She was asking questions she didn't want to hear the answer to.

'When we were together, having sex…'

Oh god, she really didn't need this level of honesty.

'... it was... empty. There was no connection there and I've never had that before. Even with the women I dated casually there was some emotion involved, but I didn't get that from Morgan. It really was just sex to her. And it did leave me feeling a little flat afterwards. So yes, I would have liked more from her.'

Willow was quiet. She had no idea what to say to that.

'But regardless of whether we had dated a bit more conventionally, I didn't love her. It was never going to be a forever thing with her. Maybe she knew that and maybe that's why she didn't give more of herself to me. Maybe subconsciously I set the tone of the relationship and she only took what I was willing to give, or maybe it was always just sex for her and I had nothing to do with it. But either way it was never going to last between us.'

Willow tried not to think about what could have been if Morgan had been a bit more emotionally available.

He pulled her to a stop, stroking his thumb down her cheek as they stood in the muted darkness.

'What we have, I've never had with anyone, not even with Sophie. *This* is what a relationship is supposed to be. This is everything I've ever wanted. Don't ever doubt that.'

She leaned up and kissed him just as someone cleared their throat nearby.

Willow looked around and saw Julia out walking Colin and Rufus.

'Don't mind me, dears, I didn't see anything,' Julia said,

giving them a theatrical wink as she squeezed past them.

Andrew laughed as he took Willow's hand and carried on walking up the alley. 'I'm sure that will be the talk of the village tomorrow.'

'I was hoping we wouldn't bump into her tonight, as one of the presents is for her. It's going to look a bit suspicious that she left her house and there was no present and when she comes back after seeing us walking towards her house, there is a present,' Willow said.

'Well, suspicious yes, but not exactly concrete proof. But Jacob's right, we probably won't be able to keep it a secret for much longer anyway, especially if we want to talk to the villagers about how they can contribute,' Andrew said.

'True.'

They emerged from the alley slowly and looked around the village to see if there were any more prying eyes but no one was around, most of the houses lying in darkness.

'Come on, let's get this done quickly,' Willow said. 'Before Julia comes back.'

They left the box of chocolate-flavoured tea on Liz's doorstep and the calendar on Roger's. They then crossed over the street to leave a book about quilting on Julia's doorstep, which they'd chosen after Andrew had overheard her talking about making one for her grandson. They left two other presents nearby and, with the three that Jacob and Ruby were delivering, that was eight people who would get surprise presents that night.

'It's a beautiful night. Let's take the cliff path back to your cottage,' Andrew suggested.

'OK.'

They followed the road out of the village and down towards the cliff tops. The moon glittered over the water, making the whole evening seem enchanting and magical.

'You know, if we're going to keep our identity as the gift-givers secret, we should probably give each other presents too so it doesn't look too suspicious that we're the only ones in the village not to receive one,' Willow said. 'What would you like?'

'I have everything I want,' Andrew smiled at her in the moonlight.

She smiled. 'Smooth.'

'Well apart from you turning up at my house stark naked, wrapped in a big bow, that would be a pretty spectacular present if you ask me.'

Willow laughed. She was sure she could think of something.

They passed the ruins of the old houses.

'No more stories about fairies and ghosts then?' she said.

'Actually I do have a story. Well, not really a story, more like a little nugget of information. This house here was known as the honeymoon house.'

'Really, why?'

'Apparently when a couple in the village got married, they would spend their wedding night here. The villagers would come out and decorate it during the day, get it all ready for them, but it was considered to be a very lucky place to consummate the wedding.'

'Blessed by the fairies?' Willow said.

'Something like that.'

In the light of the torch she could see Andrew's mischievous smile.

'Are you telling me this for some particular reason?'

He shrugged. 'Well if it's a lucky place to…'

'Have sex?'

'Yes. I think we could…'

'Consummate our relationship here?'

'Yes,' he grinned in the darkness.

'It's a bit bloody late for that if last night was anything to go by,' Willow said.

'Yes but that wasn't blessed by the fairies.'

'I'm not sure I want the fairies to watch us having sex.'

'I tell you what, we'll turn the torch off so the fairies can't see,' Andrew said, snapping the torch off and plunging them into darkness.

A thrill of excitement burst through her. She couldn't even see Andrew but she could feel his warmth as he stepped closer to her. He was still holding her hand and he placed a sweet kiss on her forehead before he stepped away and led her inside the four walls of the house.

Impossibly, it seemed even darker in here – though the house didn't have a roof and she could see the moon above them, the stone walls blocked out any further light.

Andrew cupped her face in the darkness and kissed her, gently. She ran her hands down his shoulders, feeling the muscles there, taut and strong. He slipped her jacket from her shoulders and, as it fell to the floor, he placed a kiss on her collar bone. God, that simple touch from him was enough to have her climbing the walls with need for him. He placed another warm kiss on her shoulder. There was something so incredibly sexy about being kissed in the darkness, not knowing what he was doing, just feeling his hot mouth on her body.

She could see his shadow, looming large in front of her, but she couldn't see anything else. She felt her way down his sides until she found the hem of his t-shirt and slid it up over his head.

She ran her hands gently down his chest, caressing across his stomach, and heard his breath hitch. This was heaven. She had enjoyed seeing Andrew naked but this was a whole new level of intimacy, like she was truly exploring him for the first time. She felt the slight bumpiness of a scar just under his ribcage, she felt the contours of his broad chest and placed a kiss right over his thundering heart.

He pulled down the top of her dress, exposing one of her breasts to the cool night air, but she let out a groan as his hot mouth was suddenly on it, kissing her, teasing her with his tongue.

'Christ Andrew,' Willow whispered in the darkness.

She needed this man right now.

She stepped away slightly.

'What are you doing?' Andrew said.

'Taking my knickers off,' Willow laughed.

'Planning ahead, I like it.'

'Not too far ahead, I hope,' Willow said, feeling his warm hands at her waist.

He shuffled her back gently against the wall, kissing her hard. She moaned against his lips and wrapped one leg around his hips. He didn't take his mouth from hers as suddenly his hand was right there between her legs, caressing, stroking until she was shouting out all manner of nonsense.

She felt him fumble around in his pocket, heard the tear of the foil packet as it glinted in the moonlight. The next thing he lifted her and she wrapped her legs around his waist. He kissed her hard as he slid perfectly inside of her. She wrapped her arms round his neck, pulling herself tighter against him as he moved deeper inside her. His hands were underneath her bottom, pinning her to the wall with his wonderful body.

Her heart roared against her chest, that incredible feeling building inside her again.

'Can you feel this connection between us?' Andrew said.

'Yes,' Willow moaned, teetering right on the edge.

To her frustration, Andrew stopped and that feeling started to fade away.

'I don't mean amazing sex, although sex with you is always amazing. I mean this incredible connection, this spark between us. This is what it feels like when you're in a proper relationship, when the person you're with is so incredible, so brilliant and kind and warm, it feels like this passion is impossible to contain. Tell me you feel that too?'

'I feel it,' Willow said against his lips. And so much more.

He kissed her again and started moving again and that

feeling started to build inside her again, spiralling out to every part of her body as he took her higher and higher.

God she loved this man. It was utterly ridiculous to feel like this after such a short amount of time but she knew that she loved him. She wanted to tell him, to shout it out for everyone to hear, but something held her back. Those three little words were so big and so important and so terrifying and she didn't want to casually throw them out during sex. But maybe she could tell him without saying it.

And just as that feeling burst through her she whispered against his lips. 'Elephant shoes.'

She felt him still as she fell apart around him and then he was kissing her passionately, moving against her faster and harder, holding her tight as he fell over the edge himself.

chapter 27

Andrew stroked a hand down Willow's hair as she slept on his chest. He was exhausted himself. It was already approaching nine in the morning and he had to get up and go to work. He was loath to wake Willow, and he would much rather spend the rest of the day sleeping off the night before with her wrapped in his arms, but he had a ton of stuff to do.

After making love in the honeymoon house, he'd practically marched her back to Sunrise Cottage, tumbled through the door onto the sofa and made love to her again. Then they'd kissed for what felt like hours, just kissing and stroking and touching, before he'd taken her up to her bed and made love to her again.

Christ this woman. He was never ever going to have his fill of her.

And she loved him, this incredible, smart, amazing woman loved him.

He remembered telling her that when deaf people lip-read a lot of words look the same on the lips. And that 'I love you' looks exactly the same as 'elephant shoes' or 'olive juice'. Those weren't just two random words she had uttered in the throes of passion, she had deliberately chosen 'elephant shoes'.

To hear her say those words the night before, those two words that only he would understand, well he couldn't keep his hands off her after that.

He had never felt so complete in his life before, like there had always been something missing and now she had filled that hole so it was completely overflowing.

He ached for her, which was ridiculous when he barely had the energy to open his eyes.

He'd wanted to say the words back, but when had been the right time – when his mouth was on her breast, when his hand was between her legs, when he was buried deep inside her? The words were too important for that. And he didn't want to say them now when he had to rush off for work. But equally he didn't want to go another second without telling her how he felt. She deserved to know. He would wake her and tell her now. He smiled as he pictured how heated that conversation could get. He looked at the clock again, wondering if he could spend another half hour in bed with her. Although that wouldn't be enough. He sighed; realistically he was already running late and with only ten more days before the open day, there was so much to do.

He gently rolled her onto her back and she stirred slightly, her eyes flickering open for just a few seconds. She smiled when she saw him and then seemed to drift back off to sleep again with a big contented grin on her face.

That smile was going to get him through the whole day.

He slipped from the bed and quickly got washed and dressed, watching her sleep the whole time. He loved this woman so much.

He bent down and kissed her on the cheek and then whispered in her ear. 'I love you.'

She didn't even stir this time, although she was still smiling as she carried on dreaming.

He smiled and left the house.

Willow woke to an empty bed. She sat up and looked around. It was quite clear Andrew wasn't in the house. She looked at the clock and saw it was already half past nine so he must have gone to work.

She hoped his absence didn't have anything to do with sort of telling him she loved him the night before. Although the way he hadn't been able to stop kissing, touching and making love to her throughout the whole night was a good indication that he either wasn't bothered by her words or he hadn't heard them.

He'd never said the words back but then what did she expect, she hadn't properly said them either. And to be fair, it had only been a week since they'd met. Just because she had crazily fallen in love with him, she couldn't expect him to feel the same so early into their relationship.

She needed to get up and go and see Kitty and Ken about the next part of the plan from the Secret Society of Happiness. She also needed to get to the shop – more orders had come through yesterday while she took the day off and she needed to go in and sort those out, quickly. Then she needed to do some more painting and help Ruby with the fairy lights. She felt bad because, although Andrew had agreed the fairy lights would make a lovely touch to the village, it was creating more work for him as he was the one would have to hook up the power to all of them. She only hoped that all of this effort was going to pay off on the open day.

Andrew came out of the castle on his quad bike after talking through a few renovations with Kitty and Ken. He spotted Morgan on her hands and knees as she continued to paint the screens. She hadn't been there when he'd gone into the castle earlier. He wanted to talk to her about what she'd said to Willow. He was less angry today. After the wonderful night before that had happened in spite of Morgan's meddling, he was finding it hard to wipe the smile off his face, but Morgan still needed to know it was inappropriate.

He pulled up his quad bike behind her van and climbed off. She smiled at him as she looked up from her work. She stood up and came over to talk to him.

'How's it going?' Andrew asked, although from what he

could see it looked fantastic.

'Great actually. I'm really enjoying this one. I've finished two of the screens so if you've got a spare few minutes you can help me erect them.'

'Sure, whatever you need.'

'OK, give me a moment, I need to clear these paints out the way.'

He watched her put the lids carefully back on the pots and tubes of paints.

'You were late starting today.' He cringed as soon as he said it. He didn't want to sound like the big boss, but the open day was fast approaching and the screens had to be finished by then. Although she was clearly making good progress.

She grinned at him. 'Sorry boss, it won't happen again.'

He'd known she'd take the piss as soon as he'd said it.

'I had a hot date last night,' Morgan said. 'We were at it all night and he was amazing. Very good with his hands if you know what I mean.'

Morgan was more of a bloke than he was when it came to talking about her sex life. When they had been friends, before they'd got together, she had always given him the intimate details of whichever man she had slept with the night before. He didn't really want to know.

He must have pulled a face because she laughed.

'You're not jealous, are you?'

Jealous? Nothing could be further from the truth. He had spent the night making love with the most magnificent woman he had ever met. Why would he be jealous of Morgan having no-strings-attached sex with someone else?

'No, I'm not.'

She laughed louder. 'Oh my god, you are.'

He sighed. 'I'm really not.'

'What we had was great, Andrew, but I've moved on now, to bigger and better things.'

He stared at her and laughed out loud at that one. 'Bigger and better things?'

She laughed too. 'Well I don't want to go into too much detail…'

'But I'm sure you're going to.'

'Zeus, my date from last night, he is the biggest I've ever seen. I never really thought size was important before, but it really is, and let me tell you he knew exactly what he was doing with it.'

'Zeus?' Was she actually making it up?

'He's from Greece.'

'I'm sure he is,' Andrew said, dryly. 'Anyway, while we're on the subject of sex, would you mind not discussing our sex life with my girlfriend?'

She switched to sign language.

'*Oh I feel awful about that, I thought she knew about us. There she was saying that you'd told each other everything and I just presumed she knew. I did wonder why you hadn't told her. It made me feel like a sordid little secret.*' She grinned mischievously. '*I liked it. I don't mind being your sordid little secret.*'

'You told her I'd given you multiple orgasms.'

She laughed and continued signing. '*Well you did.*'

He signed back. '*And you needed to share that level of detail with her?*'

'*I was just trying to be all girly with her. You know I'm rubbish with women. I have far more male friends than female ones. That's what girls do right, they talk about the sex they've had, compare stories. I thought we could bond over a common interest.*'

Andrew sighed. '*And what was all that stuff you told her about me having my heart broken with some woman? We've never talked about anything like that, why would you make out that we have?*'

'*You went out with that girl Amy, she broke your heart,*' Morgan went on.

'*I've never been out with a girl called Amy.*'

'*Oh, must be someone else I'm thinking of.*' Morgan shrugged as if it was no big deal, but he got the sense she had completely made it up to upset Willow, although he couldn't exactly call her a liar.

Morgan stopped signing.

'Was she jealous that we had shared that?' she asked incredulously. 'Jesus, if she's getting jealous over stuff like that, it's not exactly a healthy start to a relationship. And she's been staring at us for the last two or three minutes so I guess she's not too happy about you chatting to me either.'

He turned round and sure enough Willow was standing at the end of the road leading from the village watching them.

Crap. Why did he immediately feel guilty?

She waved and made her way over and he moved away from Morgan a little to greet her. He cupped Willow's face in his hands and kissed her. God, how could the taste of her turn him on so much?

'You were fast asleep when I left you this morning, you looked so beautiful sleeping with this big smile on your face,' Andrew said.

She stroked his cheek and smiled. 'I was dreaming of you.'

He kissed her on the forehead and then took her hand and led her back to where Morgan was standing.

'I was just on my way to see Kitty and Ken,' Willow said as she smiled at Morgan. 'And I saw you two signing, it's so interesting to watch.'

Morgan started signing to him. '*Oh I'm glad sign language is so entertaining for her.*'

Andrew ignored that. He turned his attention back to Willow.

'What were you two talking about?' Willow asked. 'I was trying to work it out from the gestures but it moves so fast.'

'What we did last night. Sex, you, multiple orgasms,' Morgan supplied, rather unhelpfully but honestly.

He watched Willow frown. She hadn't seemed to be annoyed or jealous that he'd been talking to Morgan before but she definitely seemed pissed off now, not surprisingly.

Willow dropped his hand. 'Well, I need to go and see Kitty and Ken.'

She turned and walked up the hill towards the castle.

Andrew glared at Morgan. 'What the hell?'

'I was just being truthful.'

He shook his head and ran up the hill after Willow.

'Willow, wait.'

She didn't and he didn't catch up with her until they were inside the castle walls. He grabbed her arm and she rounded on him.

'I can't believe you. I woke up this morning thinking that last night was one of the most incredible, amazing nights of my life and the whole time you're down here laughing about it. Was it really that bad?'

'God, no, I wasn't laughing about you.'

'I saw you.'

'That was something else entirely.'

'But you boasted about us, you came down here to tell your mate all the gory details about how you gave me multiple orgasms. Last night was something beautiful and private between us and you couldn't wait to get down here and tell Morgan all about it.'

'You've got the wrong end of the stick completely,' Andrew said, angrily. 'She was telling me all about her hot date last night with Zeus who apparently has the biggest penis in the world. That was what I was laughing at. And then I told her that it wasn't exactly appropriate for her to tell you all about my sex life with her.'

She stared at him.

'And why would you think so little of me? What kind of arsehole would I be to share that wonderful night with you and then tell all my mates about it after? Do you even know me at all?'

'Maybe I don't. Maybe you'd be better suited to someone like Morgan,' Willow said. 'You said yourself you have tons in common with her.'

'Maybe I would,' Andrew snapped.

'Fine.'

'Fine.'

Willow stormed off up the hill and Andrew stared after her in shock. What the hell had just happened?

chapter 28

Willow carefully poured the melted wax into ten different containers and then opened up the new box of scents she had bought. These ones were all named after different feelings. She wasn't sure what a feeling should smell like but she was intrigued enough to to give it a go.

It was raining outside right now, reflecting her mood perfectly. It had been raining ever since she had left Kitty and Ken so she hadn't seen anyone out in the village to hear about the gossip from last night and what everyone thought of their presents. But she suspected she would find out soon enough. Kitty and Ken had loved the idea of the gift-giving for the open day and now she just had to get the villagers on board. Kitty was going to call a village meeting in the pub that afternoon and Willow was going to talk through the idea with the villagers then. She guessed that most of them would realise she was behind the gifts after that.

She had planned to paint some more of the houses and help Ruby with the lights that day, but the rain had put a stop to that for now. However, it wasn't meant to last, so she was hopeful she might be able to get a few hours of village work done before the meeting. She'd texted Ruby and told her to come to the shop if she was bored, but her friend had texted to say she was busy doing online stuff for work and would catch up with her later.

Willow picked up the scent called Sadness and poured a few drops into one of the cups. Holding the wick to one side, she gave it a good stir and then leaned over and gave it a sniff. Sadness smelt a bit like honey, which wasn't a scent she would really associate with that emotion.

There wasn't any scent in the collection to reflect the other emotions that were churning through her gut: embarrassment for acting like a complete idiot, anger with herself for jumping to the wrong conclusion, regret over all the things she had said.

There had been no sign of Andrew when she'd come out of the castle and Morgan had packed her stuff away to escape from the rain.

Willow picked up the scent marked Happiness. She could do with a healthy dose of that right now. She poured a few drops into a different container and gave it a good stir. It made her smile. It smelt of summer holidays and sunshine and that wonderful coconut smell too.

'It smells nice in here.'

She looked up at Andrew hovering uncertainly by the

door and she let out a breath of relief. He was here. After all the things she'd said, he was here. He was soaking wet though and she grabbed the towel she had used earlier and passed it to him.

'That scent is Happiness apparently,' Willow said as he dried his hair and stepped closer. She held the container up for him to take a sniff. 'All of these scents are different feelings and emotions. What do you think of Happiness?'

He smelt it, his eyes on her the whole time. 'It smells of you.'

She couldn't help smiling at that. She picked up another small bottle of scent and tipped it into another container of melted wax. She gave it a stir and then held it up for him to smell. 'This one is Passion.'

He sniffed it and his eyes darkened slightly. 'This one definitely smells of you.'

She smirked and quickly grabbed another bottle, adding a few drops to a different container.

He sniffed it. 'I like that one.'

She swallowed. 'Does it smell of stupidity?'

'No, is that what it is?'

'No, this one is Love.'

He stared at her.

'Because love makes me do some crazy stupid things, it makes me overreact and it makes me scared and it makes me say things I don't mean. I'm sorry.'

He stroked his thumb down her cheek. 'Willow—'

'I am jealous of what you have with Morgan and I don't

mean sex and multiple orgasms. I mean that you grew up together, she knows what it was like for you growing up as the "deaf kid". She would have seen her brother struggle with it too. I don't feel I know that part of your life at all. I want to be there for you, for all of it, the good and the bad. But I do understand that you don't want to share or relive all of that.'

She didn't totally understand but she did respect that he might not want to talk about his childhood.

'I love you,' Willow went on. 'I know we've known each other for such a short amount of time and I don't expect you to feel the same way but I do, I love you. I held Garry back from finding happiness for so long, he was miserable with me and I don't want that for you. I want you to be happy even if you find that happiness with someone else.'

He frowned. He opened his mouth but she quickly spoke.

'Personally I don't think you would find happiness with Morgan either. You said sex was empty with her and sex should never be like that. Sex should be magnificent. I've had some good sex and some great sex and some pretty crappy sex in my life and I never knew that really it should be magnificent. Not until I came here and you set the bar so impossibly high that I don't ever want anything less than magnificent from now on. And you should aim for that too. Happiness is the most important thing in a relationship, but a part of that is sexual compatibility.'

She was waffling now.

'I'm sorry that I thought you had been boasting about us behind my back. I know you wouldn't do that, I don't know why I would think that.'

'Because Morgan deliberately made it sound like that. It sounded bad to my ears and I knew what we had been talking about. I think she has a bit of a twisted sense of humour, she likes winding people up. And you're right about one thing, Morgan is not someone I could be happy with. Sex should be magnificent, just like it was for me last night. But you're wrong about something else you said.'

'What's that?'

'I do feel the same way.'

Her heart exploded to life in her chest.

He signed something, pointing to his chest, holding his hands over his heart and then pointing at her.

Her breath was racing like she'd just been for a run. She didn't know any sign language but even she could work that out.

'Just to be clear, that means I love you,' Andrew said.

She let out a heavy wobbly breath and he moved closer, wrapping his large hands round her waist. She looked up at him as he bent his head to kiss her. 'I love you Willow McKay.'

She reached up and kissed him and he wrapped his arms around her and held her tight.

She pulled back to look at him. 'You really do?'

'Yes.'

'Do you know how utterly ridiculous this is?'

He laughed. 'Yes, it's crazy, but I suppose love does that to you.'

She kissed him again, laughing against his lips as tears ran down her cheeks.

The kiss turned very heated, very quickly, as they grabbed at each other with greedy hands. He lifted her and sat her on the table, standing between her legs as he started kissing her neck, and she suddenly realised that they were in full view of anyone walking past.

'Wait,' Willow said as Andrew pulled down the strap of her dress, trailing kisses down her shoulder.

He looked up at her in confusion.

'Not here. I have a storeroom out the back. It even has a desk.'

'Works for me,' Andrew said, lifting her off the table.

She wrapped her legs around him and laughed against his lips as he carried her straight into the storeroom and kicked the door closed behind him. He placed her down on the desk and this time he wasn't slow as he'd been the night before when he'd made love to her in her bed. This was just a desperate need and it turned her on so much to know she had this effect on him. He made very quick work of her clothes as she struggled to get him out of his. He was kissing and touching everywhere, pausing for just a second to tear open a condom, and then he was inside her, his hands tight on her hips, her legs wrapped around him as he moved against her faster and harder. That feeling started to build inside her already as she clung to his shoulders. He rolled her back gently so she was lying on the desk as he kissed her.

'I love you,' Andrew said.

'I love you too,' Willow said as her body trembled in his arms. He watched her fall apart and then he kissed her hard, groaning against her lips.

Willow was just finishing painting some flowers in the corner of a shop sign that was now painted a beautiful shade of royal blue when Ruby came sauntering down the high street towards her, carrying a large bag. The sun was out and Ruby was wearing a bright turquoise dress but she had the biggest smile on her face. It seemed that the effect of Happiness had already cast its spell on her friend.

'Hey, Rubes, how was your morning?' Willow said, climbing down the ladder. She felt bad that her friend had been stuck in the hotel room all morning because of the weather, but Ruby didn't seem too bothered by it.

'Oh it was fine, I had stuff to do, so it's been good,' Ruby said, vaguely.

Willow looked at her friend wondering what she *wasn't* saying. She was just about to ask her when Ruby spoke.

'How was your morning?'

Willow let out a heavy breath. 'Well, I had a stupid row with Andrew, spoke to Kitty and Ken about my idea that the villagers should make gifts for the open day, had amazing make-up sex with Andrew, made some candles, painted some shopfronts, so it's been a busy day.'

Ruby laughed. 'That does sound like a busy morning.

What on earth did you row with Andrew about?'

'Oh, it was nothing really, but mainly it was down to Morgan causing trouble again.'

'I haven't even met this woman yet and I don't like her,' Ruby said.

'I don't particularly like her either,' Willow said. 'But I think a large part of that is jealousy that she has all this history with him and not just sexual history. She's Andrew's friend and he might want to keep in touch with her once she finishes her work here. If that's the case I'm going to have to try to be friends with her too.'

'So you have to play nice?'

Willow thought about it. 'Nice might be pushing it, but I certainly don't want to be nasty.'

'Well fortunately for me, I don't have any such scruples or restrictions on the way I should behave around her,' Ruby said.

'Rubes, I don't need you to fight my battles for me. Don't make things worse.'

Ruby clearly thought about it.

'OK, but if you want her disposed of, I could make that happen, just say the word.'

Willow laughed at the sudden gangster approach to solving the problem. 'Anyway, did you bring the lights?'

'I did, well these are some of them, I have two more bags in my car. But we can make a start with these. What kind of effect are you looking for?'

'I think just strings of lights draped over the top of the

high street, kind of zigzagging over the road between the houses and shops. We don't want it to look Christmassy, more… like a party.'

'Are you asking me to be subtle with the lights, because I'm not sure I have that skill. You know I'm a throw-everything-at-it kind of girl when it comes to decorations.'

Willow laughed. 'I'm asking you to rein it in slightly.'

Ruby sighed theatrically. 'Well, as it's you, we'll try to keep it…' she swallowed as if she was going to say something difficult '… low key.'

'I think low key might be a bit much, but maybe we could stretch to… medium key.'

Ruby visibly brightened and plonked the bag on the floor. 'Let me show you what I've got.'

Willow sat next to Kitty and Ken in the pub nervously watching all the villagers arrive. Kitty had told her there had only been one village meeting since Kitty and Ken had taken over the castle and that had been purely for the purpose of introducing themselves. The villagers were probably wondering what was going on.

She watched them all, a hum of excited chatter as people talked about the mystery presents that had been delivered the night before.

Andrew came back from the packed bar with drinks for them all.

'Have you decided what you're going to say yet?' he asked, taking a sip of his beer. 'Are you going to out us as the mystery gift-givers?'

'No, I don't think so. There are still quite a few villagers who haven't received a present yet. It would be a shame to spoil the mystery for them, although most of them have probably guessed by now.'

Ken stood up and tried to do a head count although people were milling about so it was pretty hard to do. He turned back to Kitty. 'I think everyone is here.'

Kitty stood up and banged her spoon against her coffee mug to get everyone's attention. The pub went silent as everyone looked over in their direction.

'Thank you all for coming today.' Kitty spoke in a clear confident voice. She was obviously someone used to public speaking. 'I know some of you have been the lucky recipient of a mystery gift. I myself was given the gift of a lovely scarf and I'd like to personally thank whoever left that for me. I know some of you have your suspicions over who the gift-giver is, but I also know that the gifts haven't just been given by one or two people. Lots of you in the village have embraced this idea and given gifts of your own. Over the last few days, this village has grown into a community, filled with people who care about each other, and it's been a lovely thing to see.'

There were murmurs of agreement around the pub, people smiling at each other, and, for the first time, Willow could really see that she had achieved what she had set out to do. Even if this spirit only lasted a few weeks, she had brought happiness back to Happiness. She felt a warm glow inside at that thought.

'I'm sure you are all aware that we have the open day coming up very soon and Willow has had an idea to help the visitors see this wonderful camaraderie and see Happiness as a home. Willow, would you like to say a few words?'

Andrew gave her hand an encouraging squeeze as Willow got to her feet.

'The gift-giving has been a great success so far and those of you who have given gifts to your friends and neighbours, thank you for embracing the spirit of this.'

'Is it you?' Julia blurted out. 'Are you the gift-giver?'

Willow stalled, not having expected to have questions shouted out at her.

'Are we all going to get a gift?' someone at the back of the room shouted.

'How do we thank our gift-giver if we don't know who it is?' someone else called out.

'What's the reason behind the gifts?'

'I, erm… I do know who some of the gift-givers are. And I do know that the gifts were only given with the best intentions. I also know that all of you will get a gift. We had an idea for the open day,' Willow hurriedly tried to get the conversation back on track. 'We thought that as you are enjoying the gifts so much that the visitors on the open day would enjoy receiving a Happiness gift too. And we would like you all to get involved. We thought that you might like to make little gifts for our visitors, maybe some knitted things, or wooden toys, plants, sweets, cakes. I will be making little candles to give away on the open day. It doesn't have to be something big or time-consuming, but we were hoping you might want to contribute twenty or so little gifts each. We thought that the visitors could all be given a voucher as they arrive, which they could exchange for one free Happiness gift of their choosing. We could have tables near the main entrance to the village and people can take their gift before exploring the village and the castle.' She paused. 'What do you think?'

There was silence for a few moments and then everyone started shouting out questions and comments all at once. Willow had no idea if they were good comments or not.

Kitty stood back up and quietened everyone down with a wave of her hands.

'We want to hear your thoughts and ideas, we really do, but can we just start off by taking a quick vote? There is no point discussing it further if most of you don't want to do it. Can you raise your hand if you think it's a good idea and you would like to contribute?'

Willow smiled at Kitty's no-nonsense, get-straight-to-the-heart-of-the-matter attitude.

There were a few murmurs and whispers and then slowly hands started to rise. Willow quickly started to count, hoping at least for a majority even if it wasn't unanimous. One, two, three… she stopped as the hands were being lifted faster than she could count until everyone in the village was raising their hand. Every single person.

She couldn't help smiling at Andrew in relief.

'That's fantastic, thank you,' Kitty said. 'Let's start off with the basics first then we can get a bit more specialised in a moment. If we can start taking down some names then my able assistant will start to make a list.'

Ken cheerfully waved his notebook and pen and the villagers laughed.

'So cakes are always going to be popular – cupcakes would be good rather than big giant slabs of cake. Who would like to make those?'

A few hands shot up and Ken wrote them down.

'Cookies anyone?' Kitty prompted and again a few more hands shot up.

'OK, kids' toys next, we want all the children to have something too. Any ideas?'

'I could make some wooden shields and swords for the boys,' Joseph suggested.

'And girls,' Kitty said. 'We don't want any gender stereotypes here.'

'No,' Joseph cleared his throat. 'Of course not. My granddaughter is a right little tomboy. She loves playing knights as much as she loves being a princess. But maybe I could make some glittery magic wands too for those girls and boys that like a bit of sparkle in their role playing.'

'That sounds like a wonderful idea.'

'I could make some knitted bears,' Mary piped up. 'In non-gender-stereotype colours of course.'

Everyone laughed.

Pretty soon everyone was piping up with suggestions and Ken was having a hard time writing it all down.

Willow couldn't help smiling as she sat next to Andrew. This was really going to work.

chapter 29

Willow sat on her sofa that evening unpacking some supplies she had ordered for the shop. Ruby had gone out to see a comedy act she'd seen advertised and, while Willow had thought about going with her, apparently Jacob wanted to see the comedy act too and Willow hadn't wanted to play the third wheel if something did happen between them. She hadn't seen Andrew for the rest of the day. During all the furore of organising the villagers' gifts for the open day, he had kissed her on the cheek and told her he had to get back to work and that he'd probably be working late that night to try to finish one of the houses off, but to come by his house later if she wanted. The open day was coming round far too quickly now and she knew Andrew was starting to worry about getting everything finished on time. She was probably a bit of a distraction too.

Willow had eaten dinner alone, which had actually been

quite nice as she'd got to spend the time reading a book. She hadn't decided whether to go and see Andrew that night, he might prefer an early night. He had been working so hard lately and he certainly wasn't getting a lot of sleep in the evenings he was with her.

Willow thought she might watch a little TV, have a bath and then have an early night herself. Although after the big declarations of love earlier that day, she'd quite like to curl up and fall asleep in Andrew's arms if nothing else.

She unpacked some gift baskets and a large spool of satin ribbon. She remembered what he'd said the night before about her turning up at his house naked wearing only a bow and she grinned at the thought of surprising him in that way.

She quickly undressed and then unwound the ribbon from the spool. How should she go about wrapping herself in a ribbon? It was not something she had ever contemplated before. She tied it round her waist, but if she was going for the gift-wrapped-present look, then she hadn't quite achieved that. She slipped one length over her shoulder and the other between her legs, hoping that wouldn't chafe too much on the walk to Andrew's house, twisted the two lengths together round her back and tied it in a big bow round her belly.

She looked down at herself. It wasn't quite the sexy look she was going for but she thought Andrew might get a big kick out of it. Although there was no way she was walking up the lane dressed only in a ribbon. She grabbed her coat and pulled that on, buttoning it up to the collar, which frankly looked ridiculous in this warm weather.

She quickly left the house before she changed her mind.

Willow was hopeful she might be able to make the short distance to Andrew's house without meeting someone, although that hope was dashed when she saw Dorothy and Joseph walking towards her. To her delight she realised they were holding hands. She was so happy with this turn of events and the thought that she might have played some small role in it that she momentarily forgot that she was completely stark naked underneath her coat and hurried over to say hello to them.

'Hello, where are you two off to?' Willow asked, unable to stop smiling at their joined hands.

'We thought we'd go for a sunset walk along the cliffs,' Joseph said. 'It's such a beautiful night.'

'Yes it is,' Willow agreed, dying to ask if they were actually dating now.

'So why are you wearing a coat?' Dorothy asked, eyeing Willow's bare legs with interest.

'Oh, I just thought it might be a bit chilly later when I'm walking home,' Willow said, pulling the coat down a bit. It was quite a bit shorter than she'd realised.

Dorothy smirked as if she didn't believe a word of it. 'Yes dear, of course. Well, we better let you get on.'

They walked away with Dorothy giggling like a schoolgirl. Willow smiled as she watched them go but the ribbon really was starting to chafe a bit now and she wanted to get to Andrew's house before she met anyone else.

She hurried up his path and knocked on his door.

He opened it and his face lit up in a huge smile when he saw her. She quickly stepped inside and closed the door behind her. She was aware that the TV was on in the lounge, so obviously he'd just been chilling out before she got there.

'I'm so glad you're here—'

She stepped up and put a finger on his lips. 'I have a surprise for you.'

He frowned in confusion and she quickly unbuttoned her coat and let it fall to the floor.

His eyes bulged and he swore softly under his breath.

Suddenly there was a puppy standing in the doorway, yapping excitedly at the new visitor.

'Andrew?' came the sound of a woman's voice followed by footsteps from the lounge.

Willow looked at Andrew in confusion.

'My sister, quick in here,' Andrew muttered, opening the pantry door and bundling her inside before slamming it closed and plunging her into darkness.

'I thought someone was at the door,' said the woman's voice. His sister, Lottie.

'There was, it's nothing,' Andrew said.

'Oh, I thought we were going to meet the wonderful Willow then,' Lottie said.

Christ, no. The first time she was going to meet his sister and she was standing in the pantry wearing nothing more than a squashed and battered ribbon, the end of which had got trapped in the door. She didn't even have her coat to hide her dignity as that was somewhere in the hall. She looked around the darkened pantry for something to cover herself up but it was filled with food. There was a potato sack at the bottom of the pantry, filled with filthy potatoes. She wasn't sure if meeting his sister for the first time dressed in a potato sack would actually be worse than what she was wearing now.

Her cheeks flooded with embarrassment.

OK, it was fine. Lottie had no idea she was there and Andrew would hopefully be able to get rid of his family as quick as possible or at least smuggle her upstairs without them knowing. It wasn't like she would be here for hours with a ribbon stuck between her bum cheeks.

'Are you coming in, we're just about to put *Tangled* on,' Lottie said.

'Umm…' Andrew said.

'Poppy has been so looking forward to watching it with you. It's her new favourite.'

Through the tiny crack in the door Willow saw a little girl, presumably Poppy, come out and sign something to Andrew. He signed back and she took his hand and led him off to the lounge.

Crap. She would be here for hours.

OK, she just had to wait for the movie to start and then sneak out. Her coat would probably still be in the hall and she could put it on and get out the house without anyone noticing. It was going to be fine.

She noticed movement outside the door and she held her breath, not daring to move at all. She realised it was the puppy and that to her horror he had found the end of the ribbon and was pulling at it with all his might, yapping and growling at it as the ribbon between her legs started getting tighter. She tried to pull it back but the dog's barking and growling got louder as he put up the fight of his life.

'Max, what on earth are you doing?' Lottie was back.

Oh god.

'What have you got there?' Lottie said. Removing the ribbon from Max's mouth, she opened the pantry door to see what it was attached to.

For the longest moment no one moved, no one said anything. They just stared at each other.

The next thing Poppy came running out of the lounge. Lottie slammed the pantry door shut but Poppy had already seen her.

Willow wanted to curl up and die.

Through the crack in the door, she saw Poppy sign something to her mum.

Lottie signed back while speaking at the same time, probably for Willow's benefit. 'No honey, I have no idea why there is a naked woman in your uncle Andrew's pantry. Why don't we ask him?'

Andrew came running out into the hall looking stressed. For a moment it was clear he didn't know what to say but then decided on some honesty.

'The woman in the pantry is Willow, she came round to surprise me and didn't realise you'd be here.'

'Evidently,' Lottie said, dryly. 'Well, why don't me and Poppy go in the lounge and you can let her out the pantry.

Then she can go upstairs and put some clothes on and we can meet her properly?'

Really? She had to endure meeting Andrew's sister and niece after all this? Couldn't she just run away and hide?

Lottie and Poppy moved away and Andrew opened the door for her.

She put her face in her hands, her cheeks burning with shame, and Andrew moved forward and hugged her.

'I'm so sorry,' he whispered. 'I had no idea they'd be here tonight.'

She looked up at him. 'I'll just go home, I'll meet them properly tomorrow.'

He shook his head. 'Come and meet them now. I've told Lottie all about you. Just go and grab some of my clothes and come down and say hello. You might as well get the embarrassment over with now.'

Willow groaned and quickly ran upstairs. She ripped the stupid bow off, grabbed one of Andrew's shirts and pulled that on, then found a pair of his shorts. They were way too big but she used one of his belts to cinch them in at the waist. She looked ridiculous but at least it was a step up from wearing nothing.

She quickly washed her face to make some of the redness calm down, took a deep breath and went back downstairs.

Andrew was waiting for her at the bottom of the stairs and took her hand, leading her into the lounge. Lottie and Poppy were sitting on the sofa, Poppy clutching a doll with one eye, while Max was curled up fast asleep after he had exhausted himself with outing her.

'This is my lovely sister Lottie and my niece Poppy,' Andrew said, signing at the same time for Poppy's benefit. 'And this is my girlfriend Willow.'

'Hi Lottie, nice to meet you,' Willow said.

Lottie smiled but she didn't seem too thrilled. So much for first impressions.

'Hello Poppy,' Willow tried with Andrew's niece but, unless she could lip-read, she probably didn't understand what Willow had said.

Andrew signed for Willow and Poppy signed back. Andrew laughed. 'She says, why were you naked?'

Willow blushed. Whereas she and Lottie were steadfastly trying not to address the nudity, Poppy had no such scruples.

'I was… playing a silly joke on Andrew,' Willow explained lamely.

Andrew signed for Poppy what Willow had said and Poppy just stared unblinking at Willow.

Eventually she signed something back. Andrew laughed again. 'She says she doesn't think the joke was very funny.'

'I agree,' Lottie said, quietly.

Willow wanted to say something else, anything that might make Poppy laugh, but she felt so woefully inadequate right then. She knew no sign language, not even enough to say hello.

'Well, shall we put the movie on?' Lottie said, turning her attention to the TV.

'I should go,' Willow muttered to Andrew.

'No stay, watch *Tangled* with us.'

Right then, Willow couldn't think of anything she'd like to do less.

But Andrew sat down and pulled Willow down on the sofa next to him. Poppy immediately climbed up on Andrew's lap and she signed something at Willow, clearly expecting her to understand.

'I'm sorry, I don't understand sign language.'

'You're going out with a man who's deaf and you can't be bothered to learn any sign language?' Lottie said, her tone as disapproving as her words. 'What will you do when he loses his hearing altogether?'

'Lottie!' Andrew said.

Willow blushed. She felt awful. Even though just over a week wasn't enough time to have learned much sign language – and Andrew had hardly tried to teach her – she had to admit that she'd totally taken for granted that Andrew could hear her when he was wearing his hearing aids. But what about the times he wasn't? And what did Lottie mean, "when he loses his hearing altogether"? Of course she should learn sign language so she could communicate with him at all times and with his niece too. She felt embarrassed that she hadn't thought of it.

Even Poppy's one-eyed doll seemed to be looking at Willow judgementally.

Andrew turned his attention back to Poppy and signed to her. '*What did you say to Willow honey, I missed it.*'

Poppy signed the same gestures she'd signed before.

'She wants to know who your favourite *Tangled* character

is,' Andrew said.

'Oh, I've never seen *Tangled* before,' Willow said and Andrew signed her answer back.

Poppy stared at her as if she had three heads. In Poppy's mind not having seen *Tangled* was clearly a hell of a lot worse than not knowing any sign language.

Andrew put the movie on and Poppy made herself comfortable with her back against Andrew's chest, watching the screen avidly as subtitles played along the bottom of the film.

'How's Morgan doing?' Lottie said. 'It was so nice to see her again today.'

'She's fine,' Andrew snapped.

'I like Morgan, such a lovely girl. I always thought you two were so good together.'

'We were never together, not in that sense. We had a fling, that was it,' Andrew said.

Poppy was watching the film with wide eyes, clearly with no idea about the conversation that was happening over her head.

'Oh, it was so much more than that, anyone could see the chemistry you two had,' Lottie went on from the other side of Andrew. 'I really thought you were going to marry her.'

'Stop it,' Andrew said. 'I love you, I love seeing you and spending time with Poppy, but don't come in here and try to ruin what I have with Willow. She's the best thing that's ever happened to me. You're being a bitch and that's not who you are.'

That shut Lottie up. Willow had no idea what to say to make this awful awkward situation better. She decided she would just focus on the movie, just in case Poppy asked her questions about it later. She stared at the screen, not really taking in any of it, but after a few moments, Andrew slipped his hand into hers and they stayed like that throughout the whole film.

chapter 30

The film finally finished and Lottie started gathering her things ready to go.

'We're staying at the pub for a few days so we'll see you tomorrow,' Lottie said, deliberately not looking at Andrew or Willow. She was clearly still upset by what Andrew had said to her earlier.

'I have to work for a few hours tomorrow morning but maybe between me and Jacob we could take Poppy for a bit tomorrow afternoon,' Andrew said.

'I'm sure she'd like that, thank you,' Lottie said, giving him a weak smile.

Andrew got down on his knees to address Poppy. '*Goodnight beautiful, I'll see you tomorrow*,' he signed.

Poppy signed something back and he gave her a hug.

'It was nice to meet you,' Willow said to Lottie.

'No it wasn't,' Lottie said. 'I was a complete cow and I'm

sorry.'

Willow was surprised by this sudden about-turn. 'It's OK, we didn't exactly meet under the best circumstances. Maybe we can try again tomorrow.'

Lottie nodded. 'I'd like that.'

Willow turned her attention back to Poppy. 'It was lovely meeting you too.'

Lottie signed what Willow had said.

Poppy's hands flashed at an incredible speed as she spoke.

'She wants to know who your favourite character in *Tangled* was,' Lottie said.

'Oh, the horse,' Willow tried as she hadn't really paid attention to much of the film.

Lottie signed her answer and, to Willow's surprise, Poppy launched herself at Willow for a hug.

'Good answer,' Lottie said, 'Maximus is her favourite too. The dog is named after him.'

Little Max gave a bark of approval at hearing his own name.

Lottie gave Andrew a hug and with a little wave from Poppy they all left.

Andrew turned to her and let out a big sigh of relief.

'I'm so sorry,' he said as he pulled her into a big hug. She held him tight, stroking down his back.

'For what?'

He pulled back. 'Are you kidding? For my sister's terrible behaviour, for your embarrassing introduction to my family. For being forced to watch *Tangled* for the last two hours. For not being able to ravish you as soon as you walked through the door, which believe me was what I would much rather have spent my night doing.'

'It's OK.' She stroked his face; he looked exhausted. 'Let's go to bed.'

Andrew nodded and took her hand, leading her up to his bedroom. He got undressed and into bed and Willow did the same, snuggling into his side. He wrapped an arm round her shoulders and she slid her arm across his stomach.

'You looked amazing tonight, best present ever,' Andrew said, yawning.

It was quite clear there would be no ravishing tonight. Willow smiled because cuddling Andrew in bed was more than enough.

They were quiet for a while and she looked up at him to find he was staring at the ceiling.

'What did Lottie mean when she said about you losing your hearing completely?'

He frowned. 'Nothing, she's just being a drama queen.'

She bit her lip. He really didn't want to share that part of his life with her and she didn't know how to feel about that. She couldn't say that their relationship was surface level because they had talked in depth about many things, but if he wouldn't share something that was such a big part of him, did they really have a future together? If she couldn't be that person for him, was she really the right woman for him?

She lay in silence for a while but Andrew broke it.

'Poppy's dad walked out on them about a year ago.'

Willow looked up in shock. 'What?'

'Things hadn't been great between them for a long time. Alex got a job offer in New York and he took it. Just told them he was going and a week later he was gone.'

'So he doesn't have any part in Poppy's life any more?'

'Not really. I think he did Skype her for a while but every time he did, Lottie cursed him for everything under the sun and it dried up after that. Alex really struggled to learn sign language and as his daughter grew up he just couldn't really communicate with her. I think it drove a wedge between him and Lottie, because there was a clear bond between Poppy and Lottie and he felt like an outsider in his own family. I mean, of course there were other things that went wrong in their relationship too, it wasn't just about Poppy. They were always bickering and fighting years before Poppy was born and I always wondered why they stayed together. So I don't think she was the reason that things didn't work between them, but I suppose it added to the strain in their relationship.'

'That's awful.'

Andrew was quiet for a while. 'My dad walked out on us when we were kids. Apparently he'd had affairs with multiple women. I kind of grew up wondering if it was my fault. Of course I don't think that now but I don't want Poppy to have that feeling too. I think Lottie's been struggling with it ever since. Being a single parent is hard and I think, despite it all, she still loves Alex and misses him terribly. I'm not excusing her attitude to you tonight, but she's had this prickly outer shell since Alex left, but inside there is still this wonderful woman.

Just be a little patient with her. Once you get to know her, you'll really like her.'

'Of course. Maybe tomorrow, Poppy can come and help me make some candles in the shop. Give Lottie a break for a while. Although I'll need you or Jacob to interpret for me.'

'That would be great. I have so much work to do, but I'll bring her along and then hopefully Jacob will stay with her. I think Poppy will love you.'

Willow cringed a little. 'I'm not great with kids, I always say the wrong things. I make inappropriate jokes which they never find funny. I taught my brother's kids how to burp the alphabet. My sister-in-law was furious and rightly so.'

Andrew laughed. 'Yes, please don't do anything like that with Poppy, I want her and Lottie to fall in love with you as much as I have. But you don't have anything to worry about. You've already won her over with your love of Maximus. I'll give you one tip, she has this doll, Gertrude. It has no hair, one eye, one of the ears has melted off after she left it too close to the fire. It is the most hideous thing I have ever seen in my life and quite frankly gives me nightmares. She *loves* this thing and carries it around everywhere. Just don't insult it or look horrified if she asks you to hold it.'

'I'll tell her Gertrude is beautiful.'

'That's a great idea.'

'Will you show me how to sign that to her?'

Andrew hesitated.

'I want to learn it.'

'Ah, don't do this because Lottie gave you a hard time.'

'I'm not. This is part of who you are, I want to know this part too.'

He clearly thought about this some more. Then he sat up and slowly signed something. '*Your doll is beautiful.*'

Willow stared at the hand gestures feeling suddenly daunted. There was no way she would remember that.

He signed it again, breaking it down into little chunks. She copied each action as he did it and then tried to put all the chunks together into a sentence.

'That's it,' Andrew said, lying back down.

She practised it again, feeling like everything was hinging on these tiny little movements.

Andrew pulled her back down on top of him. 'This doesn't need to be a big deal. If you can't do it, just get me or Jacob to sign for you.'

Willow lay there listening to his heartbeat for a while. Don't be rude about the doll, don't say anything inappropriate, teach her about candles, make Poppy fall in love with her, all through Jacob or Andrew interpreting everything she said. No pressure then.

She thought about Alex, Poppy's dad, and how hard he had found it to communicate with his own daughter and how utterly heartbreaking that must have been for him.

'Is sign language hard to learn?' Willow asked.

'Yeah, it can be. I learned from a very early age so it was a lot easier for me. It's much harder to learn it when you're an adult. And as with the English language where there are many similar words, there are also many similar signs. There are also several signs that mean the same thing.'

Unease swirled in her gut. She had learned French and Spanish at school and had been awful at it. She had got an E in French in her GCSE and a U in Spanish. She couldn't even remember a single word of either language now. What if she struggled to learn sign language too? What if she spent her whole life having to have everything translated to Poppy for her? What if she had children with Andrew and they were deaf, what if she couldn't learn enough sign language to communicate with them? Would that drive a wedge between them?

No, she couldn't think like that. She would learn it. She had to if she was going to be a part of Andrew's life.

She looked up at him. 'I want to learn it.'

He stared at her for a moment. 'OK, I will teach you but try not to get frustrated with it, it's hard to pick up at first. We'll start off small.'

'OK.'

'I'm going to sleep now.'

He gave her a sweet kiss on the lips and she watched him take his hearing aids out and pop them on top of his drawers.

Then he signed something. '*Goodnight*,' he said.

She smiled and copied the gesture back.

'Perfect,' he said.

She stroked his face. 'I love you.'

He smiled and closed his eyes. 'Elephant shoes.'

She put her head back on his chest with a smile. She was going to do this, she had to.

chapter 31

After hot shower sex and breakfast, Andrew had rushed off to work with the promise to bring Poppy by Willow's shop later that afternoon. Willow had gone home to get changed into her own clothes and then decided to see if she could find Ruby before she went to work. She felt a bit guilty that her friend had come down to see her and she'd only spent one full day with her so far. Although Ruby seemed happy enough, so she didn't feel too bad.

Willow went through the back door of the pub which led straight upstairs to the bedrooms. She knocked on Ruby's door but there was no noise from inside. There was, however, laughter coming from one of the other bedrooms that sounded suspiciously like Ruby. Willow wandered down the corridor a little and listened outside the door. She had been sure Ruby was in room number six but that definitely sounded like Ruby inside number three.

Suddenly the door was flung open and Ruby walked out giggling.

'Ruby, I thought you were in number six…' Willow started.

The door opened wider and Jacob was standing there dressed only in a towel.

'I was, I mean I am. I was just borrowing some sugar from Jacob,' Ruby said, not in any way embarrassed at being caught in what was clearly the morning after the night before. She also didn't have any sugar with her.

Willow smirked. 'So good night last night? The comedy show, I mean.'

Ruby flashed Jacob a grin. 'It was a great night.'

Jacob smiled. 'I'll catch you later Ruby.'

'Oh Jacob,' Willow said. 'Andrew is bringing Poppy to my shop later this afternoon so she can make some candles with me. I know Andrew is crazy busy at the moment, would you be able to stay with her and interpret for us?'

Jacob frowned. 'Poppy's here?'

'Yes, I think Andrew was a bit surprised last night as well. They're here for a few days and Andrew said he'd have Poppy this afternoon but I don't think he really has the time so I said I would make some candles with her. Would you have the time to stay with her?'

'Of course, she'd like that. I'll see you later.' Jacob gave Ruby a wink and closed the door.

'Fancy having breakfast?' Willow said.

'Sure, that sounds good.'

They started walking down the stairs. 'Who's Poppy?' Ruby asked.

'Jacob and Andrew's niece.'

Ruby was quiet for a moment and Willow cringed a little that Jacob hadn't spoken to Ruby about Poppy.

'Why does Jacob need to translate for the two of you?'

'Poppy's deaf and she only really communicates through sign language.'

'Oh god, how awful,' Ruby said.

Willow cringed even more. 'I think Poppy's totally fine with being deaf. I don't think she would think it's awful at all.'

'But it must be, not being able to hear music or people chatting or birds singing or a child's laughter.'

'But Poppy has never heard any of those things so she doesn't think she's missing out at all. She's a very happy little girl.'

'It must be so terrible for her family though, for her parents and for Jacob.'

'What's so terrible about it? Poppy is a healthy, happy, bright, energetic little girl. Besides, I suspect her family are quite used to it. Andrew's deaf too.'

'Andrew's deaf?!' Ruby said incredulously as she pushed the door open to the pub and all eyes swivelled in their direction, including those of Lottie and Morgan who were having breakfast together with Poppy.

Ice settled into her stomach. Andrew didn't want anyone to know he was deaf and now in Willow's attempt to play down how *awful* it was for Poppy to be deaf, she'd let it slip to Ruby and her friend had inadvertently just told the whole pub.

'I can't believe Andrew's deaf,' Ruby went on, completely oblivious that she was making the situation worse.

'Sshhh,' Willow hissed. 'For god's sake be quiet. Go and grab a menu. I'm just going to say hello to Lottie and Poppy.'

'Is that them?' Ruby said, staring over at them like they were animals in the zoo.

Willow winced. Ruby was a lovely person but she was as subtle as a low-flying brick.

'Will you just go and sit down, over there?' Willow snapped. 'I'll be over in a second.'

Willow walked over to Lottie and Poppy's table. Neither Lottie or Morgan looked happy to see her. Although Poppy waved madly.

'Morning,' she addressed Lottie and Morgan. 'Hello Poppy.'

Lottie signed for Willow.

'Poppy, Andrew is going to bring you to my shop this afternoon. I make candles and we thought you might enjoy seeing how I do it.'

Lottie smiled slightly. 'Oh she'll love that.'

She signed what Willow had said and Poppy practically burst out of her seat in excitement.

'Did you just tell the whole pub that Andrew is deaf?' Morgan asked, clearly not in the mood to play nice.

Willow flushed with embarrassment. She was really hoping they hadn't heard, although Ruby had been loud enough.

'I, erm, I was just telling Ruby and…'

'And I bet Andrew specifically told you not to tell anyone?'

Morgan was right. He had told her he didn't want anyone to know and she had promised him she wouldn't tell a soul. Christ, this was all kinds of awful.

Willow looked round the pub. No one seemed to be taking an interest in their conversation and no one seemed to be excited about this latest bit of gossip like they had been over the presents or her relationship with Andrew. There were lots of little conversations going on but none of them seemed to be about Andrew.

'He's really sensitive about people finding out, he's going to hate this,' Morgan went on.

'Maybe he's a little more relaxed about it here,' Lottie said. 'This is his home.'

'I doubt it. He's tried to hide it his whole life. He doesn't talk about it with anyone. He trusted Willow and she's just let him down.'

'I think you're overreacting. Maybe it's time he embraced it,' Lottie said.

'I think that's probably Andrew's decision,' Morgan said. 'Not yours or Willow's.'

Willow had no words to defend herself. It should be her protecting Andrew not Morgan. But Morgan would never do anything so indiscreet as to out Andrew to the whole pub.

Willow cleared her throat. 'I'm going to go and have breakfast with my friend. Poppy, I'll see you later.'

Lottie signed for her and Poppy waved goodbye.

Willow returned to her table where Ruby was still watching Lottie and Poppy with evident interest.

'God, what have I done?' Willow said as she sat back down. In her head, Andrew being deaf just wasn't a big deal but of course it was for him. She'd told Ruby when she'd had no business sharing that with her. Andrew would be furious and quite rightly so.

'I wonder why Jacob didn't tell me about Poppy,' Ruby said.

'Probably because he knew you'd be really inappropriate about it,' Willow snapped and then regretted it. None of this was really Ruby's fault but she wished she would be a bit more discreet about it.

'What am I doing that's inappropriate?' Ruby said.

'You're staring at her like she's a freak.'

'I'm not. Oh my god, of course I don't think she's a freak, that's an awful thing to say. I just didn't even know Jacob had a niece until ten minutes ago and now I find out the poor girl is deaf and Andrew's deaf and—'

'Stop saying that. Christ. Andrew's really sensitive about it and I should never have blabbed it to you in the first place but you don't need to keep repeating it to the whole pub. And stop with the "poor girl" crap. Deaf people don't need or want our pity, they don't want to be labelled as an abnormality or different. They just want understanding, to have the same opportunities as us, to have access to the same stuff that we do. And sometimes that can be difficult for them but they want empathy not sympathy.'

Ruby stared at her. 'God, I am being inappropriate, aren't I?'

'Yes you are.'

'I'm sorry. It was just a surprise, that's all. I didn't mean to be an arse about it. I really should know better, what with Cal putting up with all that crap all his life, and I've just turned into one of those people who stare and make a big deal about something that really isn't a big deal.'

Willow nodded. She knew Ruby's brother, Cal, had lost his lower leg in a car accident when he was only a small child. He'd had his own battles to fight as he'd grown up. Although if anyone was a good role model for overcoming adversity, it was Cal. He was a Paralympian. Ruby really should know better.

'Right, I'm stopping now, I promise. I'll say no more about it.' Ruby picked up the menu decisively. Willow looked over to where Lottie and Morgan were sitting. Morgan and Poppy were engaged in a very animated conversation and Poppy kept laughing and giggling at what Morgan was saying to her. Lottie, however, was staring at Willow and she wondered if she had heard what she'd said. Willow thought back to what she'd said to Ruby, hoping that she hadn't said anything wrong or offensive. Andrew was right, she had no real understanding of what it meant to be deaf. She just hoped she had championed the cause in the right way.

She watched Morgan and Poppy continue to chat, the little girl had completely come alive. She didn't think she would ever be able to engage with Poppy as easily and fluently as Morgan was. Morgan was so good for her. It was no wonder Lottie liked her.

But she was going to master this and she was going to start this afternoon with Poppy.

Willow ended up leaving the pub at the same time as Morgan. Ruby was going to go back to sleep for a few hours as apparently she hadn't got much sleep the night before and Willow needed to get to work.

Willow held the door open for Morgan as she came out. Despite Morgan's frostiness with her before breakfast, Willow wanted her to know she took that part of Andrew's life seriously. For some reason she couldn't identify, she wanted Morgan's approval.

'You and Poppy seemed to be having the best conversation over breakfast,' Willow said. 'You're so good with her, she absolutely adores you.'

'That's because I understand her,' Morgan said rather testily. Evidently she was still pissed off with Willow.

'I want to learn sign language. I want to be able to communicate with Poppy properly and being deaf is a big part of who Andrew is, I want to be able to share that with him. Would you teach me a few things?'

Morgan clearly thought about this for a moment. 'OK, what do you want to know?'

'Well Poppy is coming to see the candle shop this afternoon, she loves candles. I'd love to be able to say to her something like, "Would you like to make some candles with me?"'

Morgan hesitated for a while. 'OK.'

Morgan demonstrated how to sign that sentence, slowly going through each action, and Willow copied it carefully. She repeated it a few times with Morgan correcting her if she went wrong until she had got it perfected.

'That's it and, look, I'll show you something you can say to Andrew tonight in bed.'

Morgan showed her some other sign language actions and Willow dutifully copied her.

'Perfect,' Morgan said.

'What did I just say?'

'Ah, I'll let Andrew translate that one for you, but I promise he will love it.' Morgan smiled, almost smugly Willow thought.

'Thanks so much,' Willow said and waved her goodbye as she walked into her shop.

It was a very small start but she couldn't wait to show Andrew and Poppy the sign language she had learned and how serious she was about getting to grips with that side of their life.

chapter 32

Willow was waiting nervously inside her shop for Andrew and Jacob to arrive with Poppy.

She had to talk to Andrew before anything else. She had to tell him that she had accidentally outed him to the whole village and she had no idea what his reaction to that would be. He had been angry enough that first day when she had discovered he was deaf, so how would he feel when he discovered that the whole village now knew? She only hoped that no one in the village had said anything to him, she wanted to be the one to tell him.

She was also nervous about getting the sign language right when she spoke to Poppy, but at least it would show Andrew she was willing to try.

She had all the equipment laid out ready to make some candles and she was hoping she and Poppy would have a fun afternoon.

There was laughter outside and she looked up to see Andrew and Jacob swinging Poppy between them, Poppy holding onto their hands as they swung her up into the air.

Willow rushed to the door of the shop. 'Jacob, could you just give me and Andrew a second to talk before you bring Poppy in?'

'Oh, sure,' Jacob said. He quickly signed something to Poppy and she nodded. He swung Poppy up onto his back and started prancing around outside giving her a piggyback that made her laugh.

'What's up?' Andrew said, stepping into the shop and giving her a kiss on the cheek. The affection he had for her shone from his eyes. Clearly he didn't know.

'Look, I'm really sorry, but…' She rested her hands on his chest. There was no easy way to say this. 'But I accidentally let slip to Ruby that you're deaf.'

He frowned. 'Oh.'

'And… she sort of blurted it out to the whole pub,' Willow cringed.

His eyebrows shot up in surprise and then slashed down into a furious scowl. He was definitely pissed off.

'So the whole village knows?'

'I'm so sorry, I really am. I asked Jacob if he would interpret for me this afternoon and Ruby was there and she wanted to know why he would need to translate for me and Poppy and I told her she was deaf and then I ended up telling her that you were deaf too and… I'm so sorry. I know you don't want anyone to know because you don't want to be treated differently and I've ruined that for you. That was never my intention.'

He didn't say anything, but his jaw was tense, his eyes were dark and none of the affection he had for her was there any longer.

'Are we all ready?' Jacob asked from the doorway as Poppy stood in front of him staring round at all the candles with wide eyes.

Willow looked back at Andrew and he stepped back away from her. 'We'll talk later, I have to get back to work.'

God this hadn't gone well at all but now, with Poppy eager to explore, it was really not the time to discuss it.

Jacob brought Poppy inside and Willow smiled slightly that she had brought that hideous doll with her.

'I'll catch up with you in a few hours,' Andrew said to Jacob. He knelt down to talk to Poppy. He started signing. '*I'll see you later and maybe we can go out for ice cream?*'

Poppy's face lit up and she nodded.

'You OK?' Jacob asked. Although his brother nodded, it was very clear that he wasn't.

Willow needed to show Andrew that she took this part of his life very seriously. So she quickly crouched down to talk to Poppy.

'Hi Poppy,' Willow said, and as Andrew watched she very carefully signed the sentence that Morgan had taught her, asking Poppy if she would like to make some candles with her.

'What the hell?' Andrew exploded.

Jacob let out a bark of a laugh but he was clearly shocked,

which was worrying if even Jacob was shocked.

Poppy blinked and then burst out laughing.

Crap. She must have got it wrong. She signed the words again and Poppy's laughter got louder. Even Jacob joined in this time. The only one who wasn't laughing was Andrew.

'What the fuck was that?' Andrew practically yelled. 'Is that your idea of a joke?'

Willow stood back up. 'Wait, did I get it wrong?'

'You're damned right you got it wrong. Where did you learn that?'

'Morgan taught me,' Willow said. 'What did I say?'

'"You have a very small penis,"' Jacob said.

'WHAT?!' Willow said. 'Holy shit, I didn't mean to say that. I'm so sorry.'

God, she was going to scar the poor child for life.

Poppy signed something to Willow, in between laughing almost hysterically.

'She says that she doesn't have a penis, only boys have one of those,' Jacob said.

Willow suddenly realised that she'd got the two sentences Morgan had taught her the wrong way round and what she'd signed to Poppy had been meant for Andrew, although why the hell would Morgan teach her that? She decided to try what Andrew had taught her the night before, she shouldn't go too far wrong with that.

She carefully signed to Poppy.

Poppy's laughter got louder and Andrew rolled his eyes. With that he stormed out of the shop.

She turned to Jacob. 'What did I say now?'

He pulled a face. 'Best translation I can come up with: "Your doll is making candles with me."'

Shit. This was just getting worse. 'Can you show Poppy round the shop for a moment? I need to talk to Andrew.'

Jacob nodded.

Tears smarting her eyes, she ran out of the shop after Andrew.

He was standing out on the street pacing back and forth. She raced up to him.

'I'm so sorry—'

'You just told my six-year-old niece that she has a small penis, how inappropriate is that?'

'I would never do that deliberately—'

'You should never have tried to talk to her at all unless you know more sign language, who knows what else you could have *accidentally* said,' Andrew said.

'I shouldn't have tried to communicate with her? Are you serious? I did this because I wanted to be part of your life and hers. I know I screwed it up but at least I was trying to share that side of your life with you.'

'I never asked you to do that.'

'But I wanted to. I wanted you to see that I took that part of your life seriously and how important you are to me. And you're just throwing that back in my face. And in actual fact, Morgan showed me how to sign that to her so if you have issues with my signing you take it up with her.'

'Are you saying all this is Morgan's fault?' Andrew said.

'Yes… No,' Willow said, the fight going out of her. Because he wasn't really angry at her for messing up the sign language, they both knew that. This was about her telling the whole village he was deaf and that was all on her, no matter what Morgan had deviously tried to teach her.

'Don't you dare put this on Morgan,' Andrew said. 'She wasn't the one who just blabbed to the whole village that I'm deaf. Do you know how let down I feel about that? This is my home and now you've made it awkward for me to carry on living here.'

'These people love you and care about you, they would want to help you. Why not let them in?' Willow said.

'That wasn't your decision to make.'

'That's what Morgan said, you really are well suited.'

Andrew clearly ignored that. 'I don't need their help, or anyone's.'

'That's ridiculous. You've always said that you want Poppy to grow up being proud of who she is, yet what kind of example are you setting for her pretending to everyone that you're not deaf?'

'You have no idea what it's like to be deaf, how bloody hard it is. You couldn't possibly understand what it's like to have that label permanently hanging over your head.'

'Because you won't tell me, you won't share that part of your life with me. Every time I asked you about it, you shut me out. Yet you'll share all that with Morgan. The man you are now, the most incredible man I've ever met, is a product of the life you've led, the good, the bad, the ugly, the things you love, the things you hate. And one of the most significant influences on your life, for good or bad, is you being deaf. But you won't share that with me. On our first date you made a toast to getting to know each other but you didn't really mean that, did you? You just meant the shiny stuff, the best bits, nothing else. You said you wanted us to be honest with each other but you have closed down conversations, changed the subject and lied whenever I asked you questions about that part of your life.' She took a step away from him as the full realisation of this hit her. 'I guess I really wasn't enough for you if you couldn't share that with me.'

Andrew didn't say anything, just stared at her.

'I'm sorry, I truly am, for telling the village you're deaf. I'm sorry for letting you down.' She swallowed down the lump of burning emotion in her throat. 'But I can't go through the next few years of my life feeling like I'm not enough and you shouldn't be with someone who you can't be yourself with.'

With that Willow turned and walked away, tears streaming down her cheeks as her heart broke into a million pieces.

chapter 33

Andrew slammed the tray of chips down on the kitchen unit and they bounced so hard that some of them landed on the floor.

'Jesus! Let me do that before you break something,' Lottie said behind him as Poppy sat happily at the kitchen table playing with her toys. 'Go and sit down.'

Andrew sighed and stepped back out of the way, because he had already burnt himself on the oven twice that night; his mind was clearly elsewhere.

Poppy, by all accounts, had had a lovely afternoon making candles with Willow. Jacob had said that Willow had arrived back at the shop clearly upset but somehow managed to pull it together to spend a few hours teaching Poppy. His niece hadn't stopped telling him all about it since she'd arrived at his house earlier.

'I can't believe you and Willow broke up,' Lottie said, as

she turned the chips over and returned them to the oven. 'Over nothing.'

'It wasn't nothing,' Andrew said.

'Oh yes, she accidentally let slip to her *best* friend that you're deaf. Best friends do tend to tell each other everything.'

'And Ruby then blurted it out to the whole pub.'

'And that's worth losing the love of your life over? I don't know why you're so insistent on keeping that part of your life secret anyway. You need to learn to let people in. Being surrounded by people who have an understanding of your needs, even if it's a limited understanding, has got to be better than being surrounded by people who are completely ignorant to it.'

She'd hit the nail on the head.

Andrew sighed as he sat down at the table with Poppy. 'I think that's more the real reason why we broke up. I've been shutting her out.'

Lottie shook her head in exasperation. 'And why is that?'

'I guess I don't want to appear… less.'

'Oh Andrew. You are not… less of anything. You are my favourite person in the world. Don't tell Jacob I said that.'

Andrew smiled slightly.

Poppy galloped a toy horse up his arm and he grabbed a pig and trotted it up her arm, making her laugh.

Lottie sat down with them. 'You should have heard what Willow was saying in the pub about deaf people. She was telling Ruby off for feeling sorry for Poppy, she said that deaf people need empathy not sympathy. I think she understands a lot more than you think.'

Poppy started signing something. '*I like Willow, she's funny.*'

He signed back. '*I like her too.*'

'*She's not very good at sign language,*' Poppy giggled.

He smiled sadly and shook his head.

'I can't believe she signed to Poppy that she had a small penis,' Lottie said.

'I can't believe you're not mad about that,' Andrew said.

'Why would I be mad? Firstly it's hilarious, secondly Poppy does know the names of all the body parts so it's not like it was something completely inappropriate.'

'Willow said Morgan taught her to sign that.'

'I can well believe it.'

Andrew could too, it wasn't the first time Morgan had taught someone the wrong thing to sign for a laugh.

'You said you liked Morgan,' Andrew said.

'I do but she was very annoyed with Willow for outing you to the village. She's very protective of you. It wouldn't surprise me if she did that to get her back. I think she likes you.'

Andrew sighed. 'I think so too.'

Poppy started signing again. '*You need to teach Willow how to sign properly. She really wants to learn it.*'

He swallowed the lump in his throat. '*I know.*'

Poppy continued to sign. '*Because she loves you.*'

Andrew rubbed his hand across his eyes because Poppy in her innocence had got to the heart of the matter. Willow wanted to share this with him because she loved him and if he loved her he needed to let her in.

'I need to see her,' Andrew said.

'Yes you do,' Lottie said.

'And say sorry for making her sad,' Poppy signed. *'And then bring her back here and we can share that tub of ice cream in the freezer.'*

He smiled and kissed her on the head. *'I'll be back soon.'*

Lottie gave him a nod of encouragement and he raced out of the door.

The sun was setting, making the whole world outside rose-coloured as he ran up the lane towards Sunrise Cottage. He burst through the gate and hammered on the door.

Willow answered it and it was quite obvious she had been crying.

All the words he wanted to say went straight out of his head as he stared at her, bathed in the rose-gold light of the receding sun. He loved this woman so much. He stepped forward and kissed her and for a few seconds she kissed him back, melting against him, a little sob escaping on her lips before she put her hands on his chest and stopped him.

'What are you doing here?'

'I've come to say I'm sorry.'

She shook her head and his heart dropped into his stomach.

'This isn't going to work between us,' Willow said.

Christ he was really going to lose her. 'I love you. You

said you loved me.'

'We rushed into a relationship without getting to know each other, how could we really love each other, it's been just over a week. We didn't know each other at all.'

'That's bollocks, I know how I feel for you, I don't care how long it's been. You must have felt that too.'

'I know you made me happy,' her voice was choked. 'You made me laugh and smile a lot.' She frowned. 'I know you are kind, generous, silly, determined, protective, I know you are an amazing man, and yes I think I did fall in love with you, but it wasn't enough. There was something missing—'

'There was something missing because I didn't let you in. That was all my fault. I want to change that, I'll tell you everything, whatever you want to know,' Andrew said, desperately.

She stared at him and he knew he had to give her something.

'I was bullied incessantly in school. About my hearing aids, about being deaf, about being stupid. I think the hearing children thought I was rude or antisocial when it was just easier sometimes to not get involved in group conversations in the playground or in class, everyone shouting over everyone else and speaking so quickly, I struggled to keep up with it all. I found secondary school especially hard, being with so many different children and different teachers' voices and trying to learn and understand their lip patterns when I was lip-reading. It was hard to concentrate with the other noises and I didn't get the best grades because of it. I just felt I didn't belong sometimes and it made me feel weak. I didn't tell you these things because I didn't want you to think I was weak.'

She stepped up and cupped his face. 'You are not weak, you are the bravest, strongest man I know.'

He leaned his forehead against hers, tentatively wrapping his hands around her waist. She didn't pull away.

'There is a chance that by the time I'm fifty I will have lost all my hearing completely. It's slowly getting worse and if that happens my hearing aids might not be of any use to me. I might be able to get a cochlear implant, which will help a lot, but it's not a magic fix and I might not be suitable for it anyway. And that is something I haven't really discussed with anyone, not even my family. They know, but we don't talk about it, simply because I would rather bury my head in the sand than think about what it will be like to not hear anything any more, to lose the sounds I love the most. Your laugh is one of the most beautiful sounds I've heard, it fills my heart every time I hear it and I don't want to lose that.'

'You may not be able to hear me laugh but you will still be able to see me smile. You'll still feel my touch when we make love, my breath on your lips. You won't lose that.'

He looked her in the eyes. 'Won't I?'

Tears filled her eyes and she shook her head. 'I love you. I'm not going anywhere.'

'I swear, I'll tell you everything, my hopes, my fears, my frustrations and triumphs.'

'I need to learn sign language.'

'I'll teach you, every word. I love you and I want to share this with you.'

She smiled and leaned forward and kissed him and he sighed with relief against her lips.

They were going to be OK and for the first time in his life he felt like he'd found somewhere where he truly belonged.

chapter 34

Willow came out of the castle ready for the big open day to start. They'd told estate agents and lettings agents that the village open day started officially at twelve and, as it was only quarter past eleven, they still had a short while before people started to arrive, although Willow suspected some people would come early.

The castle was going to have its official opening at the same time and she knew people in the local area were particularly curious about seeing it. The castle grounds were filled with knights and princesses who were going to engage with the visitors and there was going to be a big jousting display later.

Outside the castle walls, on the grassy slopes near the village entrance, the villagers had set up tables. They had all risen spectacularly to the challenge of providing Happiness gifts for everyone. There were cakes, toys, jewellery, plants, knitted things, sweets, biscuits, hand-painted bits of slate and pottery mugs. Even Ruby had set up a small stand with baubles hand-painted with the word 'Happiness' and pretty little flowers. They didn't look remotely Christmassy but, as Ruby pointed out, anything could look festive once hung on a Christmas tree.

Willow moved through the stalls admiring the different gifts and stopped at Dorothy's stall, picking up one of the hand-painted postcards Dorothy had painted of the village itself. Some of them were very similar to the poster that had brought Willow to the village in the first place, but this time there was nothing misleading about the picture. Thanks to all the work that Andrew, Jacob, and Jack and his team had done over the last two weeks, the village now shone. They had managed to complete twelve houses, inside and out, and repainted all the others. Willow had worked her magic by painting flowers, butterflies and other things around all the doors and painted all the shop signs too in preparation for their new owners. Willow was excited to see the visitors' reactions.

'These look fab,' she said, picking up one of the postcards that was of the beach.

'Thank you. I hope the visitors like them,' Dorothy said and it was clear she was anxious.

'They will love them.'

Dorothy let out a big sigh. 'Do you think it will work, all of this?' she gestured to the stands. 'Everyone is so nervous.'

Willow looked around as the villagers added the last touches to their stalls. They all wanted this to work as much as she did.

'I really do,' Willow said. 'I think the visitors will see the cute houses, the pretty flowers, but most importantly the amazing people who live here and this wonderful community spirit, and I think they will fall in love with the place. Everyone has come together and they will see that and hopefully want to be a part of it.'

Dorothy nodded. 'I hope you're right.'

Willow smiled and made a move to walk away.

'Thank you for my cake by the way,' Dorothy said.

Willow turned back. The last of the mystery gifts had been delivered the night before and she and Andrew had decided to be open about it, giving the presents to the villagers directly and finally letting them in on the secret, even though many of them had suspected her all along. People had been coming up to her and Andrew all morning and thanking them, although Willow had been quick to point out that they hadn't been the sole gift-givers in all of this.

'I hope you weren't too disappointed that it wasn't Joseph after all,' Willow said.

Dorothy looked over at Joseph, who had a stand a little further down, and he gave her a little wave. Dorothy visibly blushed. Their relationship had really blossomed over the last week or so and there was even talk that Joseph might pop the question soon. Mainly that talk had been from Dorothy herself, but she'd said she would say yes if he asked because

'When you find the one, why wait?' Willow completely understood that sentiment. It was probably a bit too soon for her and Andrew to be thinking of marriage just yet, but in her heart she knew that what they had was forever.

'The gift-giving brought us together, regardless of who sent the gifts, so no, I'm not disappointed at all. Thank you for what you did, Willow. I think you brought us all together.'

Willow smiled; Dorothy had finally got her name right. 'It was my pleasure.'

Willow moved on to Ruby's stand. 'Thank you for doing this.'

'Oh, no worries. Besides, as this is going to be my new home, at least for a year, I want to help if I can.'

Willow was beyond excited that Ruby had made that decision. She couldn't wait for Ruby to move in properly, but she had to wait for her own house in St Octavia to sell first.

'Well you know, Jacob is thinking of moving here too,' Willow said and watched Ruby's face light up briefly before it closed down.

'Well that will be nice for Andrew to have his brother closer,' Ruby shrugged, trying to pull off an air of nonchalance that she didn't quite achieve.

'I think he might be coming to see the fireworks tonight,' Willow tried again. Jacob had taken off the week before because he had an exhibition of his work in St Ives. Both Ruby and Jacob had insisted to her and Andrew that it had just been a one-night stand between them, well actually a two-night stand as it turned out, but Willow had the feeling that it had been more than that for both of them, though Andrew didn't agree.

'Is he?' Ruby said, clearly trying to suppress a smile as she focussed her attention on rearranging the baubles on her stall.

Willow smiled. 'Well I'll send him your way if I see him.'

'If he wants to see me, I'm sure he'll find me, the village isn't that big. But I won't hold my breath.'

Willow sighed. She wanted someone lovely for Ruby but she had to remember that not everyone was looking for the rose-tinted happy ending. Ruby seemed very happy without a man and just because Willow had found her happy ending didn't mean that her friend needed or wanted that particular conventional happy ending for herself.

She moved on to the start of the main high street and looked down the hill at the little whitewashed houses and the smartly painted shops. The gardening team had done a fabulous job of providing hanging baskets and troughs filled with overflowing flowers and, coupled with the fairy lights that were strewn across the street, the place looked magical.

She heard a vehicle trundle round the grassy slopes and she turned to see who it was. All the cars from the visitors were going to park in the large car park behind the castle but she smiled to see the words 'The Big Bang' emblazoned onto the side. This was the fireworks team and Andrew's friend Leo.

The van pulled to a stop by her side and a man with dark hair and a huge smile wound down the window.

'Hey, any idea where we're supposed to go with the fireworks?' the man asked. 'Andrew was supposed to be here to meet us but he's probably off somewhere with his new girlfriend.'

'Well, I'm the new girlfriend and he's not here. I think he might be round the back sorting out signs for the car park. Leo, right?'

His smile grew wider. 'Yes. So you're the mystery Willow, we've been dying to meet you.'

Leo got out and a woman climbed out the passenger side who was so heavily pregnant it looked like she was going to pop at any second. She was followed by a small, overexcited boy.

'This is my wife Isla and my son Elliot,' Leo said and to Willow's surprise, Isla immediately enveloped her in a big hug.

'We're so pleased to meet you,' Isla said. 'We've heard so much about you. Now that Andrew has finished most of the work here, you'll have to come round for dinner one night.'

'I'd like that.' She turned her attention to Elliot. 'Are you looking forward to seeing the fireworks tonight?'

'Yes and Daddy Leo says I can help set it all up today,' Elliot said, bouncing on the spot.

'Wow, that is exciting.'

'And the baby likes the fireworks too,' Elliot said.

'Yes, she wriggles constantly, but the only time she is still is when the fireworks are going off,' Isla said. 'I think I'll have to play firework noises in the nursery to get her off to sleep.'

Willow laughed.

'Look, we better get down there and get everything set up,' Leo said. 'Can you point us in the right direction?'

'Sure, just follow the road down to the very end and we were going to have the fireworks on the edge of the cliffs. But you set it up wherever you think is suitable.'

'Great. We'll catch up with you later.'

Willow waved them off. It was nice to meet some of Andrew's friends. She turned around and her eyes fell on Morgan. The screens had been finished two days before but Morgan had been tweaking tiny bits here and there and she was still there now, touching up one of the horses. She was definitely a perfectionist. Even Willow had to agree that the screens looked amazing.

Willow hadn't really spoken to her since the day she'd had that blazing row with Andrew. Not in any deliberately hostile way – there had been so much going on with the last-minute preparations for the open day, making her little candle gifts, making the lanterns for the parade that night and finishing off all the painting that there hadn't been any time, and Willow hadn't felt particularly inclined to seek her out anyway. She wasn't sure if Andrew had talked to Morgan about more than work, but she knew he wasn't happy with her.

But life was too short for bitter grudges and Andrew and

Morgan had so much history. She didn't want him to walk away from that so easily.

Willow took a deep breath and walked over to talk to her.

Morgan climbed down the ladder as she approached and stepped back to look at her work.

'Looks fantastic,' Willow said.

Morgan turned round to look at her. She didn't say anything for the longest time and then she nodded. 'Thanks.'

They were silent for a while as Morgan wiped her hands. 'I'm sorry.'

Willow felt her eyebrows shoot up, she hadn't been expecting that. 'For what? For teaching me to sign to Andrew that he had a small penis which I accidentally signed to Poppy instead? Or for trying to cause trouble between us from the moment you arrived in the village?'

'Yeah, both of those things.'

At that moment Andrew appeared from the car park round the back of the castle. Willow hadn't seen him for most of the morning and at some point he had clearly gone home and changed into a suit. He looked sexy and suave.

She let out an ear-piercing wolf whistle and he looked over and laughed when he saw it was her.

She carefully signed. '*You look hot.*'

He laughed again and signed back. '*Elephant shoes.*'

Her heart filled with love for him.

'Elephant shoes?' Morgan said, in confusion.

Willow smiled, not taking her eyes off him as he took up his place near the gate. 'It's kind of our thing.'

Morgan was quiet for a while and then she spoke. 'You're good for him. I literally have never seen him so happy as he is when he's with you.'

'He's good for me too.'

Morgan sighed. 'I always thought we would end up together some day. Not in the kind of way where I was head over heels in love with him. I just thought… we fitted. When I heard he had a serious girlfriend, someone he had shared things with that he'd never shared with me, I was jealous. I suppose I was jealous that I was never that person for him.'

Willow smiled. 'I was jealous of you too, the history you had shared, the friendship. The fact that you are fluent in sign language.'

'I haven't been much of a friend to him lately. But I want him to be happy. And he's found that with you.'

Andrew suddenly let out a whistle and Willow looked over.

'They're coming,' he shouted.

'I better go,' Willow said.

Morgan nodded as she quickly packed away her things and Willow raced over to her candle table. There was a last-minute flurry as everyone straightened their wares on their tables, and then suddenly the first car was pulling up at the gates.

Willow watched Andrew hand over a Happiness gift voucher to all the occupants of the car and then direct them towards the car park. As the car trundled off, it was replaced by another.

Willow took a deep breath and crossed her fingers behind her back. After everything they had done, this had to work.

Willow couldn't help but smile as she passed out the lanterns she had made to the visitors and they started making their way towards the end of the village. There was an excited buzz about the firework display from the visitors, many of whom had stayed the whole day.

The open day had been a big success. There had been quite a few visitors to the castle who had loved exploring the ruins and watching the jousting entertainment and most of them had then gone to investigate the village. But there had been almost two hundred people that had come to specifically look at the village itself. A few people had even reserved houses there and then. Kitty and Ken had been rushed off their feet taking down details from interested parties. Many of them might go away and decide Happiness was not for them but Willow was quietly confident the village would at least be half filled in a few months' time.

Everyone had been charmed by the little village and most of all its people who had made the guests feel very welcome, chatting to them and giving them their little gifts. The visitors were thrilled with their presents and it really helped to show

Happiness in its best light.

She watched people walk past, the villagers mingling with the visitors, everyone happily chatting to each other. They had achieved something wonderful and really put Happiness back on the map.

Across the street, Willow could see Ruby and Jacob talking, standing very close to one another as the sea of visitors and villagers swarmed around them. Jacob whispered something in her ear and she smiled and nodded. Then he took her hand and together they marched off towards the pub. It seemed that they might miss the fireworks and Ruby didn't seem to care.

Willow smiled. She didn't know what the future held for the two of them but as long as her friend was happy, then Willow was happy for her.

Kitty and Ken approached and she gave them a lantern. There didn't seem to be anyone else coming down the high street towards them as all the visitors were already making their way to the cliff tops, so she grabbed one of the last lanterns for herself and joined them on the walk down.

'I think the day has gone off with a bang,' Willow said.

'It really has,' Kitty said, linking arms with her. 'All thanks to you.'

'Oh god no, everyone has worked so hard for today, you guys have been rushed off your feet and so much work has gone into getting the village ready. And the presents that everyone has made, I can't take credit for any of that.'

'But it was your idea,' Ken said.

'But it took the whole village to make it work. How many houses did you manage to fill today?' Willow said, quickly deflecting the attention away from her.

'Eight definites and six more that are going to let me know on Monday. But there were lots more that were really interested so we may hear from them once they've had time to think about it,' Ken said.

'It will be lovely to have some new faces here and some new shops too,' Willow said.

Just then she saw Andrew moving towards them through the crowds, a big smile on his face.

'Sorry,' he said, signing it at the same time. 'Just helping Leo make sure everything is ready for the fireworks.'

She watched his hands as he spoke and smiled. The biggest change in the village over the last week or so had been Andrew's attitude to his deafness. He had started teaching her sign language straight away and, although she was a long way off being able to sign whole sentences, she knew many key words now. He had started to sign almost every time he spoke so she would get used to it and that meant he would sign to her in the pub, out on the street, in her shop, where everyone could see it. The villagers had been interested in this change, of course, Willow had seen them watching him on several occasions, but beyond that no one had treated him any differently and they had quickly got used to it. As Dorothy said, most of the elderly villagers were deaf or hearing impaired too and there had been talk of offering a sign language class to the whole village which a lot of people were interested in. Even

Ruby had said she wanted to learn it, which Willow liked after all the fuss she had made about finding out both Poppy and Andrew were deaf.

Because Willow didn't yet know the signs for '*Don't worry*' or '*No problem*' she leaned up and kissed him instead. Sometimes actions spoke louder than words.

They followed the golden glow of the lanterns out of the village and past the old ruined houses until they came to where hundreds of people were standing against the temporary barricade. It had been erected so no one could get too close to the fireworks but Andrew lifted the rope for her and tugged her underneath.

'Aren't we supposed to stay that side?' Willow said, looking back at the crowds who were watching them disappear into the darkness as they approached the cliff edge. She could see all the fireworks were ready to go in tubes pointing out towards the sea and Leo running around doing last-minute checks.

To Willow's surprise, Andrew led her to the top of the steps leading down to the beach.

'I thought we could watch the fireworks from down here, it's a better view without all the crowds,' he said.

'Oh, that's a lovely idea,' Willow said as they started picking their way down the steps. She was glad of the lantern she was carrying but it didn't throw out too much light and, as they stepped away from the lights of the rest of the village, Andrew pulled his mobile phone from his pocket and turned on the torch too.

When they reached the bottom, Willow could see the tide was out and there was a picnic blanket laid out on the sand, surrounded by tiny little solar lights.

'Oh, this is why you were late?' Willow laughed and Andrew grinned at her over his shoulder.

The picnic blanket was laid out with a hamper to one side and a bottle of champagne chilling in an ice bucket.

'This is lovely, thank you for doing this,' Willow said, sitting down on the blanket and using the sign for '*Thank you*' as she spoke.

'It's my pleasure. I've been so busy over the last few weeks and I want to spend some quality time with you,' Andrew said, uncorking the champagne and pouring out two glasses. He passed one to her and sat down next to her. 'It was here on this beach, as you ran off with my clothes and I could barely breathe I was laughing so much, that I knew I was going to marry you one day. I think I loved you even then, though I didn't want to admit it to myself. You have turned my life around and I love you so much.'

She smiled and leaned forward and kissed him. 'I love you too,' she whispered against his lips before kissing him again.

She put her champagne glass down in the sand and lay down on the blanket, staring up at the stars twinkling above them. Andrew lay down by her side and held her hand. They listened to the sounds of the waves for a while and beyond that there was silence. She had never felt so completely and utterly blissfully content in her whole life as she felt then lying next to the man she loved.

Andrew rolled onto his side and placed a kiss on her bare shoulder. 'You know, the last time we made a toast we toasted to making love under the stars?'

She laughed. 'Oh that's your game, bringing me down here? Is that picnic basket filled with condoms instead of food?'

Andrew sat up, opened the picnic hamper and pulled out a condom. She laughed loudly.

'There is food in there too,' he said. 'For after.'

She shook her head. 'You're so sure of yourself.'

'I am now. That's because of you.'

She smiled with love for him and as he lay back down next to her she kissed him, slowly undressing him as he removed her own clothes. He rolled over on top of her, still kissing her.

He moved back onto his knees as he ripped open the condom and a firework exploded in the night sky above them.

'Oooh,' Willow said as the sky glittered with gold.

Andrew leaned over her, bracing himself on his forearms as he positioned himself between her legs.

'You're going to miss the show,' Willow said, watching another firework send cascading silvery stars through the darkness behind Andrew.

'I've got something much more beautiful to look at. You can tell me all about it.'

As the fireworks exploded above them, one after the other, Willow signed the words for the different colours that sparkled above the sea. Although she stopped when she realised Andrew was just watching her, smiling.

'Did I get it right?'

'You are perfect, in every single way.'

He slid carefully inside and she wrapped herself around him. As the fireworks lit up the sky in a riot of colour he started to move against her, his eyes locked on hers the whole time.

'I never did give you a Secret Society gift, did I?' Andrew said. 'It doesn't seem right that you're the only one in the village not to get one. I'll have to rectify that.'

'But you did,' Willow said, reaching up and stroking his face. 'You gave me the gift of happiness.'

the end

afterword

If you enjoyed *The Little Village of Happiness*, you'll love my next gorgeously romantic story, *The Gift of Happiness,* out in October.

To keep up to date with the latest news on my releases, just click on the link below to sign up for a newsletter. You'll also get two FREE short stories, get sneak peeks, booky news and be able to take part in exclusive giveaways. Your email will never be shared with anyone else and you can unsubscribe at any time

Sign up here!

Website: https://hollymartin-author.com/

Twitter: @HollyMAuthor

Email: holly@hollymartin-author.com

Facebook author page:
https://www.facebook.com/hollymartinauthor/

Sunshine, Seaside and Sparkles – The Holly Martin Reader Group:
https://www.facebook.com/groups/483957115452985/

a note about andrew

When I started writing Andrew's character, I knew almost straight away he was going to be deaf. As vividly as I knew he had dark hair and blue eyes, I knew he was going to be deaf too. But then I got worried about doing his character justice. I'm not deaf, I have no deaf people in my family, could I really comprehend what it was like to be hearing impaired or to have no hearing at all? But a very good author friend said that if we are scared to write what we don't know, then when will it stop? Should I not write about men because I'm a woman, should I not write about children because I'm an adult, should I not write about dogs and cats because I'm a human? She said being fearful of misrepresenting a certain way of life could drive further wedges between our differences, keeping us apart rather than bringing us closer to a society of true understanding and equality. And I knew she was right and I had to write Andrew as I always envisaged him.

So then I researched the hell out of it, more so than I ever had before for any other character. I had a deaf friend at university and while we are not really in contact anymore, I remembered what she told me and some of that helped to shape Andrew's past. I spoke to a lot of people in the Deaf community who were more than happy to share their experiences of growing up deaf, using hearing aids, sign language and all the good and the bad stuff in between.

A lot of people obviously had very different experiences of being deaf. For example, one person said it would be very unlikely that a person that had been born deaf could be cured so well with hearing aids that they had no problem speaking, she said that it was more likely that Andrew had learned to speak and then went deaf when he was older. Other people I spoke to said it was fine that Andrew was diagnosed very early in his life before he could talk. So while for some, Andrew might not be a true representation of their experience of being deaf, he is a character made up of lots of people's experiences.

The one sticking point I had while telling the story was with British Sign Language (BSL). The language has its own structure, so for example when you're describing something you always start with the setting. 'There was a small boy called Rob standing on the bridge in the park,' would be signed something like, 'Park, bridge, small boy, Rob, standing.' I obviously couldn't have conversations like that in my book as the reader wouldn't understand what the characters were saying so I had to use a bit of poetic licence while interpreting the sign language.

I have to say that the research paid off, at least for me. While writing Andrew's character and trying to ensure he was as real as possible, I completely and utterly fell in love with him and I hope you did too.

also by holly martin

The Summer of Chasing Dreams

Sandcastle Bay Series

The Holiday Cottage by the Sea

The Cottage on Sunshine Beach

Coming Home to Maple Cottage

Hope Island Series

Spring at Blueberry Bay

Summer at Buttercup Beach

Christmas at Mistletoe Cove

Juniper Island Series

Christmas Under a Cranberry Sky

A Town Called Christmas

White Cliff Bay Series

Christmas at Lilac Cottage

Snowflakes on Silver Cove

Summer at Rose Island

Standalone Stories

Fairytale Beginnings

Tied Up With Love

A Home on Bramble Hill

One Hundred Christmas Proposals
One Hundred Proposals
The Guestbook at Willow Cottage

For Young Adults
The Sentinel Series

The Sentinel (Book 1 of the Sentinel Series)
The Prophecies (Book 2 of the Sentinel Series)
The Revenge (Book 3 of the Sentinel Series)
The Reckoning (Book 4 of the Sentinel Series)

a letter from holly

Thank you so much for reading *The Little Village of Happiness*, I had so much fun creating this story and the beautiful village of Happiness. I hope you enjoyed reading it as much as I enjoyed writing it. If you did enjoy it, and want to keep up-to-date with all my latest releases, just Sign up here. Your email will never be shared and you can unsubscribe at any time.

One of the best parts of writing comes from seeing the reaction from readers. Did it make you smile or laugh, did it make you cry, hopefully happy tears? Did you fall in love with Willow and Andrew as much as I did? Did you like the gorgeous little village of Happiness? If you enjoyed the story, I would absolutely love it if you could leave a short review. Getting feedback from readers is amazing and it also helps to persuade other readers to pick up one of my books for the first time.

My next book, out in October is called *The Gift of Happiness* and is set in the same village, this time following Ruby and Jacob's story.

Thank you for reading.

Love Holly x

acknowledgements

To my family, my mom, my biggest fan, who reads every word I've written a hundred times over and loves it every single time, my dad, my brother Lee and my sister-in-law Julie, for your support, love, encouragement and endless excitement for my stories.

For my twinnie, the gorgeous Aven Ellis for just being my wonderful friend, for your endless support, for cheering me on, for reading my stories and telling me what works and what doesn't and for keeping me entertained with wonderful stories. I love you dearly.

To my lovely friends Julie, Natalie, Jac, Verity and Jodie, thanks for all the support.

To the Devon contingent, Paw and Order, Belinda, Lisa, Phil, Bodie, Kodi and Skipper. Thanks for keeping me entertained and always being there.

For Sharon Sant for just being there always and your wonderful friendship.

To everyone at Bookcamp, you gorgeous, fabulous bunch, thank you for your wonderful support on this venture.

To Kirsty Greenwood, thanks for answering all my questions with unending patience.

Thanks to the brilliant Emma Rogers for the gorgeous cover design.

Thanks to my fabulous editors, Celine Kelly and Rhian McKay.

Thanks to Alexandria for help with formatting.

A huge thank you to Cath, Helen Edwards, Audrey Dickson for all your help. Thanks to BATOD, BDA, Action on Hearing Loss and the Royal Association for Deaf People for pointing me in the right direction.

To all the wonderful bloggers for your tweets, retweets, facebook posts, tireless promotions, support, encouragement and endless enthusiasm. You guys are amazing and I couldn't do this journey without you.

To anyone who has read my book and taken the time to tell me you've enjoyed it or wrote a review, thank you so much.

Thank you, I love you all.

Lightning Source UK Ltd.
Milton Keynes UK
UKHW010604111219
355129UK00001B/135/P